His repu... that of a rake.
Hadn't he better prove it?

⊢ ▪▪▪ ⊣

"You must be sensible, little Penny," he murmured. As her velvety brown eyes widened in surprise, Julian bent his head and kissed her swiftly on the lips.

At least he had meant it to be a swift kiss. When their lips met, however, all rational thought flew from his head. There was only softness and warmth and an incredible sweetness.

His sudden move took Penelope by surprise. Her startled "oh" was lost and then forgotten under the touch of his firm mouth. She wanted to be held closer, to drink in the masculine scent of his shaving soap, to feel his hands caress her back.

Breathlessness forced her to pull away, thereby breaking the spell. She became instantly aware of whistles and catcalls shrilling in the air, of jeering and clapping. She whirled out of Julian's arms to stare with horror at urchins, jarveys, vendors, crossing sweeps, and indignant matrons, who had all gathered in Newgate Street to watch the gentleman and his lady love.

Her eyes flew to Julian's face. *He was grinning!*

▪◄►◄

AN HONORABLE AFFAIR

Also by Karla Hocker

A Bid for Independence
A Madcap Scheme
A Daring Alliance

Published by
WARNER BOOKS

AN HONORABLE AFFAIR

Karla Hocker

WARNER BOOKS

A Warner Communications Company

To Niki and Jasmin

WARNER BOOKS EDITION

Copyright © 1988 by Karla Hocker
All rights reserved.

Warner Books, Inc.
666 Fifth Avenue
New York, N.Y. 10103

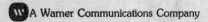A Warner Communications Company

Printed in the United States of America

First Printing: November, 1988

10 9 8 7 6 5 4 3 2 1

chapter <u>ONE</u>

"**D***id* you see Henrietta Spatterton's turban?" Lady Belmont said indignantly as the carriage pulled away from the brightly lit portals of the Russian Embassy.

Penelope Langham directed a glance of mingled amusement and indulgence at her aunt. "Black with gold plumes? Yes, Aunt Sophy. How could I not have seen it?"

"A monstrosity that made Henrietta look like a gilded ostrich!"

"I certainly am glad you chose the lavender lace cap. Only think how you would have felt had you bought the turban you described to me last week. Black with gold feathers, was it not, Aunt Sophy?"

"Yes. I had my heart set on it, until that clever girl at Balena's Hat Shoppe told me I should always wear lavender or mauve with my silver-blond hair. I daresay she knew that Henrietta planned . . ." Lady Belmont's voice trailed off. She peered uncertainly into her niece's face, then laughed. "You're an abominable tease, Penelope! You knew all along that I could have scratched Henrietta's eyes out for wearing the turban *I* wanted!"

"You look very fetching in lavender, Aunt Sophy," Penelope said soothingly.

She clung to the leather strap suspended from the ceiling of the coach as they turned rather sharply into Oxford

Street, then into Davies Street, with the rumble of a second carriage following close behind them. "It appears Hunter made a wager against Lady Margaret's coachman again," she said, laughter dancing in her voice.

"The wretch! And I don't know why you should be laughing, Penelope! Don't think I haven't noticed how you raise your brows when I lose a few pennies at silver-loo. Yet when our groom gambles with our very lives, you— Oh, for heaven's sake, Penelope! Tell him to slow down," Lady Belmont cried as they rattled on at such a pace that the well-sprung carriage swayed precariously.

Penelope blinked but said nothing. *A few pennies!* She had seen her aunt lose as much as a hundred pounds in one night.

She turned and opened the small panel behind her just as the carriage swung into Berkeley Square, its familiar outline illuminated by the hazy glow of numerous gas lanterns. Before she could relay Lady Belmont's message, however, Hunter slowed down on his own accord, then stopped.

"There be summat amiss!" he shouted. "I can see Belmont House lit up from top to bottom, Miss Penelope, an' there be a crowd like we had the two-headed leddy of Bartholomew Fair sittin' on our steps!"

"Thank you, Hunter. But that's no reason *not* to take us home. Proceed, if you please." Penelope shut the panel and braced herself for bumps and jolts as Hunter whipped up the horses for the home stretch.

Lady Belmont scooted to the edge of her seat and peeked out the window. Hunter had indeed described the scene in front of her house correctly. If anything, the crowd she saw in the light of the gas lanterns was even thicker than that at Bartholomew Fair.

"I hope the house isn't on fire!" the plump little lady wailed. "Dawson warned me that the chimney in the kitchen needed sweeping! Oh, whatever could be the matter?"

"Aunt Sophy," Penelope said gently, "we've arrived, and see, the house is still standing. If you let go of the door, Hunter can open it and let down the steps for you."

Lady Belmont almost tumbled from the carriage in her haste and was immediately engulfed in a voluble if unintelligible stream of explanations from Sweetings, her dresser, and from the housekeeper Mrs. Dawson, as they accompanied their mistress into the house.

Before Penelope stepped down, she surveyed the throng of shouting men and women. Her aunt's servants were milling around, as were dozens more from the neighboring houses. Something was, indeed, amiss. Penelope took a deep breath and, beckoning her aunt's butler to follow her, brushed through the shouting, gesticulating crowd.

In the relative calm of the foyer she faced the old retainer. "Sit down, Dawson," she said after one glance at his pale, gaunt face and his trembling hands. "Tell me what happened."

Dawson tottered to the nearest of several ladder-backed chairs flanking the entrance hall. He sat down heavily. "It's the opals, Miss Penelope," he said, his thin, old-man's voice quavering more than usual. "The Belmont Opals are gone!"

A picture of her aunt replacing the opal necklace and tiara in a velvet-lined box, then taking out her diamonds, flashed through Penelope's mind. "Nonsense, Dawson," she said bracingly. "I saw the opals myself less than four hours ago."

Dawson shook his head. "The opals are gone! They were stolen. I tell you, Miss Penelope—" Stiffly the butler got to his feet when a burly individual dressed in a gray frieze coat and a wide-brimmed hat came stomping into the foyer.

"This, ah, gentleman here is a Bow Street runner, Miss Penelope. I sent for him," Dawson said apologetically.

"Dare's the name. Theobard Dare, miss." The runner snatched off his hat and bowed. "If ye would kindly direct me to the Dowager Countess of Belmont, miss? It's my dooty to take a statement."

If Penelope still maintained doubts about the theft of the opal necklace and tiara, they were swept aside by a piercing shriek dwindling to a wail from above.

"Pray excuse me," she said to the Bow Street runner, who had pulled from his coat pocket a much-thumbed occurrence book and the stub of a thick pencil. "I fear Lady Belmont won't be able to see you now."

As Penelope rushed up the two flights of highly glossed

oak stairs, she reflected that eight years ago when she first
arrived at her aunt's house, she might have felt a thrill of
excitement at the sight of a Bow Street runner, for then her
first thought would have been for the possibility of an
adventure—a burglar hunt. Now, at the ripe age of three-
and-twenty, she could only think of the shock her aunt's
frail nerves must have sustained when she found her opals
missing.

Slipping off her evening cape and handing it to Nancy,
her own maid who had joined the housekeeper and dresser
in Lady Belmont's bedroom, Penelope stepped briskly to the
daybed at the foot of the wide four-poster bed where her
aunt reclined against a multitude of silken cushions. Sweetings, waving sal volatile and still crying out incoherent
explanations, hovered over Lady Belmont.

"Take the smelling salts away, Sweetings," Penelope
ordered. "My aunt is not unconscious." For a moment she
studied Sophy's pale face, the tightly closed eyes, and the
compressed lips. "Do you have the headache, Aunt Sophy?"

When Lady Belmont nodded, Penelope turned to her
maid. "Open the windows, please, Nancy, and then take
Sweetings to the servants' hall for a cup of tea." To the
housekeeper she said, "Mrs. Dawson, please send up some
tea for Lady Belmont as well. The Bohea, I think."

When Penelope was finally alone with her aunt, she
splashed lavender water on a handkerchief and dabbed it
against Lady Belmont's forehead and temples.

"Dear Penelope," the dowager countess murmured. "You
always know just what to do when I suffer one of my
spasms."

"Yes, indeed, Auntie. But don't tell Sweetings so, for I
fear she takes it as a slight on her own capable ministrations. Now, Aunt Sophy, do you feel up to talking or would
you rather wait until you've had a dish of Bohea to sustain
you?"

Recalling her loss, Sophy let out another wail. "My
necklace! My tiara! Oh, Henry," she cried, gazing through
tear-filled eyes at a large portrait on the silk-hung wall
opposite her four-poster bed. "Whatever shall I do?"

Predictably, Sophy's late husband, the Sixth Earl of

Belmont, vouchsafed no reply. He stared down haughtily from his high position where he guarded the safe hidden behind the ornate picture frame.

"The safe is closed, Aunt Sophy," Penelope said. "Are you certain—"

"The opals weren't in the safe! I told Sweetings to leave them out until I'd returned and taken off the diamonds." Overcome by her emotions, Lady Belmont fell back against the cushions and covered her face with her hands. Her plump shoulders encased in lavender satin shook, and tears trickled through her diamond-covered fingers.

Penelope was relieved when a knock on the door heralded the arrival of the tea tray, sparing her the necessity of an immediate reply. *Careless, negligent,* and *foolish* were the least objectionable comments that popped into her mind, but while she went through the ritual of measuring and pouring and stirring, Penelope's equanimity returned.

"There's a Bow Street runner downstairs, Aunt Sophy," she said. "No doubt you'll have the opals restored to you within a day or so."

Taking her aunt's cup, she moved back to the daybed. "Sit up now, Auntie, and drink your tea before it cools. Then you must see the runner and give him a description of the necklace and the tiara. His name is Theobald Dare. A singularly appropriate name for one who plans to challenge our wretched thief, don't you think?"

Lady Belmont, however, was past the state when Penelope could coax or cajole her. With streaming eyes the elderly lady looked up at her niece. "My dearest Henry gave me the opals!" she wailed. "He personally traveled to Hungary when he heard that some impoverished count had put them up for sale, and he snatched them right from under the Emperor Francis's nose."

Heart-rending sobs made her next words unintelligible, and Penelope understood only the end of her aunt's disclosure, "—the very finest and largest opals, from the Dubnyk mine!"

"Yes, I know, dear," Penelope said, perching herself on the edge of the daybed and patting her aunt's soft, plump hands while at the same time holding the fragrant Bohea temptingly close to her aunt's nose.

Sophy, crying harder and working herself into a fine state of hysterics, pushed away the tea. "Sweetings!" she cried. "I want Sweetings! I must have my elixir!"

Penelope's eyes grew troubled. She prayed that distress over the theft wouldn't make her aunt dependent on Dr. Wise's prescriptions once again. Aunt Sophy had done so well these past two months or longer and had stayed away from the noxious stuff dispensed by the doctor.

"My opals! I need my medicine, Penelope! Please!"

Penelope set the teacup onto a glass-topped table nearby. She stepped into Lady Belmont's dressing room and opened a small, lacquered cabinet. Standing on tiptoe, she could see at the back of the upper shelf an innocuous-looking brown medicine bottle. Dr. Wise's elixir. Laudanum.

After eight years with her aunt, Penelope should have been accustomed to Sophy's weakness, but she wasn't. Her insides still twisted into a painful knot at sight of the medicine that promised escape from trouble and worry.

Hesitantly Penelope's hand closed around the bottle. It might be best if she gave her aunt a small dose now. Sweetings, unfortunately, could not be trusted to put her foot down and say no if Lady Belmont asked for more than was good for her.

Penelope measured a few drops of the liquid into a spoon, then returned to the bedchamber. "Take your medicine, Auntie," she said calmly. "I shall attend to the Bow Street runner for you."

Lady Belmont's sobs ceased. "Yes," she said. "I must take my medicine, mustn't I? My nerves are overset and my poor head is bursting." She peered shortsightedly at the spoon. "You measured wrong again, Penelope," she complained. "Dr. Wise said that a lady of my sensibilities must take *at least* a full spoon."

"This is enough, Aunt Sophy. It'll make you quite sleepy, you'll see." Penelope met her aunt's distraught gaze steadily, and after a while Sophy swallowed the small dose, then lay back against the cushions.

Sweetings, much restored as Penelope saw by the usual

dour look the dresser bestowed on her, returned shortly. "Mayhap you'd best see to matters downstairs now, Miss Langham," the woman said, watching with jealous eyes when Lady Belmont reached for her niece's hand.

Miss Langham, Sweetings thought angrily, might look like a lady with her beautiful face and dainty figure, but when all was said and done, she was still the same brazen hussy who had come to Belmont House clad in the trousers and shirt worn by Turkish women.

Permitting herself a disdainful sniff, Sweetings stalked to the walnut bureau under the window and pulled open a drawer. She took out a frothy pink nightcap, shaking out the ruffles with loving care while she reflected on Penelope's unorthodox arrival eight years ago.

Sweetings had predicted then—and it was horribly confirmed now, wasn't it?—that no good would come from the young hoyden whose parents had irresponsibly allowed her to travel with them among heathens and then had contracted typhoid fever in Constantinople. Mr. and Mrs. Langham had lived only long enough to arrange for a passage home for their daughter and to write a letter consigning the girl to her aunt's care.

Sweetings sniffed again as she picked up a white and pink bed jacket before approaching the daybed. Well, *she*'d never call her Miss Penelope as the other servants affectionately did. She shot a sour look at the young lady who still held her aunt's hand clasped in hers.

"That Bow Street runner has called everyone to the servants' hall, Miss Langham. Asking questions about where we was and what we did. I doubt not as he'll have everyone up in arms in no time at all," the dresser pointed out with great satisfaction.

"Thank you, Sweetings. If you're sure you can manage alone, I'll go down and see what I can do. But my aunt, I fear, is rather drowsy from a dose of Dr. Wise's elixir. If you need help, please call."

Penelope received no reply. After another look at her sleepy aunt, she patted the plump fingers, then left the room. The corridor was dim and cool. Goose bumps formed on her bare arms and shoulders, reminding her that she still wore her ball gown of gossamer Indian silk.

Mayhap it's my conscience that makes me shiver!

Penelope stepped briskly along the woven runner to her room where Nancy had left a small lamp burning. The delicate French clock on her dressing table showed it was past three o'clock, and in the large, round mirror behind it, Penelope saw her eyes staring back at her—wide and apprehensive; more black than brown.

She spun away from the mirror. After one longing glance at her bed, Penelope changed into a simple frock with a matching spencer, then descended to the nether regions of Lady Belmont's spacious London home.

She was responsible. She was in charge—as she had been for the past six years.

The moment she parted the green baize curtains in the rear of the entranceway and opened the door to the back stairs, her ears were assailed by a great din of shouts and shrieks. Steeling herself against mayhem, Penelope started down the flight of plain wooden stairs lit by lanterns affixed to the whitewashed walls.

She heard a shout, followed by a crash as though a chair had been tossed across a room, but her steps did not falter. The heels of her dainty shoes tapped steadily along the tiled basement passage.

Penelope ignored the doors on her right leading into the various kitchens, sculleries, and storerooms; she passed the first doors on her left leading to the Dawsons' and the French chef's quarters, and advanced toward the ruckus behind a set of sturdy double doors. With a firm push she flung them wide open to reveal the servants' hall before her.

Ten men and women were seated or standing around the long refectory table, but their yelling and shrieking was loud enough for a gathering of twice their number. To add to the din, some of the men signaled outrage by hammering their fists on the scrubbed tabletop. Two of the women were crying.

Penelope stood quite still just inside the open doors and a little to the left of Mr. Theobald Dare, the Bow Street runner, who had his back to her and was shouting as loud as

Lady Belmont's staff. Rachel, the upstairs maid, saw Penelope first. She broke off in midscream, nudging Ben, the first footman who had jumped up and looked as though he were about to lunge at the Bow Street runner.

Suddenly they all fell silent and rose. Only Mr. Dare's shout of "my dooty to take a statement!" boomed and echoed in the long chamber. Then he, too, was still. Penelope walked to the head of the table, where Ben quickly placed a chair for her between the Dawsons.

"Pray be seated," Penelope said, and when the Bow Street runner had squeezed his bulk into one of the vacant chairs at the foot of the table, she looked sternly from one disgruntled servant's face to the other. "It is late. In three hours you are supposed to start your tasks. Let us hear what Mr. Dare requires. After all, he is here to recover Lady Belmont's opals. Then you may all go to bed, and I don't think Lady Belmont would mind if you slept an hour late."

Penelope received shy smiles and grateful nods from most of the staff, but the first footman scowled and jumped to his feet again. "Miss Penelope," Ben said in a rumbling voice, "this here runner as much as told us that we stole them jewels, and I tell you, Miss Penelope, we didn't do it! He should be out in Seven Dials lookin' for the thief!"

"I understand, Ben," Penelope said soothingly, "but no doubt Mr. Dare wishes to know where you all were in case one of you heard or saw something pertinent to his investigation."

"That's what I said, miss." The runner nodded importantly. "I must have the pertinent facts, I told them. But they ain't even all here," he grumbled. "I asked the butler—all in the course of my dooty, miss—that the three missing persons be summonsed. But did he do so? Not he! Mr. Dawson refused to obey an officer of the law, miss!"

Penelope quickly surveyed the tired faces around the table. "Sands, our coachman, hasn't been able to leave his bed for several days, Mr. Dare. He suffers from arthritis. Miss Sweetings is sitting with Lady Belmont, and the only other person missing is Miriam, our scullery maid. The girl is thirteen, Mr. Dare. She works very hard and needs all the sleep she can get. As does everyone else."

Again her eyes skimmed around the table. She nodded. "You may all go now. Dawson, I'll speak to the staff later in the library. Please see that a fire is lit by nine o'clock."

The Bow Street runner opened his mouth to protest but, encountering Penelope's quelling stare, prudently changed his mind.

"And now, Mr. Dare," Penelope said when the door had shut behind Hunter, the last to leave the servants' hall, "you may tell *me* what you require, and I shall see to it that you have everyone's statement by noon tomorrow, or rather," she added with a pointed look at the large clock affixed to the wall, "today."

"It is my dooty also to have a statement from you and her ladyship," the runner said stubbornly. "And I must search the premises. It is—"

"Your duty," said Penelope, rising to her feet. "I quite understand, and you shall do so when you return at noon."

Mr. Dare could do no less than rise as well, and before he knew it, he was firmly and inexorably led to the back door and ushered outside even while he was explaining what pertinent facts should be contained in the servants' statements.

With a sigh of relief, Penelope bolted and locked the back door. It was so dashed difficult to show a calm front at all times. How close she herself had come to screaming with impatience at the runner's officiousness. Or banging her fists on a hard surface. But she had long outgrown such childish behavior. Hadn't she?

No, I haven't.

She had made a good pretense of it, though, Penelope thought as she went up to her bedroom. She didn't bother to disrobe but lay down on her bed atop the soft quilt. In a few hours, after she had interviewed the staff, life would flow once again along its usual, calm channels, she told herself. Soon the opals would be restored to her aunt, and then Sophy again could reduce the amount of laudanum she took and be her cheerful old self.

Sophronia Belmont, like her younger brother, Penelope's papa, was easygoing, a bit of a gambler, just a mite irresponsible, and above all so very likable and charming.

She had opened her home to her orphaned niece and had showered her with kindness and affection.

Why, then, am I so ungrateful? Why are there still moments when I wish I need not behave like a lady?

Penelope's thoughts became muddled as she finally drifted off to sleep. She awakened to the rich, sweet smell of hot chocolate. A cup rattled in its saucer, then Nancy's cheerful humming drifted past and came closer again as the little maid moved about, clanking the hot water jug and opening drawers and doors.

Reluctantly Penelope opened her eyes. It was morning, a bright, sunny May morning, and she must ready herself to interrogate her aunt's faithful staff.

At nine o'clock, Penelope entered the book-lined room tucked away between the Chinese drawing room and the card room on the first floor. At eleven o'clock, she finished writing out the last statement, that of little Miriam, the scullery maid, who was shaking and crying as though she were facing the hangman and his noose instead of her dear Miss Penelope.

"Thank you, Miriam. Now I only require your signature, and then you may go." Penelope blotted the page before turning it around and beckoning the young girl closer to the desk.

With an unsteady hand, Miriam produced an *X* and a large inkblot on Lady Belmont's finest crested writing paper.

Penelope tried to look stern, but her eyes twinkled at Miriam's woebegone little face. "It's all in the line of our civic 'dooty,' child."

Miriam's crimson face confirmed that the other servants had regaled her with a good imitation of Mr. Dare's bluster. Encouraged, Penelope pressed, "Why are you so afraid that you seem to have forgotten how to write your name? Come now, you wouldn't want that Bow Street runner to think he can intimidate the Belmont staff!"

Miriam said nothing, and after a while Penelope continued gently, "You are afraid, Miriam. What is it? Don't you trust me? Take your time, child, and read the document. There's nothing in it that would confine you to Newgate."

The girl tossed her head and looked at Penelope. "I already did," she whispered. "The paper says just what I told ye. But—but I should've heard the thief," she burst out. "I weren't sleeping, ye see. I were reading t' book ye gave me, an' I'm so ashamed!"

"You were reading in your room?"

The girl nodded, and Penelope said, "Well, then even if you weren't asleep you could not possibly have heard anything unless the thief was extremely careless and made a lot of noise, which I'm sure he didn't. So you have nothing to be ashamed of, Miriam."

Taking a deep breath, the girl picked up the pen again, dipped it in the inkwell, and signed her full name beneath the *X*.

"Very good. Now promise me not to spend *all* night reading again, Miriam, and then you may go to the kitchen and ask Mrs. Dawson to give you a cup of broth. Oh, and have someone bring me a sandwich and a pot of tea, please."

When Miriam had scurried from the library, Penelope spread out the statements and studied them. Even the arthritic Sands had limped over from his rooms above the coach house in the mews to report that he had heard and seen nothing. In fact, most of the staff had neither heard nor seen anything; they'd had the night off and had been out, pursuing their own diverse pleasures. If the Bow Street runner couldn't find a clue or a trace of the opals—they were after all of a very rare size and beauty—the chances of recovery were not very good.

For Aunt Sophy's sake, the opals must be recovered!

Penelope pulled a clean sheet of paper from a drawer. Heading it with the previous day's date, May 19, 1818, she started to list what little information she could glean from the statements, stopping only when Dawson arrived with a tray and set a plate of ham sandwiches conspicuously on top of her list.

"The Bow Street runner has arrived, Miss Penelope," Dawson said while pouring her tea. "What would you have me do with him?"

"Well, don't serve him to me for lunch. You had best show him over the house, Dawson. It's Mr. Dare's duty to search the premises, I was informed last night."

"Yes, Miss Penelope. I'll have him start in the cellars, and he can work his way to the attics."

Penelope stared at the old butler. She had rather expected some vigorous protestations, or at least a silent show of hurt feelings, but Dawson looked quite willing—even smug, if such an expression was possible on his seamed face.

"And what about the journalist, Miss Penelope?" he asked, backing to the door. "He's wanting to see her ladyship."

"A journalist! You didn't disturb my aunt, did you, Dawson?"

"No, Miss Penelope. I took the liberty of ascertaining from Sweetings that her ladyship was not herself this morning."

"Thank you." Distractedly Penelope wound one of the short curls framing her face around her finger. "You had best show him in here. I'll find out what he wants."

"He's a reporter for *The Times*, Miss Penelope. Undoubtedly he wants to report on the theft of the opals."

"Oh, very well. I'll tell him what I know."

Against her will, Penelope was intrigued by the notion of being interviewed by a newspaper reporter. They were wily fellows she had heard, and not above twisting words to suit their own purpose.

She sat up, straightening her shoulders, when Dawson returned to announce the man from Fleet Street.

"Mr. Julian Rutherford."

chapter TWO

The Honorable Julian Rutherford's first impression when he stepped into the narrow room was of a pair of large, dark eyes widening in surprise.

What had she expected? A gaunt, bespectacled scarecrow of a man—or a sleazy, snaky type of fellow? Well, his reception was no worse than his father had prophesied it would be in the homes of the rich and the noble.

He strode toward the desk. "Beg pardon for intruding upon you, miss. I hoped to be able to speak with Lady Belmont for just a few minutes. Perhaps you can intervene for me?" Julian revealed white, even teeth in a smile reputed to be utterly irresistible to the frailer sex.

Penelope felt an unfamiliar warmth invade her body as clear gray-green eyes studied her and the rugged features of the tall, muscular intruder lit up in a disarming grin. So unlike her notion of a reporter! He looked as though he should be wielding a rapier at Angelo's rather than a pen in Fleet Street.

Just in time, she exerted pressure on the corners of her mouth, which wanted to respond all too spontaneously to his grin. She extended a slender hand across the desk. "How do you do, Mr. Rutherford. I'm Penelope Langham, Lady Belmont's niece."

Her voice—full and rich, almost husky—surprised him. Her delicate looks had led him to expect higher, clearer tones. Her handshake was firm but brief.

"Undoubtedly you were informed by our butler that my aunt is indisposed. I assume you have come about the theft of the Belmont Opals, Mr. Rutherford?"

"I have, Miss Langham." Julian's eyes followed a beam of sunlight that dipped in the window and onto her hair, painting it the color of honey in a glass jar. "I have only a very few questions. Perhaps if I were to return this afternoon, Lady Belmont—"

"There's no need to come again, Mr. Rutherford. Pray take a seat. I'll do my best to answer your questions satisfactorily."

Julian shifted his gaze to her face, admiring the shape of her mouth with its most kissable lower lip. "Will you sup with me, Miss Langham?"

The enticing mouth grew prim. There was an infinitesimal pause before she said stiffly, "Questions pertaining to your business at Belmont House."

"Ah, yes. The burglar business." Quite unabashed, Julian whisked a chair closer, sat down beside the desk, and crossed his long legs encased in immaculate fawn pantaloons. He pulled a wad of paper from his coat pocket, flicked the sheets open, and laid them on the shiny mahogany surface. "Do you have a pen I might use, Miss Langham?"

Again her eyes widened. They were a deep dark brown, he noted, and fringed by long, curling lashes. Most unusual and absolutely charming with her warm peach complexion and light brown, gold-tipped ringlets.

In fact, Miss Langham was a stunner. A diamond of the first water! Julian moved still closer to the desk, admiring her straight little nose and the elegant curve of chin and throat as she leaned to open one of the drawers.

She directed a haughty look at him when she handed him the pen, a look calculated to put him in his place. "Dawson mentioned you're from *The Times*, Mr. Rutherford. Shouldn't a reporter be just a little better equipped for an interview than you are?"

Julian grinned. "He should. And generally *this* reporter is, Miss Langham. It so happens that it's my day off, which every other week I spend in Bow Street. I transcribe the magistrates' reports of recent crimes into understandable English so that they may be published in the *Hue and Cry*. You have heard of the police gazette, Miss Langham?"

Penelope shook her head. She was fascinated by his voice, which, no matter how mundane a statement he made or how impertinent a question he posed, always sounded as though it caressed the listener.

"The *Hue and Cry* was established in 1786 by one of the Bow Street magistrates. In each issue are published brief accounts of the examination of suspects at all the police courts and of crimes committed, together with a description of goods stolen and of suspected or escaped thieves. Hence my knowledge of the theft of the Belmont Opals."

"And does this police gazette help with the apprehension of criminals, Mr. Rutherford? Thieves in particular?"

"It does if the thief tries to sell the stolen goods to an

honest shopkeeper who reads the *Hue and Cry*." Julian picked up one of the ham sandwiches sitting temptingly close to him on an elegant, gold-edged platter. "It is a different matter altogether," he said after he had swallowed a bite, "if the thief can rely on one of his accomplices to fence the goods for him."

"You mean they'll remove the opals from their setting," Penelope said, "and sell them separately so that no one will recognize them"

"It could mean that. Or the fence might sell the jewels to a foreign buyer. Or both." Julian pushed the platter closer to Penelope. "Here, have a sandwich, Miss Langham. They're quite good."

Penelope blinked, dazzled by the brightness of his smile, and reached for one of the dainty triangles of white bread.

As Julian expounded on the different methods used to dispose of stolen goods, Penelope ate and listened, drawn by the magic of his voice into a world of London about which she knew nothing. He spoke of thieves, robbers, pickpockets; of fences, receivers, and pawnbrokers; of courts and alleys in Seven Dials where even the Bow Street runners did not dare penetrate.

Between them they made short shrift of the sandwiches and shared a smile as they both reached for the last one. Penelope broke it in half and passed a portion to Julian.

"I'll order more," she said, then hurriedly withdrew her hand when his fingers brushed hers and her skin started to tingle as though she had come in contact with one of Sir Humphry Davy's electrical contraptions at the Royal Society.

"No, thank you. Not for me," Julian said politely. "But your tea must be cold."

"So it is." Penelope looked at her cup as though surprised to see it sitting on the desk. "I'll ring for a fresh pot and another cup."

Julian, whose beverage generally consisted of ale or wine—depending on the time of day—inclined his head. "I would appreciate a cup of tea, Miss Langham."

While they waited, Penelope showed Julian the list she'd been trying to compile. "As you see," she said, "my aunt and I left the house shortly after nine o'clock last night and did not return until almost two. Hunter, our groom, drove us and was, of course, away from Belmont House for the same length of time. My aunt gave the rest of the staff the night off."

"Are those the times of the servants' departures and returns?" Julian asked, pointing to two columns of numerals.

"Yes." Again the thought flitted through her mind that his hands—strong and tanned from some kind of outdoor activity—looked more suitable for the pursuit of gentlemanly sports than the writing of dull newspaper reports. "The last of the servants to leave the house was Arthur, our second footman. He went across the square at eleven-thirty and waited for his girl at the side entrance of Gunter's where she is employed to wash the cutlery. Arthur walked her home at midnight. They saw nothing unusual when they left Berkeley Square.

She pushed her notes a little closer to him, but Julian was more interested in the young lady herself than in her accounting of the servants' activities. He counted four freckles on the tip of her nose. They, and the short curls tumbling about her face, gave her the look of a little girl with the naughty habit of escaping from her governess. Yet her manners were those of a self-assured lady.

"No one was left in the house, then?" he murmured absentmindedly as his eyes lit upon a fifth freckle.

"Oh, yes." Penelope hunted for her handkerchief, which she felt quite certain, she had tucked into the sleeve of her gown. "Miriam, the scullery maid, was sleeping in her attic room."

"I hardly think she would have heard anything," Julian said dryly. "If nothing else can be said about the homes in Berkeley Square, their attics are sound."

Penelope wondered how a reporter would have knowledge of the houses in this distinctly aristocratic square. A clandestine visit with a comely maid?

Very much aware of Mr. Rutherford's eyes still on her, Penelope tried to concentrate on her notes. What could be the matter with her nose that he stared so? And where the dickens was her handkerchief?

"Sweetings, my aunt's dresser, stayed at home, as did

Maurice, our French chef," she continued. "They played backgammon in the housekeeper's sitting room until the Dawsons, our housekeeper and butler, returned at a quarter to one. They were the first to return to Belmont House."

Having made his own notations on one of the sheets of rumpled paper he had spread on the desk, Julian said, "That leaves about an hour and fifteen minutes when no one was coming or going. Are the Dawsons quite certain of the time?"

"Mrs. Dawson reported that the hall clock struck just as she and her husband crossed the kitchen passage."

Julian sat back in his chair to better observe the varying expressions flitting across her face. "I don't suppose she could have been mistaken?"

"Not Mrs. Dawson." Penelope kept her eyes firmly on her notes. "She's very observant, and if you think she might have indulged in a little drink while she was out, you may safely put that notion from your mind. Dawson—yes. He likes a glass of port or brandy now and again; but not Mrs. Dawson."

At that point, they were interrupted by Dawson himself bringing in the tea. "Lady Margaret has arrived, Miss Penelope," he said as he placed the tray on the desk.

When Penelope only nodded and started to speak to the reporter again, Dawson cleared his throat and, after a baleful look at Julian, said, "Lady Margaret has gone to sit with her ladyship, and I thought you might wish to make certain her ladyship don't overtire herself, Miss Penelope."

Penelope raised a finely arched brow. "I'll go up a little later, Dawson. Mr. Rutherford and I have not yet concluded our business.

"Very well, miss," the butler replied, and busied himself with the teapot, a task that he would generally not lower himself to perform. "May I remind you that you promised her ladyship to bear her company in the event that Lady Margaret made a visit?"

"Thank you, Dawson. You may go. I'll pour myself."

Julian's lips twitched. When the butler's shuffling footsteps had receded on the stairs, he said, "I believe he doesn't trust me, Miss Langham. It goes sadly against the grain with him that he must leave you unprotected in my contaminating presence.''

Penelope regarded him thoughtfully. ''What might I catch, pray tell?''

''Oh, for instance, my profligate ways might rub off, or you might catch my reprobate manners.''

''I haven't noticed anything amiss with your *manners,* Mr. Rutherford.''

''I'm on my best behavior for the nonce.'' Julian, his eyes filled with mischief and laughter, accepted the cup she offered him. ''And I promise not to continue in my profligate ways. No more outrageous invitations to supper, I swear!'' he said, enjoying the delicate blush spreading across her face.

Not until I'm certain of your acceptance. The thought, fleeting though it was, took Julian by surprise. There was little chance he'd issue another invitation to the young lady.

''Let's return to your list before the redoubtable Dawson thinks of another excuse to remove you from my presence. Did you note anything else of significance, Miss Langham?''

''Ah . . . yes.'' Penelope lowered her gaze to the sheet of paper before her. *What's the matter with you!* she scolded herself. *Staring like a moonstruck halfling! No wonder he always looks at you as though he's greatly amused.*

And Dawson's interference! His transparent excuses! As though Margaret Cleve-Abbots would ever tire Aunt Sophy! More likely their outspoken neighbor would coax Auntie out of her fit of despondency. Why, then, did Dawson . . . ? After all, he never behaved this way when Penelope's long-time suitor Gilbert Bromfield sat with her and bored her for hours with details of his delicate health.

Only once before, when she was sixteen, had Dawson been quite that obvious with his disapproval and his attempts to oust her visitor. That visitor had been Harry Swag, the dashing, gambling, and yes, womanizing captain of the Prince of Wales's own hussars, Penelope remembered. And she had believed herself desperately in love with him.

Penelope felt a wave of heat rush into her face. This time Dawson presumed too much! She had been a naive schoolroom miss then, and besides, Mr. Rutherford was a reporter. After this interview, their paths would never cross again.

She took a sip of tea and realized she had not added any sugar, and neither, apparently, had she answered Mr. Rutherford's question, for he said a little impatiently, "What else did you find, Miss Langham?"

Gathering her wits and dignity, she said, "Yes, here it is"—quite as though she'd spent some time looking for it—"Sweetings's statement. She is Lady Belmont's dresser and went upstairs at one o'clock to place a hot brick in my aunt's bed."

Penelope glanced up and met Mr. Rutherford's eyes. He was still watching her in that disconcerting way of his.

"A hot brick in the middle of May? Why would she do that?"

Penelope raised her chin. "Lady Belmont has a very sensitive constitution. When she's been out at night, she has trouble falling asleep. She finds that a hot brick at her feet is very soothing."

He held up his hands as though warding off her displeasure. "I believe you, Miss Langham! And that's when the woman discovered that the opals were gone?"

"Yes."

"We must assume, then, that they were taken between the time"—Julian briefly consulted his notes—"Arthur left the house and the Dawsons returned. Between eleven-thirty and a quarter till one. Was anything else taken from the safe?"

"The opals weren't in the safe," Penelope confessed. "The case was sitting in plain view on my aunt's dressing table." She saw Mr. Rutherford's jaw drop, but he said nothing, merely scratched a notation in his bold, almost illegible hand.

"How do you suppose the thief—or thieves—got in?" she asked.

His black brows climbed until they touched the shock of unruly dark hair that kept falling onto his forehead. "Don't you know? Surely signs of forced entry were found on one of the doors or windows."

"If they were, Mr. Rutherford," she said stiffly, "the Bow Street runner neglected to tell me of his findings."

Julian's lips twitched. "Theobald Dare got under your skin, did he? Give him time, Miss Langham. Mr. Dare is one of the more perspicacious runners I've known—and I've met them all. If anyone will, he'll catch the thief."

"We shall hope your confidence is not misplaced, Mr. Rutherford. Well, if that's all?"

Julian looked into the brown eyes that gazed at him so coolly—just as though the companionable interlude had never taken place at all. Something stirred in him. It might have been regret that once he left Belmont House he'd have no excuse to call on her again. Mayhap it was pique at her reserve.

She wasn't so damned stiff when she listened to my tales of crooks and thieves, he thought, then warned himself to be careful. This was a young lady of quality, Lady Belmont's niece she had told him—and unmarried to boot. Just the type of young lady he had learned to avoid. And yet—

There's something about this one that makes her an irresistible challenge. A guinea to a gooseberry that I can break through her reserve!

"There is, unfortunately, no guarantee that Dare will catch your thief," Julian said. "Not even a good chance. Unless—" He shook his head. "No, I don't suppose you'd even consider it."

"Consider what, Mr. Rutherford?"

A flash of emerald green appeared in his eyes. Then it was gone, and a pair of quite commonplace gray-green eyes looked at her with a definite challenge in their depth. "The notion popped into my mind, Miss Langham, that we might form a team to catch the thief ourselves."

Startled, she opened her mouth to protest, but all she actually said was, "Oh, dear," as Lady Margaret Cleve-Abbots's strident voice preceded that lady along the corridor.

"Now let's have a look at that rag-mannered, nosy reporter you've been complaining about for the past twenty minutes, Dawson," Lady Margaret said. "See if I don't send him on his way with a flea in his ear!"

Then Lady Margaret stood in the open door. Where Lady

Belmont was plump, Lady Margaret Cleve-Abbots was majestic. Her iron-gray hair was topped by a mannish, gray felt hat, and her wide frame was encased in a severely cut gown of the same drab shade. She raised a lorgnette to her eyes, and through it the magnified orbs stared at Julian.

He promptly rose, bowing with an appreciative grin on his face.

"Julian Rutherford!" Lady Margaret exclaimed. "Had that bumbling Dawson told me it was you, I would never have gone upstairs to see Sophronia. What are you doing here, you scrapegrace? Trying to seduce the child?" Her pugnacious chin pointed at Penelope, but her eyes, now that she had removed the lorgnette, peered at Julian with affectionate appraisal.

"Handsome as ever, you young devil!" Lady Margaret muttered. She sailed toward one of the chairs, seating herself in the manner of one determined not to be routed for quite a while and addressing Penelope with the informality of long acquaintance. "Well, child? What have you to say for yourself? You threw the faithful Dawson into quite a pother when you thwarted his attempts to oust Rutherford."

Penelope's initial mortification was replaced by annoyance at Lady Margaret's meddling. "How do you do, Lady Margaret? But I need not ask. You appear to be in fine fettle."

She glanced from her neighbor to Julian and back to Lady Margaret again. "You and Mr. Rutherford have met? When your home was burglarized last month?"

Julian's smile deepened. "We've known each other longer than that, haven't we, Lady Margaret?"

"Hrrumph! Knew you when you were still in leading strings." Lady Margaret turned piercing eyes on Penelope. "And he was a scapegrace even then! The hens wouldn't lay for a week after one of his visits, and the maids were in hysterics after only five minutes of his company. 'Twas when we lived at Cleve Court for the most part of the year, and his mother used to bring him along when she made the rounds. Let it be a warning to you, Penelope!"

Wide-eyed, Penelope gazed at Julian. An obstreperous child, making the rounds of the local mansions with his mother? Was his mother a seamstress? A midwife? A vicar's wife?

Julian, meeting her look with a mischievous twinkle in his eyes, resumed his seat at the desk and turned to the dowager marchioness. "It had quite slipped my mind that you were robbed as well, Lady Margaret," he said. "How did they get into your house? That was the question puzzling Miss Langham and me in this robbery, and we had not arrived at a satisfactory conclusion when you came in."

"Must have had a key to my home, the demmed gallows bait! No door was forced, no window broken, and they took the silver service. The one Queen Anne gave my great-grandmother when my ancestress found herself in an interesting condition and had to resign her position as lady-in-waiting." Lady Margaret scowled. "Could have forgiven almost anything, but not the theft of my heirloom silver! I'll see the louts swinging on Tyburn for that. I'll have them drawn and quartered!"

Penelope blinked. "That's the punishment for traitors, not thieves. Dear Lady Margaret, please calm yourself."

"Afraid I'll succumb to the lure of laudanum as well?" The dowager marchioness snorted. "Never fear, Penelope. My constitution is made of sterner stuff than Sophronia's. Shouldn't pamper her so much, child. Let her face up to her responsibilities for once! And so I told her to her face."

With difficulty Penelope kept her voice calm. "We're boring Mr. Rutherford, Lady Margaret. Personal details can be of no possible interest to him. And now, if you will excuse me, I must check on Mr. Dare's progress."

"The Bow Street runner?" asked Lady Margaret. "Your footman was taking him to the attics when I went up to Sophronia's room."

Penelope remembered Ben's anger the night before. She rose and stepped around the desk. "I had better hurry."

"Allow me to go with you, Miss Langham." Smoothly Julian got to his feet. "We're partners in crime now, aren't we? And I'd like to ask Theobald Dare if he has found anything."

"Partners in crime?" Lady Margaret said in scandalized tones.

"Short for 'partners in solving a crime.' What did you believe, Lady Margaret?" Julian said reproachfully.

The protest Penelope had been about to utter before the dowager marchioness entered the library was forgotten. She smiled at Lady Margaret. "We're going to recover Aunt Sophy's opals," she said. "Pray excuse us."

Feeling inexplicably happy and carefree, Penelope left the book room with Julian following close behind. Partners in crime . . . Perhaps, for a short while, there could be some spice in the staid, humdrum life she led for her aunt's sake.

Her pleasant feelings lasted until they reached the topmost floor, where Mr. Dare, having finished his search of the attics, stood arguing with Ben and Sweetings. Could the staff never meet Mr. Dare without snarling at him like a pack of hounds?

"But it is my dooty," the battered and harassed-looking Bow Street runner said obstinately.

"Over my dead body!" Arms akimbo, Sweetings took a threatening step toward the runner.

Mr. Dare raised a fist, swathed in a large handkerchief, and shook it in the air. "I've had my fingers cut to the bone by mousetraps! Whoever heard of mousetraps among the wine bottles! I've had my life endangered by rafters falling in the attic, but"—he lowered his voice to a booming whisper—"I shan't be swayed from the path of dooty!"

Ben crouched in the manner of a pugilist. "Come on then," he crooned as he danced on the balls of his feet. "Come on! I'm just itchin' ter put ye through yer paces. Put up yer deuces!" he ordered, swinging his fists dangerously close to the runner's ample midsection. "Puny, lily-livered prattlebox! Put 'em up, I say!"

"Ben."

At the sound of Penelope's cool voice, Ben dropped his hands. Blushing furiously, he spun and faced her. With some difficulty he resumed the more dignified manner and speech befitting the first footman of a noble household. "Miss Penelope, this here Bow Street runner wants to search milady's rooms now," he said indignantly.

"Over my dead body!" Sweetings repeated.

"Go to your mistress," Penelope told the abigail, "and

help Lady Belmont dress. I give you thirty minutes, Sweetings.''

With a dour look on her face, the abigail turned on her heel. She knew very well that Miss Langham was as good as her word. If Lady Belmont wasn't dressed in half an hour, her niece would have no compunction about dismissing the faithful servant from her aunt's rooms and assisting the dowager countess herself.

"Come, Theobald," said Julian, slapping the runner on his muscular shoulders, "you might as well search the first floor instead. Have you found anything yet?"

"Nay, sir. It's just like all them other burglaries. No sign of forced entry."

"Others!" Penelope looked sharply from Julian to the runner. "Were there more? Besides the robbery at Lady Margaret's?"

"As I were saying, miss, they weren't no robberies as such. No violence, not as much as one door forced and—"

"You didn't tell me!" Penelope looked accusingly at Julian.

"That's why I suggested our little partnership, Miss Langham," Julian said smoothly. "I'm planning to make a list of all the previous burglaries to show you tomorrow. It's Carlton House to a Charley's shelter that we'll find some clues."

Frowning, Penelope followed the Bow Street runner, who edged past the scowling Ben and started down the stairs. Whichever way she looked at it, Mr. Rutherford's explanation was not a very satisfactory one. Even if he didn't have all the information at his fingertips, he could at least have mentioned the other burglaries—especially after Lady Margaret reminded him of the theft of her heirloom silver set!

She turned her head to observe the man beside her and encountered such a whimsical look of mingled plea and apology that she felt herself blushing as though it had been she who was found out in some neglect.

The rueful look changed to a dazzling smile. "It is agreed then, Miss Langham? We'll meet tomorrow morning."

They had reached the foot of the stairs. From the corner of her eye, Penelope saw the runner tiptoe into the Chinese drawing room. Ben had disappeared long ago. She was very much aware of Mr. Rutherford's presence, an aura of strength and power and a certain daredevil air surrounding him, to which her adventurous spirit, so long repressed, responded instinctively.

Those same qualities she had admired in her father, and they had drawn her to Harry Swag, she reminded herself. The heady excitement of a burglar hunt mustn't betray her into doing something rash or foolish!

"*I* may be able to make time for *you*, Mr. Rutherford, but what about you? Shouldn't you be at work for *The Times* tomorrow morning?"

"Naturally I shall be working for *The Times*, Miss Langham. Don't you think it would make an excellent article? 'Lady and and Reporter Catch Dastardly Thief.' Or should it be, 'Lady and Reporter Solve Mysterious Burglaries'? In any case, it's all in the line of—"

" 'Dooty,' " Penelope finished for him.

The appreciative gleam in his eyes drew an answering smile from her. Sternly Penelope reminded herself to beware of his charm, which must be considerable if as a brash village lad he had come to be on familiar footing with Lady Margaret, a very high stickler indeed!

"Good day, Mr. Rutherford." Penelope inclined her head in cool dismissal. "I shall expect you tomorrow at nine o'clock."

"I shan't disappoint you, Miss Langham!"

He gave her a cocky, two-fingered salute, the way she had seen jarveys greet each other, but with him it brought to mind the way a Corinthian would touch his whip handle to the brim of his hat. Then Julian Rutherford descended to the foyer two steps at a time.

chapter
THREE

A Corinthian! What an odd comparison to draw.

Penelope stood on the first-floor landing and stared at the oaken staircase as though she could still see his tall, muscular figure bounding down the steps.

A man rounded the newel post in the foyer below and started up the stairs. For an instant, Penelope's heartbeat quickened—but it was only Dawson.

"Miss Penelope," he said when he reached the top, and from the tone of his voice she could tell that he was steeling himself to give her a lecture or a scold. "That reporter said"—Dawson took a deep breath, necessitated partly by the exertions of the climb, partly by indignation—"he said you'd be seeing him again tomorrow!"

"Yes, indeed. Mr. Rutherford and I are planning to put our heads together and see if we can't catch the thief."

"That, Miss Penelope, is the work of the Bow Street runners!"

"And so you may tell the staff, Dawson! In particular, warn Ben that I won't tolerate any more mousetraps among the wine bottles, or falling rafters in the attics." She raised a brow. "How on earth *did* he make a beam fall?"

"I wouldn't know, Miss Penelope. About Mr. Rutherford—you know that her ladyship won't be down at nine o'clock. I'll ask Mrs. Dawson to chaperon you."

The butler bowed and started to shuffle down the corridor toward the stairs leading to the west wing of the second floor, where Lady Belmont had her rooms.

"Dawson! I believe I'm old enough to conduct a business

meeting without the benefit of a chaperon, and I'll thank you not to embarrass me again in front of Mr. Rutherford," Penelope said, catching up with the old retainer.

Dawson had a way of being silent and yet conveying his disapproval more eloquently than mere words could express. Penelope read the signs easily—an almost imperceptible lift in his already haughtily arched brows, the pinched nostrils of his long, thin nose, and the disdainful downward curve of Dawson's prim mouth. In fact, Dawson was becoming starchier than a governess.

"Really, Dawson! If you could have heard yourself! Your excuses to remove me from the library were the flimsiest—" Penelope broke off. A bubble of laughter threatened to escape her when Dawson's cool disapproval changed to outrage. "Oh, what's the use? You'll do as you see fit, no matter what I say."

"Someone has to look after you," the old man said severely. "Seeing as her ladyship is poorly again and in no shape to leave her chambers! And that someone has been me ever since you rode in Hyde Park dressed in a pair of Hunter's breeches!"

Penelope laid her hand on his arm. "If you would only look at me, properly look at me, Dawson," she said coaxingly. "I am fifteen no more! I am a staid old maid now, rather long in the tooth and quite settled down."

"You're a beautiful young lady, Miss Penelope. And Mr. Rutherford, if I may say so, does not strike me as one to know his place."

Penelope agreed cordially. "He's quite outrageous, I know. But again you forget, Dawson, I am a schoolroom miss no more. I can deal with Mr. Rutherford."

"You may think you're up to snuff, Miss Penelope, and able to handle anything that comes your way, but the truth is you've no more notion how to look after yourself than a newborn babe!"

Penelope drew herself up. "Just because I don't mix with the younger set doesn't mean I don't know how to deal with gentlemen. And don't forget Mr. Bromfield. He has given me plenty of opportunity to master the art of a polite yet firm set-down."

"There's gentlemen, and there's *gentlemen*," Dawson muttered darkly.

Deep inside, Penelope had to agree, for there was something very disturbing about Julian Rutherford and the thought of a second meeting with him. "Oh, véry well! If it'll make you feel better, I'll arrange further meetings with Mr. Rutherford at an hour when Aunt Sophy or Maria Hilbert can be present."

"Miss Hilbert is a sensible lady," Dawson acknowledged, "but Lady Elizabeth Howe ain't one for giving her companion time to visit you. And what about tomorrow, Miss Penelope?"

A mischievous twinkle appeared in her eyes. "I doubt not you'll find a reason to enter the library at strategic intervals. And now, will you please see if my aunt has left her rooms? Mr. Dare would like to complete his tour of inspection."

Admitting defeat, the old retainer shook his head as he continued to Lady Belmont's rooms.

Penelope turned left to slip up the east stairs to her own room and a much needed nap. She had one foot on the bottom step when Lady Margaret, bored with her own company, emerged from the library.

"If Sophronia isn't prepared to come down and entertain me properly," said the formidable old lady, "I might as well go home. Really, Penelope, I don't understand why you permit your aunt to take such large doses of laudanum that she can't rise from her bed!"

Penelope felt the blood drain from her face. Slowly she turned. "Lady Margaret! You can't mean to imply that I encourage Aunt Sophy in her habit!"

"No, child. Of course I mean no such thing."

"If you had seen Aunt Sophy after she heard of the theft—" Moving toward her aunt's friend, Penelope raised her face and squarely met the older woman's troubled look. "Aunt Sophy was hysterical," she said in a quiet voice.

"And when Sophronia loses her composure, she gets one of her frightful headaches and must have laudanum. I understand, child. She has been like that ever since Henry died. I believe she has never forgiven him for leaving her to cope with all manner of unpleasant affairs."

Penelope nodded. "If I don't measure the dose for her, I'm afraid . . . I'm afraid she might take too much. As she did six years ago."

Lady Margaret took a deep, rasping breath. "So you know about that incident. Thought we had hidden it from you. You were but a child then."

"I was seventeen! Old enough to know better, but I never stopped to think."

"What are you talking about, child?" Lady Margaret sank down upon one of the chairs strategically placed, along with the occasional, ornately carved and gilded small table, against the walls between the various doors.

"The scandal, Lady Margaret!" Penelope started to pace along the corridor. "When I made such a cake of myself over Harry Swag!"

"What utter nonsense! There was no scandal!"

"But Auntie feared there would be, and so, to forget, she took laudanum. Too much."

"Sit down, Penelope," Lady Margaret said sharply. "You make me giddy, and when I'm giddy I can't think."

Penelope ignored the request. As though it were yesterday she remembered Sweetings's panic when the woman was unable to rouse Lady Belmont from her laudanum-induced sleep. Penelope suffered again the agonies of fear and guilt as she had suffered during those long hours outside her aunt's door, locked against her by Sweetings and Dr. Wise.

With a swish of skirts, Penelope turned and started back toward Lady Margaret. "I almost caused Auntie's death," she said in a tightly controlled voice. "I can never forgive myself for that."

"Thunder and turf," Lady Margaret uttered weakly.

Then, as she realized she had found the answers to several questions that had puzzled her for years, she raised her lorgnette and stared at Penelope. "And believing that, you changed overnight from a mischievous, adorable imp into a model of propriety and started to mother your own aunt," she said, horrified. "You withdrew from your friends— you even refused to have a come-out! Great Scot! If only I had known."

Her iron-gray brows drew together in a fierce frown.

"And what lunkhead was so considerate to lay the burden of guilt upon—Never mind, child! It was Sweetings, wasn't it? And Sophronia's spiteful daughter-in-law."

"Yes, it was Drusilla. And it was the only decent act she ever performed."

"Despicable!" Lady Margaret's voice grew more strident as the enormity of what she'd just learned dawned on her. "First of all, let me make it clear that the overdose was accidental."

"How can you know that?" Penelope cried.

Lady Margaret gave a snort. "Sophronia and I have been friends for more years than I care to own. I know her as well as I know myself. Believe me, child, no one can lay that unfortunate incident in *your* dish! It was all Drusilla and Henry's doing."

Penelope did sit down then. "Henry?" she asked numbly. "Aunt Sophy's son?"

"The same."

"But—why?"

"Your aunt had suffered some heavy losses at the faro table. Thirty thousand pounds to be precise. And Sophronia's dutiful son threatened to have her declared mentally unfit to administer her own accounts."

Penelope sat quite still, seemingly unmoved by what she had learned, but inside she felt as though she had passed from bitter winter into midsummer. A bright, glowing warmth touched the guilt stored in her heart and melted away painful memories.

Watching Penelope, Lady Margaret said, "All these years, child! You must have felt awful! Why did you not speak about it?"

"How could I, Lady Margaret? I was quite aware that Aunt Sophy wanted it kept from me. I believed at the time that she wished to protect me, that she didn't want me to know how much I had hurt her."

"But you hadn't! Sophronia knows that young girls make mistakes. After all, she raised a madcap daughter of her own." After a slight pause, Lady Margaret said insistently, "You were *not* responsible, Penelope. Drusilla lied to you."

"Yes," Penelope said in a low voice. "Drusilla lied. And

Henry,'' she added, her eyes blazing in sudden anger. ''He must have devastated Aunt Sophy! Mentally unfit! What a cruel thing to say!''

''Thirty thousand pounds boggled his mind, I daresay. Boggled mine, too. But Sophronia hasn't been near a faro table in years. Her game now is silver-loo or whist. Nothing wrong with that.''

Lady Margaret rose and tugged on the folds of her gown in a decidedly militant manner. ''However, Sophronia must be made to realize the folly of taking that opiate. I shall speak to her again. Gracious! The many times I scolded her already! Do you remember, Penelope? A few months before your twenty-first birthday your solicitor and Sophronia's lawyer both believed there was no way they could fight the Crown for your inheritance.''

''Papa had left such a mess of debts and investments.''

''And Sophronia guzzled laudanum as though it were tea!''

''But finally the court granted me control of my fortune. Thank God!'' said Penelope. ''There's no telling what would have happened to Aunt Sophy otherwise.''

''Nothing would have happened, child. I had a nice little chat with Dr. Wise. Told him I'd make certain none of his patients would call him again if he didn't reduce Sophy's supply.'' Lady Margaret drew herself up. ''It is time to have another talk with the old quack!''

''No,'' said Penelope, the light of battle in her eyes, ''let me speak to the doctor!''

Penelope parted from Lady Margaret and went up to her own room just as her aunt and Dawson descended the west stairs. She could hear them talking about Theobald Dare, and then Lady Margaret's voice drowned out Sophy's and Dawson's softer tones.

''Let us take a bite of luncheon now, Sophronia. A bit of food and a glass of wine will make you feel much more the thing,'' Lady Margaret said bracingly.

Penelope hesitated, wondering if she should go to her aunt. But Lady Margaret was there. Her old friend would be better company for Sophy than an utterly exhausted niece, who desired nothing but solitude and rest.

The bright sunshine that had awakened Penelope earlier

no longer penetrated through the windows of her chamber. The four-poster bed, hung with cream-colored silk drapes, beckoned with inviting dimness. Penelope took off her gown and in her petticoats slipped between the sheets.

Nancy had placed several sprays of white lilacs in a brass urn on the mantel. Their fragrance filled the room, sweetly soothing.

Relaxing, Penelope snuggled deeper into the soft pillows. She thought about her aunt—quite possibly Sophy could be cured from her laudanum addiction.

Quite possibly recovery of the opals would help Auntie!

A smile tugged at the corners of Penelope's mouth. It would be exciting and no mean feat if she and Julian Rutherford were to beat Mr. Dare to the thief.

How Maria Hilbert would stare when she learned of Penelope's intention to catch the jewel thief! But how to arrange a meeting? Penelope hadn't seen her friend in weeks, and she missed Maria's quiet companionship. She must think of something that would persuade Lady Elizabeth Howe, Maria's crotchety employer, to give her companion an afternoon off.

Still grappling with the problem, Penelope finally fell asleep only to be awakened, moments later it seemed, by the opening of her bedroom door.

Nancy poked her head into the chamber. "Are ye awake, then, Miss Penelope?" she asked, bouncing inside. "An' did ye 'ave a good lie-down?"

"Thank you, Nancy. I feel quite rested," Penelope lied.

"An' will ye be ridin' this afternoon, Miss Penelope, or shall I lay out t' new sprigged muslin?"

Penelope swung her legs over the edge of the bed. "The muslin, please."

She went to the washstand and splashed cool water into her face while the maid bustled about the room, tidying and straightening up. Nancy's mouth was as busy as her hands. Penelope tried in vain to block out the shrill young cockney voice as she again searched for an excuse to lure Maria away from Lady Elizabeth. Nancy's next words, however, caught her full attention.

"An' Maurice said as 'e would sleep with the meat

cleaver under 'is pillow tonight," the maid said with wide-eyed awe. "Imagine 'im bein' that afeared! But 'e thinks we'll all wake up murdered in our beds as long as them pesky thieves can walk in an' out of 'ouses as they like."

"Keys," muttered Penelope. "Hurry with those buttons, Nancy. I must see Dawson immediately!"

"Just what I been thinkin', Miss Penelope. Now do turn around an' 'old still, if ye please!"

Penelope controlled her impatience while Nancy did up the row of tiny buttons on the back of her gown and tied the pale blue velvet sash in a bow, but when the maid picked out a matching ribbon for her hair, Penelope shook her head and started for the door. "No time for such fripperies, Nancy. I have too much to do."

And indeed, the afternoon passed in a rush of frenzied activity. After a brief consultation with Dawson, Hunter was dispatched in Lady Belmont's elegant town carriage to fetch Mr. Samuel Abel, the locksmith, from Fetter Lane. Penelope herself supervised the master smith and his apprentice while they installed new locks on the front and back doors. Then Mrs. Dawson called upon Penelope to speak to Rachel. The maid, saying the theft had upset her, was doing slipshod work and, to boot, had dropped a plate of Lady Belmont's Sevres dinner service.

Finally Sophy herself required Penelope's assistance. A search had to be made of Sophy's private desk for some insurance papers her late husband had implored her to keep in a safe place. After a feverish hunt, Penelope at long last retrieved the document from beneath a pile of unpaid bills that had been stashed at the very back of a drawer.

Penelope scanned the pages, filled with legal clauses and restrictions that seemed to have the sole purpose of giving the reader a pounding headache.

"Uncle Henry insured this house and its contents—including the Belmont Opals, your pearls, and your diamonds—against loss through fire," Penelope said finally. "I'm sorry, Auntie. There's no mention of theft. In fact, I don't believe you can purchase insurance against theft."

"As though I cared a jot about money," Sophy said, her eyes filling with tears. She looked small and lost in the large armchair behind her desk. "All I want is my opals, and that stupid Bow Street runner can think of nothing better than to search my own house!"

"We may not have to depend on Mr. Dare alone, Auntie."

Hope flickered in Lady Belmont's eyes. "Did the magistrate assign more runners to the case?"

Leaning against a corner of the handsome walnut desk, Penelope admitted, "Well, no. Not that I know, Aunt Sophy. It's Mr. Rutherford, you see. He promised to help."

"Rutherford? The name sounds familiar. Let me think—"

"He's the reporter from *The Times*, Auntie. You must remember that I told you of his visit."

"Oh. The reporter."

Lady Belmont sounded so disappointed that Penelope had to smile. *Just wait, Auntie, until you meet the dashing reporter! Until you see the lithe grace with which he moves. The shock of dark hair falling onto his forehead . . .*

Lud! Those characteristics would not be a recommendation in Aunt Sophy's eyes. And if she learned that he had asked Penelope to sup with him!

Penelope's wayward thoughts dwelled on a pair of gray-green eyes that could startle her with a disturbing gleam, and on strong, tanned hands whose fleeting touch could set her skin atingle.

Catching Sophy's puzzled look, Penelope resolutely banished Mr. Rutherford from her mind. She could not, however, stop a rush of color to her face. Fanning her cheeks with one of Sophy's bills, Penelope said, "Could you ask Lady Elizabeth to tea, Aunt Sophy? I haven't seen Maria in ages."

"Of course I will," Sophy said in quick sympathy. "I expected to find Maria at the ball last night. And so did Mr. Rugby, but Elizabeth no doubt had the poor thing sit at home, doing some wretched accounts."

"Mr. Rugby should know better than to expect generosity from Lady Elizabeth. He's fortunate to be working for Mrs. Welby. But listen, Auntie." Penelope pushed away from the desk and went to stand beside Sophy's chair. "There's something else I should like to talk about. Something Lady Margaret—"

With a jerk, Sophy thrust her chair back and rose. "It can

wait until the morrow, can't it, dearest? I'm afraid—I'm afraid I have one of my headaches coming on."

She pressed a shaking hand against her forehead and fled into her adjoining bedchamber. Before Penelope could recover from her astonishment, Sweetings appeared in the connecting doorway.

"My lady must have absolute quiet, Miss Langham. I'll let you know when my lady is ready to see you again," she said, relishing her position, which for once gave her the upper hand over Lady Belmont's niece.

Slowly Penelope left her aunt's sitting room. Obviously, Lady Margaret had made some mention of her conversation with Penelope, and Sophy felt unable to discuss her dependency on laudanum. But the time would come, Penelope felt certain, when she and Sophy could talk. With the burden of guilt lifted off her shoulders, Penelope felt equal to any task, even a battle with Dr. Wise, that sinister man who wielded such power over her aunt.

But first the opals! Recovery of the jewels would ensure Sophy's happiness and make it easier for her to forgo the solace of the opiate.

Inevitably, thoughts of the opals brought Julian Rutherford to mind, and the exciting chase they would give the jewel thief.

A tingle of anticipation raced over her skin. Anticipation, she admitted, that was not caused by the prospective jewel hunt alone. Mr. Rutherford himself had a great deal to do with it.

Dash it, Penelope! You told Dawson you were a schoolroom chit no more, yet you indulge in fancies like a green girl. Your meeting with the dashing reporter is a matter of expediency. Nothing more!

On the following morning, keeping the purpose of Julian Rutherford's visit firmly in mind, Penelope chose a long-sleeved gown of somber moss-green hue, cut severely and without embellishments except for a lace Bertha around the modest scoop neckline. Gazing at her austere appearance in the cheval glass, she smiled with satisfaction. She felt prepared to meet even the most dazzling smile, the most outrageous remarks, with cool dignity.

Shortly before nine o'clock, Nancy brought word that Dawson had shown the reporter into the library. Penelope nodded and, after one last look into the mirror, walked briskly from the room. The large clock in the foyer was booming the full hour when Penelope swept into the library.

Julian rose. He looked at the no-nonsense gown, and an appreciative gleam lit up his eyes. "How delightfully, ah, efficient you look this morning, Miss Langham."

"Good morning, Mr. Rutherford. Pray be seated." Penelope slipped into the deep leather chair behind the desk. "Thank you for being on time," she said, placing her elbows on the desk and steepling her fingers the way she had seen her solicitor do when he wished to indicate that the preliminaries of polite chitchat must be at an end. "Were you able to copy the complete list of thefts?"

"Yes, indeed, Miss Langham." He resumed his seat close to her desk, affording her an excellent view of his hawklike profile while he whipped out the same wad of papers he had carried during their last meeting. Again he spread the sheets on the polished mahogany surface; only this time they revealed neatly written, dated accounts of burglaries instead of the scratched notations he'd made during the interview with her—which, she suspected, were on the reverse side.

Julian watched her eyes narrow a little, and prepared himself for an accusation and a demand for an explanation, but she only turned the papers to a more readable angle for her.

"Which one was the first, Mr. Rutherford?" she asked in her charmingly husky voice.

"This one." His long finger tapped on the heading, January 18, 1818. "A pearl necklace was stolen from Lady Spatterton in Mount Street. Then, on February fifteenth, three valuable paintings were taken from Lady Arbuthnot's home in Grosvenor Square."

"I know," Penelope muttered, trying to ignore the disturbing nearness of his hand. "One Reynolds and two Romneys. Lady Arbuthnot told me." She looked at the next entry and read, "March seventeenth, a diamond brooch and a large sum of money taken from Mrs. Gertrude Welby's safe. Bruton Street."

"Then we have Lady Margaret Cleve-Abbots, your neighbor, whose heirloom silver service was taken on April sixteenth, and your aunt, whose opals were stolen on May nineteenth."

Penelope looked up with a frown. "I knew of several of these thefts," she said, "and I certainly am acquainted with all of the ladies, but until now I never realized——Why, it looks as though the thieves are preying on affluent, elderly ladies. All of them widowed!"

Julian nodded. "None of the houses showed signs of forced entry, and if you discount Mrs. Welby's broken safe, there was none of the deliberate destruction that thieves so often leave behind when they have searched the drawers and closets."

"And look at the dates." Penelope dipped a pen into the inkwell and wrote a neat column. "The dates are all about a month apart. And there is something disturbingly familiar about them."

"All but one of the ladies were out, attending some function or other, at the time of the burglaries," Julian said after consulting his notes. "Only Lady Spatterton was entertaining at home when her pearl necklace was taken."

"January eighteenth," Penelope murmured. She opened the wide center drawer of the desk and withdrew the engagement calendar she kept for her aunt. In a moment she found the entry she wanted. "Yes, I thought so. It was the day of Lady Spatterton's card party. She holds one every third Sunday of the month."

Julian raised a brow. He watched with delight as Miss Langham's composure slipped and a delicate blush tinted her cheeks.

"It is all very respectable," she said. "The stakes are no higher than a penny a point, I assure you."

"But on a Sunday, Miss Langham?"

Her chin went up. "Does White's or Brooks's Club close its gaming tables on a Sunday, Mr. Rutherford?" she asked, and immediately wished she could retract the words. Mr. Rutherford would hardly have entrée to those strictest of gentlemen's clubs where members only could gain admission.

"My aunt and I attended Lady Spatterton's party in

January," she continued in a cool and dignified manner, "as did Lady Margaret and Mrs. Welby. On February fifteenth, when Lady Arbuthnot's paintings were stolen, Lady Arbuthnot, Lady Spatterton, Mrs. Welby, Lady Margaret, my aunt, and I all attended a dinner at Lady Elizabeth Howe's home in Brook Street."

"What, no gentlemen were present at the dinner?"

"Of course there were gentlemen. And also Miss Barbara and Miss Helena Twittering, and—"

"Thank you, Miss Langham. For the nonce we had best concentrate on those ladies who have been visited by our thief. It seems to me—" Julian leaned across the desk, again placing his hand next to hers on the papers. He slowly moved his index finger from one date to the next, brushing his palm across her knuckles.

Penelope felt as though she had been touched by fire. Quickly she withdrew her hand to the safety of her lap, just as Dawson appeared in the doorway with a tea cart laden with plates of sandwiches and small cakes and a large silver coffeepot.

Grinning, Julian leaned back in his chair. "Your hospitality is exemplary, Miss Langham. And Dawson, it seems, fully understands the value of a timely entrance."

His back stiff with disapproval, the butler looked at Penelope.

She nodded. "You may go, Dawson. We'll help ourselves." She waited until Dawson had left before addressing Julian again. "Forgive the interruption, Mr. Rutherford. You were saying?"

"It seems to me that we must look for the thief among those persons who would have prior knowledge of the ladies' movements."

"Someone who would have access to the keys of the house," Penelope said.

"Someone like a friend, a servant, a secretary or companion."

"A daunting prospect." Penelope looked at him with troubled eyes. "The list will be a long one, and it will include names I'd be loath to have come to anyone's ears."

"I hope you don't mean to imply that I would divulge

any names before our investigation is concluded," he said,
and for a moment he looked as dangerous as Penelope's
papa had looked when he believed his honor slighted.

"No, I don't," Penelope said. And she meant it. Julian
Rutherford might not be a part of her own social circle, but
he was a gentleman nevertheless. "So you needn't fly into a
huff, Mr. Rutherford."

The grim expression was wiped out by his dazzling smile.
"Let's get started," he said, holding his pencil poised.

For an hour they worked, listing every person Penelope
could remember seeing on those five dates, and with every
minute that ticked by, Julian felt her earlier reserve melt.
Caught up in the spirit of the burglar hunt, Miss Langham
was as warm and friendly as he could wish. Only he didn't
really wish for friendliness. He was rather hoping for
something a bit more thrilling, but it was early days yet.

While they refreshed themselves with lukewarm coffee
and sandwiches, they whittled down the depressingly long
list of names to those that appeared repeatedly.

"It doesn't make sense," Penelope said finally. "Only in
January the burglary took place while the guests were on the
premises. How could any of these people we listed have
taken Mrs. Welby's brooch and money from the safe while
they attended Lady Jersey's rout?"

"Accomplices," Julian pointed out. He got up and walked
about the narrow room to stretch his legs. "Come for a
drive with me, Miss Langham," he said abruptly. He pointed to the window. "It's too lovely a day to stay cooped up
inside."

Julian knew instantly that he had made a mistake. He saw
the stiffening of her shoulders and a reappearance of the
reserve that their work had so successfully banished.

"Thank you, Mr. Rutherford. How kind of you, but I'm
afraid I must decline."

"Tomorrow then," he said recklessly. "You can point out
the houses that were burglarized." He could see that she
was about to decline again when he heard the butler's
shuffling footsteps approaching. *Perfect timing, old fellow!*
"There's Dawson again. Coming to evict me, no doubt."

Penelope was sufficiently distracted to leave her refusal

unuttered. "What is it?" she asked when Dawson appeared in the doorway.

Dawson's mouth stretched in a smile. He positively beamed at her. "Mr. Bromfield has called, Miss Penelope."

A sensation of gloom settled over Penelope. More than half willing to deny herself to Gilbert Bromfield, she looked at Julian. But Mr. Rutherford would press his invitation for a drive, and she'd really rather not share the intimacy of a carriage with him!

She was about to decline his second invitation as well when he said, "I won't take up any more of your time, then, Miss Langham. I'll call for you in my carriage at—let's say ten o'clock tomorrow morning?"

He sketched a bow, then quickly left the library.

"Wait!" Penelope jumped up and rushed after him. "I didn't . . ." *I didn't say I'd drive with you,* was what she had planned to say, but she swallowed the rest when she heard his voice drift up the stairs to her.

"Don't bother," he said, and she could have sworn that he was laughing. "I'll see myself out."

Penelope trailed back to the library. What a shabby trick to play on her! But, oh, so smoothly executed! Her lips twitched, but under Dawson's reproving frown she soon assumed a grave mien. "And where have you put Mr. Bromfield?" she asked resignedly.

"He is with her ladyship in the small salon."

"I'll just tidy myself a bit, Dawson. Tell Mr. Bromfield that I'll see him in fifteen minutes."

The bulter bowed a dignified approval. It was, after all, only right that Miss Penelope should want to present herself to her suitor looking her very best, he mused as he made his slow way to the salon at the other end of the first floor.

Penelope whisked up the sheets of paper she and Julian had so diligently covered with endless lists of names and carried them to her room. From the back of her wardrobe she dragged a miniature sea chest given to her by her parents on her seventh birthday—so that her dolls might travel in style—and into it she placed the incriminating papers. She locked the chest, then threaded the tiny key onto the gold chain she wore around her neck with her parent's likenesses in a gold locket.

The remainder of her fifteen minutes Penelope spent reclining in a chair by the fireplace. She stared into the empty grate, preparing herself for the ordeal of a visit with Mr. Gilbert Bromfield. She had known him for almost five years. He was ten years her senior, a well-meaning man of placid disposition—and, oh, so ponderous and boring! And Gilbert was working himself up to his fifth proposal of marriage! A proposal a year—each one refused so far. But she was getting no younger. Mayhap she should . . . ?

The high lace collar of her gown seemed too tight suddenly. Marriage to Gilbert—she didn't want to think about the possibility! Penelope rose and started for the door. After all, she had endured so many of his visits, she could face one more.

chapter
FOUR

Penelope stood for a moment in the open door of the small salon. Sophy and Gilbert Bromfield were seated near the windows, their chairs turned slightly toward each other and Sophy's favorite Sheraton satinwood table between them. So engrossed in conversation were they that they had not noticed Penelope's arrival.

How heavyset Gilbert was! Penelope's eyes widened, and she studied him as though she were seeing him for the first time.

Compared with Julian Rutherford's dark magnificence, Gilbert was unimpressive. His rather florid countenance did not offset his drab brownish-blond hair or his lackluster hazel eyes. Not once had she encountered a gleam of emerald in Gilbert's eyes—or a gleam of *anything*! Where the planes of Mr. Rutherford's face appeared to be chiseled by a master's hand, Gilbert Bromfield's round chin and round jowls must have been shaped by a dispirited apprentice.

Compared to Julian Rutherford—

Startled by the impropriety of her thoughts, Penelope stepped forward, greeting Gilbert with more cordiality than she would ordinarily have done.

"Penelope!" Beaming, he led her to a chair near her aunt, then drew his own chair closer. "How charmingly you look, my dear. A delightful gown!"

Penelope smoothed the demure folds of her moss-green skirt. She smiled, remembering Mr. Rutherford's "delightfully, ah, efficient," and the gleam in his eyes—as though he quite understood why she had chosen her most severe and unadorned gown.

"I take it you heard about the opals, Gilbert?"

"Yes, indeed. A horrible business!" Gilbert leaned closer. "My valet had to dose me with one of his special elixirs when I learned of it. An exceptional man, my Harvey. He takes excellent care of me, I assure you."

Gilbert's hand covered Penelope's in what he undoubtedly meant to be a comforting gesture, but she was aware only of the clamminess of his soft palm. So unlike the electrifying sensation Julian Rutherford's fingers evoked with their touch!

She pulled her hand away, careful to keep it out of Gilbert's reach.

"Penelope?" Sophy looked searchingly at her niece. "Are you feeling quite the thing, dear?"

"It's the theft," Gilbert Bromfield declared. "The horrifying experience of returning to a burglarized home would overset the strongest constitution. Made her jittery, no doubt."

"The 'horrifying experience' took place two days ago, Gilbert," Penelope pointed out. "Even if I had been overset then—which I wasn't—it would not take me two days to recover."

"My niece isn't such a namby-pamby miss that she must be coddled like you," Lady Belmont said indignantly. "Why, Penelope has great strength of character—"

"Yes, indeed. Too much at times," said Gilbert, primly

pursing his fleshy mouth and quite oblivious to his companions' indignant looks. "But not all of us can claim an iron constitution," he rambled on. "I for one did not feel sufficiently restored until this morning to undertake a drive in my closed carriage. I came instantly," he said, bowing to the dowager countess, "to offer my condolences to you, dear Lady Belmont."

"I'm honored," Sophy muttered.

"If there's anything I can do for you, ma'am, anything at all in your hour of despair, don't hesitate to call upon me for assistance," Gilbert said earnestly. "Not that my delicate state of health permits—"

"Don't worry, Gilbert," Penelope interrupted, "we shan't need to call upon you. Everything is being taken care of."

"Ah, yes." He allowed himself a little smile. "Your dear aunt was telling me that a runner is investigating the matter. Very efficient chaps, these Bow Street runners."

He pulled a large gold watch from his waistcoat pocket, snapped open the lid, and peered shortsightedly at its face. "Past noon already!" he exclaimed. "Penelope, my dear, if I'm to be home in time for my luncheon, we had best go on a very short drive only."

"I don't recall having agreed to go for a drive with you, Gilbert! And definitely not in your closed carriage. Not on a day like this!" Penelope motioned her hand toward the window where bright sunshine highlighted the cabbage-rose pattern in curtains of Brussels lace and the whisper of a May breeze rippled the sheer fabric.

With a pang of regret, she remembered her refusal of Mr. Rutherford's invitation to take her for a drive. Surely he wouldn't have expected her to languish inside a closed carriage. What type of carriage *did* he drive? she wondered. Or was a reporter obliged to hire a vehicle?

Gilbert Bromfield's voice broke into her musings. "Oh, but Dawson said—did he not say, ma'am," he asked Lady Belmont in some confusion, "that Penelope was wishful of taking a drive?"

"Dawson takes too much upon himself," the dowager countess said. "Now, Mr. Bromfield, if you don't wish to displease your chef and your valet, you had best be on your way.''

Gilbert Bromfield lumbered to his feet. "Yes, indeed, ma'am. Harvey understands my delicate system. Knows just what's good for me. My dear—" He bowed over Penelope's hand, squeezing it delicately between both his moist palms. "I'll send over some tincture of Valerian root which Harvey blends with several of his secret ingredients. Mix a spoonful in a glass of barley water and drink it this afternoon and again before you retire. You'll be in fine fettle on the morrow, you'll see," he assured her gravely.

Penelope withdrew her hand. "Spare yourself the trouble, Gilbert. I have no need of your valet's brews, nor, I might add, would I ingest such quack medicine were I indeed feeling poorly. Good day to you.''

Lady Belmont barely waited until the door had closed upon his portly figure before saying, "As if it weren't bad enough that we cannot deny him entrance, now we must suffer his patronizing ministrations as well! If it isn't just like Henrietta to have such a pompous gudgeon for a grandson.''

Penelope's eyes danced. "Auntie," she said in mock reproof, "I believe you're still put out by Henrietta Spatterton's wearing the turban you coveted.''

"Now there you're wrong!" Sophy shot a triumphant look at her niece. "I'm going to have my own turban made at Balena's this very afternoon. Lavender with a silver plume! Would you care to go with me and help chose the material?''

"I am sorry, Aunt Sophy. I—"

"You have some urgent correspondence to deal with. I quite understand, dear," said Sophy.

It was not the first time that Penelope had declined an invitation to accompany her aunt to the modiste or to a milliner. Penelope appreciated fashionable apparel as much as any lady. She was, however, lacking the requisite love of fingering and discarding bolt after bolt of luxurious materials to enjoy the hours Sophy would wish to spend in the tiny establishment that had become all the rage during the past few months.

After luncheon, therefore, Lady Belmont ordered her carriage and set out for Balena's Hat Shoppe at the corner of Oxford and Quebec streets. Penelope settled herself with a book in the front parlor, but for once the delightful collection of letters from Constantinople written by Lady Mary Wortley Montague failed to capture her full attention. And it wasn't even that her mind drifted on memories of her own travels with her parents!

With the slender volume in her hands, Penelope stared blindly at her aunt's collection of Dresden figurines in a glass-fronted cabinet while names from Mr. Rutherford's list of suspects filled her head.

He had named every servant of the households visited by the thief, from Miriam, the young scullery maid, to Benjamin Rugby, Mrs. Welby's trusted agent. Why, Mr. Rutherford had even included Penelope's friend Maria Hilbert simply on the grounds that Maria was Lady Elizabeth Howe's companion and had accompanied the same to Lady Spatterton's card party in January! Any one of the servants, or one of the more impecunious friends of the widowed ladies, Mr. Rutherford insisted, could have slipped off and nabbed—

Now why did that preposterous word of thieves' cant stick in her mind? Mr. Rutherford's vocabulary was not one she should strive to emulate. In any case, none of Aunt Sophy's friends, no matter how straightened their circumstances, would nab or steal, and then smilingly face the victim across the dinner or the card table! Not Miss Barbara or Miss Helena Twittering. Not—

The sound of the door knocker was a welcome distraction. Company, even if it were a second visit from Gilbert, would be preferable to the suspicions Mr. Rutherford had sown in her mind.

It was not Mr. Bromfield, however, whom Arthur, the second footman, addressed in haughty tones. "H'I regret to h'inform you, Dr. Wise, but 'er ladyship h'ain't in."

"Then, my good man, have the kindness to deliver this to her ladyship's maid," the doctor replied.

Penelope's book flopped unheeded to the floor as she jumped up and rushed out into the foyer. "Dr. Wise!" Snatching the wrapped bottle from Arthur's gloved hand, she thrust it back at the cadaverous-looking man who stood in the front door. "My aunt requires your services no longer, Dr. Wise."

"My dear Miss Langham." His voice was smooth and thick as oil, but his eyes pierced her with dagger looks. "I'm afraid there must be a misunderstanding. I am but responding to your aunt's urgent plea for more of my restorative."

"And I tell you she won't need any more of your poppy syrup! I must request you to leave, Dr. Wise. And don't bother to return!"

"You'll change your tune fast enough, miss, when your aunt screams for release from her agony. And suffer she will if she isn't supplied with her daily dose, mark my words!"

Dr. Wise turned on his heels and like a vulture in a black frock coat retreated to his carriage, content to wait for a more propitious moment to peddle his wares.

"Arthur, that man is not to be admitted again."

"Yes, Miss Penelope. But h'if 'er ladyship sends for 'im?"

With a heavy heart, Penelope said, "I'll see to it that she won't, Arthur. And do not accept any of his medicines. They are very harmful."

"H'I know, miss. H'opium." Nodding sagely, he closed the front door, then returned to his chair by the wall, where he stood stiffly at attention until Penelope had gone into the front parlor.

Absently Penelope picked up her book and smoothed a creased page before setting it aside, her mind busy with the new problem facing her. If only Aunt Sophy were willing to discuss her addiction—or the need to find a new physician. If only Sophy wouldn't shut her out when she broached the subject of Dr. Wise's elixir.

When Sophy returned from Balena's, she was bubbling with happiness. The new turban she had bought was all the crack! It would completely cast Henrietta Spatterton's into the shade!

Penelope did not have the heart to spoil her aunt's mood. She waited until that night when Sophy had retired and

Sweetings had withdrawn to her own quarters before confessing that she had shown Dr. Wise the door.

Sitting on the edge of Sophy's bed, Penelope said, "I did not accept the laudanum he brought, Auntie, and I told him never to come again."

For a moment, Sophy's expression was quite blank, as though she did not comprehend Penelope's words, then her face puckered and she burst into tears. "First Margaret. Now you!" she said between sobs and hiccups. "Why, Penelope?"

"You don't need Dr. Wise's elixir, Aunt Sophy! I want you to give me whatever laudanum you have left."

"I can't, Penelope! It's too painful. Please leave it here in my room! I must have it during the night!"

"Please try! For my sake as well as your own!"

Something flickered in Sophy's eyes, but Penelope could not recognize the fleeting expression, drowned as it was in a new spate of tears.

Finally Sophy nodded. "Take it, then," she said, and turned her face away.

Feeling elated and guilty at the same time, Penelope rose. "Thank you, Aunt Sophy. Call me if you wake up. I'll sit with you."

She took down the bell pull that summoned Sweetings to her aunt's bedside and attached it to the lever that was connected to a small bell in her own room. This had been installed a few years back when Lady Belmont suffered from a severe attack of bronchitis and Penelope had helped nurse her aunt.

"Good night, Auntie. Sleep well, and God bless."

Weary, Penelope prepared for bed and fell immediately into a deep, dreamless slumber. She came awake with a start, only minutes later it seemed. She lay in the dark, motionless, listening. Yes, there it was again. A scraping sound as of a drawer being opened or shut, then the rustle of stiff fabric dragging on the floor.

Someone was prowling in the small dressing room adjacent to her bedchamber!

Noiselessly Penelope slid her legs out from under the cover and sat up. She fumbled for the tinderbox on her bedside table, but when she turned her head toward the dressing room, she saw she had no need of her candle. The door was ajar, and through the crack shone a wide sliver of light.

"Aunt Sophy," she called. "Why didn't you ring for me?"

After a moment of breathless silence, Lady Belmont stumbled out of the dressing room. Her face matched her ivory-colored silk dressing robe, and her mouth was trembling.

"Where is it?" she asked, her eyes darting about Penelope's chamber. "Where did you hide it?"

With some difficulty, Penelope coaxed the distraught woman back to bed. Throughout the long night, she sat with her aunt, talking or reading, or simply holding her in her arms. She made numerous trips down to the kitchen to warm up milk and honey—even milk and a drop of brandy—then taking it up to her aunt along with hot bricks for Sophy's feet. To no avail.

Sophy grew more and more fretful, until at five o'clock, fearing an attack of hysteria, Penelope promised to fetch a spoonful of Dr. Wise's elixir.

In her own chamber, Penelope unlocked the doll chest. She took out the bottle of laudanum, measured half a teaspoon into a glass of water, and carefully relocked the chest. She looked with loathing at the contents of the glass in her hand. "I'll beat you yet," she whispered. "Just you wait and see!"

Finally, when her aunt had dropped off to sleep, Penelope crept back into her own bed. It was not surprising that Nancy, when she carried up a cup of chocolate at eight o'clock, found it rather difficult to rouse Penelope.

"Lovely mornin' it is, Miss Penelope," the maid said cheerfully as she looped back the drapes, allowing bright sunshine to flood the room.

"Go away, Nancy."

"Cor, Miss Penelope. Are ye sickening?"

Penelope's eyes flew open. No, she wasn't sickening, but she must find a physician for her aunt! "Nancy, lay out my blue dimity gown, then fetch me something from the breakfast parlor. I need to go out this morning, and I'll just have a bite to eat up here.''

As soon as the maid had left the room, Penelope removed the list of suspects from the doll chest and tucked it into her reticule, then measured a small dose of laudanum for her aunt. A half hour later, she knocked softly on Lady Belmont's door. Sweetings opened it a crack and peered out.

"Her ladyship's asleep," she whispered angrily.

"Please step into the corridor, Sweetings. I wish to speak with you."

Briefly Penelope explained to the abigail how she was trying to help her aunt. "But I need your assistance, Sweetings. Here is a small measure of laudanum. Give it to Lady Belmont if you must, but try to make it last until afternoon when, I hope, the new physician will call on her.''

The abigail took the glass Penelope held out to her. "But her ladyship never had no problem with Dr. Wise's medicine," she said defensively, "and she doesn't usually take anything during the daytime.''

"No, Sweetings? Then pour it out," said Penelope, and under her steady gaze the abigail's eyes flickered uncertainly, then shifted to the floor. Without another word, Sweetings turned and disappeared into Lady Belmont's bedchamber.

Penelope stared at the closed door, asking herself if she was doing the right thing. Perhaps she should not have interfered. After all, for much of the time, when nothing upset her, Aunt Sophy seemed to have the habit under control.

Penelope turned on her heel. No matter how right or wrong her actions, if she didn't get a note off to Mr. Rutherford soon, he'd show up expecting her to go for a drive with him.

In the library, she quickly spread out a sheet of writing paper, dipped her pen in the inkwell, and then sat there, frowning, while the ink dried on the nib.

She must see Julian Rutherford again soon if they were to help Bow Street find the thief, or better yet the opals. That would certainly cheer Aunt Sophy!

First, however, she needed a few days to resolve the laudanum problem. Quickly, before she might change her mind, she dipped her pen and started writing. *Mr. Rutherford, I find myself unable to meet—*

The library door opened after a most perfunctory knock. Julian Rutherford stood in the opening. "I thought I'd find you here, already hard at work," he said with a grin.

He closed the door, and with that simple act the room seemed to shrink to half its size. His presence surrounded her. She felt his energy as he strode toward her and pulled up his chair. The masculine scents of shaving soap and the blacking on his highly glossed Hessians teased her nose, and his deep voice sent a tingle down her spine.

"You're early," she said accusingly. "And where's Dawson? You should have let him announce you."

"Your footman tried to tell me the same thing, but I convinced him that I could find my way alone. Were you planning to deny yourself to me, Miss Langham?"

Penelope feared that she was blushing, but she forced herself to meet his quizzing look. "As a matter of fact, I was just writing you a note. Some circumstance has arisen that prevents me from meeting with you for a few days, Mr. Rutherford. I will let you know when I'm free to continue our investigation."

"Your pen is dripping, Miss Langham. I'm afraid I cannot read what you started to write to me, except for *Mr. Rutherford*. No *dear* Mr. Rutherford?"

Penelope picked up the sheet of paper and crushed it in her hand. "There is no need for you to read it since I already told you that I'll be busy for a few days," she said, tossing the wad into the wastebasket. "And now, Mr. Rutherford, since you let yourself in, you may see yourself out."

Julian made no move to rise. He was not about to miss two or more days of her company. She was such a delightful surprise, this Miss Langham, and he wondered why she wasn't married or at least betrothed, and why he hadn't met her before—five or six years ago, when he had still been mixing with the younger set of the London *ton*.

"Perhaps I can help you," he suggested.

Penelope shook her head. "I'm afraid not. This concerns my aunt."

The smile that played about his mouth disappeared. He said nothing, merely looked at her. Again Penelope felt that, no matter what his station in life, he was a man who could be trusted.

"I must find a physician to replace Dr. Wise," she said.

He raised one dark brow. "The opium peddler. So that's why Lady Margaret was concerned. How long has he been 'treating' Lady Belmont?"

"At least eight years. Probably quite a bit longer."

"Then there's no time to be lost."

"Aunt Sophy generally takes the laudanum in very small doses. Only lately—"

"You don't have to explain, Miss Langham," Julian said gently. He rose. "Fetch a shawl, and I'll drive you to a friend of mine. Peter Ludlow was an army surgeon. He has helped many of the poor devils who became addicted to laudanum during their recovery from amputation."

Swept along by his decisive manner, Penelope stepped out into Berkeley Square a few minutes later. Her eyes widened, for there, in the sun-dappled shade under the plane trees, stood a curricle drawn by a pair of magnificent bays. No job-horses these! If they indeed belonged to Mr. Rutherford, he must have spent a pretty penny on them, and on the curricle as well.

Julian helped her into the seat, tossed a coin to the boy who had been watching the bays for him, and swung himself up beside her. With a flick of the reins he set the horses in motion.

For several minutes Penelope reserved judgment on his driving skills, even clung to the side of the carriage as they whisked around slower-moving drays and fourgons in busy Piccadilly, but finally she had to acknowledge that Mr. Rutherford was an expert whip. If he weren't a reporter, surely he'd be offered a membership in the Four-in-Hand Club. Penelope relaxed and settled back in the well-upholstered seat.

"Enjoying yourself?"

"Yes. I am now." She turned her head, meeting his amused glance. "How was I to know that you can drive?"

"Never underestimate a man, Miss Langham. And speaking of underestimating, have you heard from Theobald?"

"Mr. Dare hasn't seen fit to show himself since he turned the house upside-down in his search."

"No doubt he's taking a few sparring lessons before he faces your plucky footman again."

"That's all very well, Mr. Rutherford, but I rather wish he'd look for the opals." Penelope frowned. "I know Lady Margaret's silver service was not recovered, and neither were Lady Arbuthnot's paintings. But what about the other items? Have the Bow Street runners recovered any of the stolen goods?"

"None. That's what makes me believe they've been sold across the Channel just as soon as they were taken." Judging to a nicety a gap in the oncoming traffic on the Strand, Julian turned his horses to the right onto Waterloo Bridge.

Becoming aware of her surroundings, Penelope asked, "Where does Dr. Ludlow live?"

"Just yonder, in Narrow Wall."

Penelope drew a ragged breath, but before apprehension and doubts could overcome her, Julian Rutherford laid his hand over hers. "You're doing just as you ought," he said.

Penelope gathered warmth and strength from his confidence, and after a while she turned her hand palm-up to be held in his in a firm yet gentle clasp.

Dr. Ludlow owned a tall brick building at the corner of Waterloo Street and Narrow Wall. He had transformed three of the spacious ground-floor rooms into a dispensary, but when the maid took in Julian's card, the physician sent word that he'd see them in his study on the first floor.

Penelope barely had time to pace twice between the window overlooking the cobbled street below and the fireplace on the opposite wall before the doctor's hurried footsteps sounded in the corridor.

"Well, Julian!" he boomed as he entered, filling the doorway with his wide shoulders. "And with a lady! What a surprise."

Dr. Ludlow listened calmly to Penelope's account of her aunt's laudanum addiction, then looked at her with a smile and a twinkle in his clear gray eyes. "Well now, Miss Langham, that's a problem I'm well equipped to tackle. Would you like me to call on Lady Belmont?"

"I'd appreciate it, but"—Penelope returned his look steadily—"my aunt may not."

He chuckled. "I am not easily intimidated, Miss Langham. And now, if you have no questions, I'll get back to my patients. Influenza. Always strikes the poorest first—and the hardest."

"You'll come to see my aunt this afternoon?" Penelope asked anxiously.

Dr. Ludlow nodded his large, shaggy head. "Or early evening. Depends how long I'll be needed at St. George's Hospital. I'm glad you came to me, Miss Langham. I'll help your aunt, never fear."

Penelope returned to Belmont House much buoyed by Dr. Ludlow's assurances. "Won't you come in and take some refreshment, Mr. Rutherford?" she asked as Julian brought the curricle to a halt in Berkeley Square.

"If I find someone to walk the bays."

An urchin appeared at the horses' heads before he had quite finished speaking, and with a pleased grin Julian handed Penelope down. "I don't know where they hide," he muttered, "but, thank goodness, they always pop up when they're needed."

"I believe these little boys smell where they can earn a penny. I'm convinced, however," Penelope said with a chuckle, "that you'd have found a way even if he hadn't popped up. You look like a man who'd do anything for a draft of ale." Briskly she rapped the knocker against the gleaming brass plate.

"No tea today?"

"That was thoughtless of me, wasn't it? I should have known that a man prefers—Oh, good morning, Dawson," she greeted the butler, who had come to open the door. "Is Lady Belmont down yet?"

"Her ladyship is in the Chinese drawing room with Lady Elizabeth."

Penelope turned to Julian. "Will you come up and meet any aunt, Mr. Rutherford?"

"My pleasure, Miss Langham." Slowly Julian followed her up the stairs and into the drawing room.

At first he saw only the red and gold opulence of the chamber, the claw-footed, dragon-headed furniture, and the many precious jade ornaments. Then he noticed two elderly ladies huddled in deep, comfortable chairs before the fireplace. Their eyes skimmed over him before fastening onto Miss Langham.

"Penelope, my love!" the plump, silver-blond lady cried. "You can have no notion—something absolutely awful has happened!"

chapter
<u>FIVE</u>

*P*enelope's eyes darkened with apprehension. Rushing across the expanse of ivory and gold rugs, she said anxiously, "You look pale, Aunt Sophy. Are you . . . did you . . . ?"

"No, dear." A tremulous smile curved Lady Belmont's mouth. "I'm in fine shape. It's Elizabeth who has distressing news."

Thank God, Penelope thought, *not a laudanum crisis!*

Lady Elizabeth Howe, a tall, dark-haired, stern-faced former beauty, stiffened her already straight back. "Outrageous news!" she said icily. "Maria Hilbert has been arrested."

"Beg pardon, Lady Elizabeth. What did you say?"

"You heard quite right, Penelope," the old woman snapped. "Miss Hilbert was arrested. This morning. By a Bow Street runner calling himself Theobald Dare!"

"The very same runner," Lady Belmont interjected, "who turned my house upside-down."

"He charged Miss Hilbert with theft and took her away." Lady Elizabeth's narrow face tightened angrily. "The effrontery! As though *my* companion has a need to steal! What on earth am I to do without Miss Hilbert?''

"Dash it, Lady Elizabeth!" Penelope, her mind spinning, pressed her fingers to her temples. "You should be wondering what to do *for* Maria!"

Lady Elizabeth gasped. "Well! I know you entertain feelings of friendship for Miss Hilbert, Penelope. So unsuitable! But I shan't say a word about that. It's your tone of voice I object to. Your language! You can't shout at me, young lady."

Lady Belmont rose to stand at her niece's side. "Penelope does not shout, Elizabeth. And besides, she's quite right. With all your lamentations about the loss of your overworked, underpaid companion, you haven't said where the runner took her."

Grasping this opportunity to remind the ladies of his presence, Julian stepped forward. "He would first take Miss Hilbert before the magistrates in Bow Street, ma'am."

"Mr. Rutherford!" Penelope brightened. Thank goodness she had agreed to his scheme to catch the thief! "Aunt Sophy, Lady Elizabeth, allow me to introduce Mr. Julian Rutherford."

Lady Belmont extended her hand. "You must be the reporter Penelope mentioned to me."

Lifting the plump fingers to his lips, Julian bowed.

"A reporter!" Lady Elizabeth's voice rose, drowning Julian's reply. "Don't say a word to him, Sophy, unless you want to find it twisted and garbled in tomorrow's gossip sheets!"

"Mr. Rutherford works for *The Times*, Lady Elizabeth," Penelope pointed out. "He also collaborates with the Bow Street magistrates on the police gazette."

"Indeed," said Julian, "I am well acquinted with the chief magistrate Sir Nathaniel Conant, ma'am. I can find out—"

"Sir Nathaniel! The blackguard! Why, he's the man who had Miss Hilbert arrested, and without a moment's notice I might add!"

"How inconsiderate," said Sophy.

Hearing the note of sarcasm in her aunt's voice and

observing her trembling hands and pale face, Penelope suggested, "Perhaps Lady Elizabeth should take a drop of brandy, Aunt Sophy, and I did promise Mr. Rutherford some refreshments."

"We could all do with a drop." Recalled to her duties as hostess, Sophy bustled into action, and a short while later the two dowagers sat facing Julian and Penelope. A generous measure of the finest French cognac in exquisite Waterford crystal glasses did much to relax the strained atmosphere in the room.

"Did you accompany Miss Hilbert to Bow Street, Lady Elizabeth? What did Sir Nathaniel say?" Julian asked.

Lady Elizabeth looked startled. "Of course I did not go to Bow Street. However, I sent a footman to inquire what had become of Miss Hilbert. He informed me that Sir Nathaniel examined her and sent her to Newgate Prison."

Penelope's glass slipped from her fingers. For a moment she watched helplessly as a dark amber stain spread across the soft pile of her aunt's precious rug. Then she picked up the glass, set it on a table, and rose. "I must go to Maria. She'll need me."

"Penelope!" Paling, Lady Belmont clasped a hand to her bosom. "You can't—you mustn't go to that dreadful place! I'll send . . ."

"Yes, Aunt? Whom will you send? A footman?"

Julian tossed down the last of his cognac. "I shall see to it that your niece comes to no harm, Lady Belmont. Will you entrust her to me?"

The dowager countess studied him as he stood up, stretching his limbs to their full length. He easily topped six feet, and the muscles rippling under the cloth of his coat and breeches soothed her anxious heart. With him to champion Penelope, the girl would come to no harm even in that awful prison.

Sophy nodded, knowing she wouldn't be able to sway Penelope from her set course. "Guard her well, Mr. Rutherford. I couldn't bear it if Penelope—"

"I shan't leave her out of my sight," Julian promised. With a flourish, he proffered his arm and led Penelope from the room.

Lady Elizabeth's sharp voice followed them. "Penelope!

I came to ask if you would pen the invitations to my soirée, which Maria planned to finish today. The soirée is on the . . .''

But Penelope didn't stop.

"What's wrong with writing them yourself, my lady?" Julian muttered as he and Penelope approached the staircase.

The grim set of Penelope's mouth relaxed a little as she pictured Lady Elizabeth laboring at her desk, but instantly the image was replaced by one of Maria in some dark, stinking hole in the bowels of Newgate.

Descending the last step, Penelope saw Dawson hovering in the hall. "Miss Penelope," he said anxiously, "is it true? Lady Elizabeth's maid is belowstairs, and she told us about Miss Hilbert. A terrible thing, and all a mistake, I'm sure!"

A lump formed in Penelope's throat. "I *know* it's a mistake. I am going to Miss Hilbert now, Dawson, but there's something for which I require your help."

The butler listened attentively to Penelope's brief explanation of Dr. Ludlow's expected visit later in the afternoon. A ray of hope lit up his tired eyes, and his voice was unsteady as he said, "If only it would work—Oh, Miss Penelope, I'll be happy to ask her ladyship to see the doctor when he comes."

"Thank you, Dawson. I hope I'll be back by then, but Miss Hilbert—" She touched Dawson's arm in a gesture of gratitude before hurriedly joining Julian, who had gone ahead to the curricle.

"I apologize for having kept you waiting, Mr. Rutherford. Maria's plight had momentarily driven Dr. Ludlow from my mind. Besides, I wouldn't wish to mention it before Lady Elizabeth, but Dawson will see that my aunt understands the purpose of his visit."

"Peter will know what to say to Lady Belmont, Miss Langham. You need have no fears on that account." Julian helped her into the vehicle, swung himself up beside her, and lightly flicked the reins. The bays responded promptly, and soon they were once again rolling along Piccadilly at a fast clip.

For a while Julian was occupied guiding the horses through the bustle of mail coaches and post chaises leaving or approaching the various coaching inns situated along this busy street, but every now and again he shot a worried glance at Penelope, sitting stiff and silent beside him. Finally, as they approached the Strand, traffic thinned a little. Transferring the reins to one hand, he placed the other over Penelope's tightly clenched fingers. She gave a start, as though he had torn her from deep thought, and turned to look at him.

"I am sorry," she said with an attempt to smile. "I fear I must be dismal company for you, Mr. Rutherford." Gently but firmly she freed her hands from his clasp.

"Miss Hilbert is a friend of yours?"

Her eyes darkened. "Yes. My only true friend."

Trying to hide his astonishment, Julian quickly transferred his attention to the street. Miss Penelope Langham, a beautiful young lady with connections to the highest circles of London society had only one friend? And a companion at that? "Tell me about Miss Hilbert."

"Maria is the sweetest, kindest person I know. She is a little older than I am, and when we first met eight years ago she must have looked upon me as a troublesome little sister in dire need of guidance. She helped me through—"

Penelope caught herself, reluctant to disclose such personal information to a man she had known for only a very few days, and a reporter at that. Yet, somehow, she never felt as though Mr. Rutherford were a stranger, and before she realized what she was about, she said more to him than was prudent.

"Helped you through the briar patches and quagmires of your youth?" Julian suggested.

A gleam of mischief appeared in her eyes. "Those are fairly accurate metaphors, Mr. Rutherford. Your own experiences must have prompted your choice of words."

He heaved an exaggerated sigh. "Dear Lady Margaret! She did me no good turn with her reminiscences of my youthful adventures. Pray remember, Miss Langham, that elderly ladies are prone to exaggeration."

"I shall try, Mr. Rutherford." Penelope gripped the side rail of the seat to avoid swaying against his shoulder as the curricle turned into Old Bailey. They had almost reached the prison. So fast—too fast!

How could she give strength and courage to Maria when she herself felt shaky and confused? She hadn't had time to collect her thoughts, hadn't had time to come up with a plan to free Maria.

The corner of Newgate Street! And there was the prison—huge, stark, and utterly intimidating. The only windows staring back at her were those in the keeper's house in the center of the building; the gracefully arched window openings in the prisoners' quadrants to the right and left were bricked up.

And Maria inside somewhere!

Penelope squared her shoulders and put up her chin. She placed her hand in Julian's and allowed him to help her down. There was no shortage of boys here in front of the prison to hold the horses, and almost before she had time to draw breath, they were admitted into the gloomy interior of the women's quadrant.

A matron, topping Penelope shoulder and head and weighing about twice as much as the young lady, led them in grim-faced silence down a dark passage. The rattle of her keys, footsteps echoing on the flagged stone floor, and the hastily stifled cry of a child were the only sounds to break the oppressive stillness that hung over the place. The stench of cheap food, dirt, and worse closed around Penelope. For the first time in her life, she wished she carried a bottle of smelling salts in her reticule.

Goose bumps raced up and down her spine. She felt her soul shrivel at the sight of small children everywhere. They stood in the open doors of the cells, their huge eyes staring at the visitors from thin, pale faces; they sat or lay motionless on threadbare blankets in narrow, dimly lit cubicles where their mothers were occupied with sewing.

And then, suddenly, the stillness was shattered. Shouting imprecations at the top of her lungs, a woman, followed closely by several other prisoners and a wardress, came storming from a cell ahead.

"To 'ell with Mistress Fry's reg'lations!" the ragged blasphemer shouted. Shaking her fist, she rounded on the wardress. "She may bring us bread 'n rags, but who wants ter pray 'n listen to sermons? Not me, I won't! Gor'blimey! I wants ter sing! Jolly, bawdy tavern songs!"

"Not in here ye won't, slut!" The wardress grabbed the woman's arm and twisted it sharply back and up. "I warn ye, Meg! I'll have ye in chains if ye so much as open yer mouth again!"

Shrieking, Meg tore herself free and started to run toward Penelope and Julian, but the husky matron who accompanied them stepped into her path. A blow from a hamlike fist staggered Meg.

Instinctively Penelope rushed forward. Her hands closed around frail arms. She had no difficulty preventing the woman's fall. The poor thing was as thin as a reed and light as thistledown, and Julian's hurriedly offered assistance was not required.

Unable to tear her eyes off Meg's gaunt face, Penelope slowly released her. Close up, she could see that the prisoner was much younger than she appeared, that, in fact, she was barely past girlhood. Yet her face was old and bitter.

"Are you all right? Can I do something for you?" Penelope asked, compelled by the knowledge that this pathetic creature was, for the time being, Maria's companion in misery.

A look of great cunning flitted over Meg's dirty features. "Oh, aye, miss. If ye gimme an alderman, it'll keep me 'n me babe in vittles fer a sennight."

Penelope threw a helpless glance at Julian.

He reached into his pocket. Without looking at the woman, he tossed her a coin. "An alderman—a half crown," he said to Penelope. "And she's lying. She won't buy food, but gin or ale."

"Thank 'ee, kind sir!" Meg curtsied, then, arms akimbo, pushed out her hip and looked Julian up and down with a leer. "There be an empty cell ahead, sir. With a cot 'n mattress 'n all. Cost ye but a yeller George, or mebbe two."

Julian took Penelope's arm and bustled her off. "Come along, matron!" he said briskly. "Surely the wardress can manage that bundle of bones herself!"

"What'll happen to her?" Penelope asked the matron when she plowed past them to resume her position as guide.

The woman snorted. "A day or two in chains. If that don't help, a good flogging will soon teach Meg the prison code. We'll not allow the likes of her to undo the good brought by Mrs. Fry an' her Ladies Committee. The keeper an' the sheriffs are just waiting for an excuse to take away the cots, the blankets, an' the sewing. An' wouldn't they be pleased to dismiss me an' the other females in favor of male wardens!"

Penelope shivered. If the cold, stark interior of the prison seemed unbearable now, it must have been pure hell before the courageous Elizabeth Fry and her Quaker friends had demanded female guards for the women prisoners.

"How much farther before I can see Miss Hilbert?"

"Just around the corner, miss. The magistrate ordered her put into a cell by herself."

"Oh, thank goodness!"

The matron stopped before a closed door with a small, barred window at eye level. The rattling and clanking as she picked and discarded key after key stretched Penelope's nerves to snapping point. Then, finally, metal grated in the lock. Hinges creaked in protest as the door swung open.

"Fifteen minutes, miss, and not a moment longer!" the matron said harshly, but Penelope paid no heed to the warning. Her eyes were fixed on Maria.

She barely recognized her friend in the stooped woman sitting motionless, half turned away from the door. Maria wore half mourning for her father, who had passed away eighteen months ago, and the gray bombazine of her gown was sadly crushed and stained. Never before had Penelope seen Maria other than impeccably gowned and coiffed, yet now her pale blond hair was in disarray. Several long strands had escaped from Maria's chignon and fell onto her shoulders, obscuring her face. And Maria had done nothing to correct the matter.

Sadder still was to see Maria's shoulders slumped in utter dejection. Graceful Maria, who prided herself on her deportment . . . who did not believe in showing her feelings to the world.

In two quick strides Penelope crossed the narrow expanse of stone floor. She sank to her knees beside the stool while behind her the heavy door swung shut and the key turned in the lock. For a moment Penelope couldn't breathe. It seemed as though the brick walls were moving inward, trying to crush her. Then she felt Julian Rutherford's hand on her shoulder. His touch, warm and ressuring, dispelled her fears.

Penelope wrapped her arms around her friend. "Maria! Maria, look at me! It's Penelope! Oh, my dear, what have they done to you?"

Slowly, Maria's head came up as she turned to face her visitor.

"Penelope," she whispered, her tired gray eyes brightening. A smile curved her pale lips. She looked as though she were about to return Penelope's embrace, but the smile faded, the eyes grew wide and frightened. A dull red spread across her face, then receded, leaving her paler than before.

"You shouldn't have come." Maria tried to move away, but Penelope's arms tightened around her.

"Nonsense, Maria. Of course I had to come. And I'll get you out of here, too!"

"Please go, Penelope!" Maria struggled against an almost overwhelming desire to throw herself into her friend's arms and confess her shame and anguish. "If I had known you'd come to this dreadful place! Oh, this is worse than anything! Please go, Penelope! Go now!"

"Don't worry about me. I am not alone. Mr. Rutherford has accompanied me. Nothing will happen, Maria. And I'll get you out," Penelope said fiercely. "I'll get you out just as soon as I can. I promise!"

Maria's mouth started to tremble. Tears spilled down her blanched cheeks.

"Miss Hilbert"—Julian's voice was warm with compassion—"can you tell us why the Bow Street magistrate felt he had to make the arrest?"

Maria turned her face to the wall and did not reply.

"Maria, tell us what happened," Penelope urged. "Mr. Rutherford and I want to help you, but we must know why you were arrested."

Maria Hilbert did not reply. It was as though she had become deaf and dumb and quite unaware of anything that went on about her.

Hoping to shock or anger her into some kind of reaction, Julian fired question after question at her. "Has someone laid information against you, Miss Hilbert?

"Were you seen at one of the homes at the time a theft occurred?

"Were any of the stolen articles found in your possession?

"Have you come into a large sum of money recently?"

Maria Hilbert remained mute.

"Are you the thief, Miss Hilbert?"

Penelope, still holding her friend in a close embrace, felt Maria flinch. Encouraged by this sign of awareness, Penelope shook her gently. "Tell him, Maria! Tell him he's a presumptuous, insufferable flat if he believes you to be a thief!"

After a moment, Penelope looked up at Julian and shook her head. "They've crushed her spirit. Maria *always* reprimands me when I use a cant expression."

"And so should *I*, Miss Langham. I've been called all manner of things, but never in my life a flat."

Her eyes widened. "I beg your pardon, Mr. Rutherford. You must know I didn't mean it. I merely—" She broke off and grimaced a little ruefully. "And now I'm being the flat."

"Never," he said gallantly.

"For a moment there I believed Maria was reacting to your questions, but"—Penelope shrugged helplessly—"it's as though she's turned to stone. What shall we do, Mr. Rutherford?"

Julian extended his hand to help her up. "I have several plans, Miss Langham. Let's discuss them outside."

Shaking out her skirts, Penelope looked helplessly down at Maria. She heard Julian knock on the door, heard the key turn in the lock and the squeal of the hinges as the heavy door swung open. Her stomach tightened into a painful knot. In a moment Maria would be locked in again—alone in this dreadful place. Something must be done to set her free. Fast!

Penelope gently touched Maria's hair, smoothing it away

from her face. "Nothing's as bad as it seems at the moment. Remember that, Maria. It's what you used to tell me when I was down in the dumps. *Au revoir,* dear friend."

Hoping for at least a glance from Maria, Penelope backed out of the narrow cell, but her hope was in vain. Her last glimpse of Maria as the door creaked shut was still that of a stooped back and bowed head.

Maria stayed thus, motionless, listening to the voices outside her cell. The man was speaking, and the matron. She did not hear Penelope.

When the murmur ceased and she heard footsteps moving away, Maria jumped up from the stool. She flew to the door and pressed her face against the bars. "Penelope," she whispered. "Dearest friend, I'm afraid it is *good-bye.*"

With dry, burning eyes, Maria stared after Penelope. Her tears were spent. She had cried for hours after the matron had locked the cell door this morning, and a few more tears had been surprised from her when Penelope had so unexpectedly come to the prison. Now Maria was done with tears. She had accepted that she wouldn't see her two dearest friends again. Benjamin, dear Benjamin. And Penelope.

She was resigned to her fate—almost. There was still Susannah. But she mustn't think about Susannah. The pain was unbearable!

Just before Penelope reached the bend in the corridor that would take her out of sight, Maria saw the tall, dark gentleman's arm go around her friend. Maria's eyes opened a little wider. Penelope had not even permitted Mr. Bromfield such a familiar gesture, and Mr. Bromfield considered himself as good as betrothed to Penelope. Yet, somehow, it was comforting to see the stranger close to Penelope. . . .

Penelope felt the strong arm encircling her waist, guiding her along the corridor, and she was grateful. Blinded by tears burning in her eyes and throat, she did not see where she was going. She did not see the ragged children she knew to be staring at her, or the dank stone walls, as Julian led her out of Newgate Prison, but when the great, studded door opened before her, it was the sudden brightness that made her head spin.

Julian felt her stumble as they stepped out into the

sunshine and the hustle and bustle of Newgate Street. He noted her wan face and the stricken look in her eyes. Without stopping to think, he pulled her into his arms and cradled her against his chest, wishing to protect her, to soothe away her hurt.

To his astonishment, Miss Langham did not slap his face or fire up at him indignantly. She burrowed into his coat, and her arms fastened around his waist as though she never wanted to let go.

His body responded to her heady proximity with the familiar stirrings of desire; his common sense, however, told him rather sharply that Miss Langham was looking for warmth and comfort, not passion.

Julian was in a turmoil. He had the delectable young lady where he had wanted her since he first noticed her kissable lower lip, yet he was strangely reluctant to claim the kiss he craved. And he could snatch it with impunity, he felt certain of it.

With a rueful grin he studied the crown of her elegant hat. A cluster of lifelike silk forget-me-nots nestled against ivory satin, and a wide, blue bow was tied rakishly just below her left ear.

"I have arranged with the matron to have Miss Hilbert sent to the master's side," he said rather gruffly in an effort to disguise the emotion in his voice. "She'll have a proper bed and an armchair, a rug on the floor, and food brought in from an inn."

With a start, Penelope realized that the warm haven she had found was in fact Mr. Julian Rutherford's chest. The heart beating under her cheek and soothing her with its strong rhythm was Mr. Rutherford's, and the hands stroking her back and caressing the curls at the nape of her neck belonged to Mr. Rutherford as well. Before embarrassment could throw her into utter confusion, however, his words penetrated her numbed mind.

"The master's side!" Disappointment and anger deepened Penelope's husky voice even more. Her hands left the lean waist in a hurry, pushing against his chest as she raised her face to his. "I promised Maria to get her out of there, not to arrange her move to another cell!"

"We *shall* get her out of Newgate." Julian refused to be pushed away. He stepped closer, retaining his grip on her shoulders. "But until then, would you wish her to suffer in that cold, bare cubicle?"

The rebellious flame in Penelope's eyes died at Julian's calm words. He sounded so certain that Maria would be released. "When?" she asked, relieved and eager to know the particulars. "How do we go about it?"

"I suggest I first take you home to your aunt, Miss Langham. Then I shall go to Bow Street and try to speak with Theobald Dare and Sir Nathaniel Conant."

"We'll pass Bow Street on our way to Berkeley Square. Take me with you!"

Instead of pushing against him, Penelope's hands now moved pleadingly to his upper arms. Her eyes clung to his face, and her mouth was, oh, so temptingly close. Julian's pulse quickened. He had nothing to lose. His reputation was that of a rake. Hadn't he better prove it?

"You must be sensible, little Penny," he murmured. As her velvety brown eyes widened in surprise, Julian bent his head and kissed her swiftly on the lips.

At least, he had meant it to be a swift kiss. When their lips met, however, all rational thought flew from his head. There was only softness and warmth and an incredible sweetness.

His sudden move took Penelope by surprise. Her startled "oh" was lost and then forgotten under the touch of his firm mouth. She wanted to be held closer, to drink in the masculine scent of his shaving soap, to feel his hands caress her back.

Breathlessness forced her to pull away, thereby breaking the spell. She became instantly aware of whistles and catcalls shrilling in the air, of jeering and clapping. She whirled out of Julian's arms to stare with horror at urchins, jarveys, vendors, crossing sweeps, and indignant matrons, who had all gathered in Newgate Street to watch the gentleman and his lady love.

Her eyes flew to Julian's face. *He was grinning!* Shame and anger swept through her, driving hot color into her face.

She had behaved like a strumpet—like Meg inside the prison!

But he! Oh, he was a cad! No gentleman would have taken such shameless advantage! She had been thinking of Maria, how to help her, and had let down her guard. And he had behaved like a black-hearted, lowdown . . . reporter!

Julian leaned toward her and with deft fingers straightened her hat and retied the velvet bow. His thumbs caressed her cheeks. "Penny, my love," he murmured, and for a moment she feared he would kiss her again.

"How dare you!" She took a hasty step backward, away from the disturbing fingers. *Tare and hounds!* How the man could stir her senses! But thanks to Harry Swag she was well versed in the ways of rattles and rakes, and how to deal with them.

"Take me home this instant, Mr. Rutherford!" she said coldly.

Spinning away from him, Penelope carefully raised the hem of her gown to avoid contact with the filth littering Newgate Street, and with a haughty toss of her head swept past the gaping onlookers to the waiting curricle.

chapter SIX

Without a word, Julian helped Penelope into the carriage. *Damn!* he thought as he took his seat beside her and set the horses in motion. *Damn, but you're a fool! What the devil do you think you're doing, trying to dally with a lady of quality? An unmarried lady of quality!*

But had he been dallying? The kiss had felt so right, and for a moment she had responded. There could be no doubt about that. He had wanted to keep on holding her, keep on kissing her.

Damn again! You're losing your touch, old boy! You want a flirtation. Nothing more! Frowning, Julian stared over the bays' heads, as though he'd find counsel on the rutted surface of the road.

Covertly Penelope studied his profile. The mouth that mere minutes ago had touched her own with such startling sweetness, was stern. His chin and jaw had an implacable, chiseled look, and he stared straight ahead as though his smoothly trotting horses required his full attention.

"Mr. Rutherford!" Penelope gripped the handrail and held on tightly. "If you were a gentleman, you'd apologize to me!"

At the precise moment of her indignant outcry, Julian was wondering whether he had taken shameless advantage of her vulnerable state after the prison visit. He was—*perish the thought!*—considering an apology.

Startled by Penelope's unexpected attack, Julian dropped his hands. His well-trained pair of bays instantly picked up speed, and he was obliged to postpone his response until he had adjusted the horses' pace and guided them around a cumbersome dray pulled by six plodding draft horses just as a yellow and black post chaise came thundering toward them.

He turned to Penelope with a grin. "Not only am I no gentleman, apparently I'm no whip either."

"The latter I can forgive, Mr. Rutherford."

"Ah, yes. I forgot. You had anticipated my lack of driving skills. After all, a mere reporter cannot be expected to show the expertise of a Corinthian."

A trace of color mounted in her cheeks. "Mr. Rutherford, that is very much beside the point. I merely wished to show you that you did not behave in a gentlemanly manner."

"You have made that quite clear, Miss Langham." Julian maneuvered the curricle into Piccadilly, and when he spoke again, his voice was solemn, but his eyes held an unmistakable gleam of deviltry. "I sincerely apologize for my poor judgment in choosing that particular locale for our first kiss,

Penny, my love. Too public by half. No wonder you ripped up at me."

Penelope caught her breath. This was intolerable!

"But I shan't apologize for the kiss itself," he continued softly, throwing her into utter confusion. "The memory shall warm my heart—until the next occasion."

"Mr. Rutherford—"

"Julian. After all that we've shared, you must call me Julian, Penny, my love."

"Don't call me that," she said irritably. "Penny makes me feel like the female lead in a farce."

"But I may call you my love. Thank you, *Penelope, my love.*"

His voice was a caress. Striving to maintain her composure, she spoke more sharply than she had intended. "You are impertinent, Mr. Rutherford. The length and nature of our acquaintance does not warrant any type of informal address."

There! That had put him in his place! Resolutely Penelope turned her head, pretending an interest in the windows and storefronts lining the wide thoroughfare. Thank goodness they'd be in Berkeley Square soon! She had no wish to continue this conversation.

She maintained her silence until Julian pulled up before Belmont House, then spoke in an admirably cool voice. "I shan't ask you to come inside, Mr. Rutherford. You must wish to get to Bow Street as soon as possible."

Penelope held out her hand, which he shook solemnly. "Thank you for coming to the prison with me, Mr. Rutherford. You have been all that is kind."

Julian chuckled, and with some disquiet she noted the emerald gleam in his eyes. He jumped down from the curricle, then helped her onto the sidewalk. "Servant, Miss Langham."

His bow was blatant exaggeration, and Penelope had the uncomfortable feeling that instead of having put *him* in his place, he had, somehow, neatly turned the tables on her.

He still held her elbow when he looked across the square at a horse and phaeton being led by a groom. "Ah," he said. "There's Peter Ludlow's tired cob. The sick at St. George's Hospital did not keep him as long as he feared."

Penelope tried to pull free of his firm grip. "In that case, I must hurry. Thank you again, Mr. Rutherford."

The glint in his eyes deepened. His fingers slid down her arm. Slowly he raised her hand, turned it over, and pressed a lingering kiss onto her wrist where the short glove exposed her skin.

"I shall call for you tomorrow morning. Might as well take advantage of the weather and go for a drive while we discuss Miss Hilbert's case. So long, Penny, my love."

Penelope remained standing in front of Belmont House long after his curricle had rolled out of sight. She knew she ought to be vexed; yet she couldn't help the smile that tugged at the corners of her mouth. After all, Lady Margaret had warned her. Julian Rutherford was a rogue of the first stare, a devil-may-care, a here-and-thereian, and he would try to flirt with her.

He had snatched a kiss—as though she were the merest straw damsel. Admittedly, his kiss had been pleasant. Very much more pleasant, she acknowledged, than the slobbering imprints Gilbert Bromfield bestowed occasionally on her hand.

Julian. Trying his Christian name in her mind, Penelope thought it very pleasing—like the man himself. It had a strong sound to it and yet conveyed a certain gentleness. Like the man himself?

Lud! What a perfectly mawkish thought! She must stop thinking about him in that manner, else she might make a cake of herself as she had done with Harry Swag! She must think only of his genuine helpfulness; at least there he was quite unlike Harry Swag.

Penelope rubbed a finger against her tingling wrist while watching Dr. Ludlow's groom as he stopped the phaeton before the house. The man stared first at Penelope, then at the ornate front door. After a moment, when the door remained firmly shut, he tugged at the horse's reins, beginning another slow circuit of the square. Penelope's eyes followed him, riveted to the left side of his coat where an empty sleeve was neatly tucked into the coat pocket.

A gruff, male voice made her jump. "That's Jessup. Lost his arm at Waterloo."

"Dr. Ludlow. I didn't hear you come out of the house."

"I don't doubt it. You were preoccupied."

A blush warmed Penelope's cheeks. "I didn't mean to stare, Dr. Ludlow. I was wondering whether he, too, is one of the laudanum addicts you're helping."

"Jessup hasn't needed my help for two years. It's I who need him. I'm so absentminded, I might end up in Richmond when I want to drive to Chelsea."

Penelope smiled. "Then you and Jessup are both lucky to have each other. How did you find my aunt, Dr. Ludlow?"

"In a fret about you, Miss Langham. I understand Julian took you to Newgate."

"Yes . . . a dear friend of mine is incarcerated there. I had to see her."

"There has been an outbreak of fever at the prison, Miss Langham."

"Gaol fever!" Penelope blanched. Had Maria caught it already? Was that the reason for her strange behavior? But no, Maria had only just been admitted into the prison.

Dr. Ludlow looked at Penelope from beneath his bushy brows. "I don't suppose it'll do any good to ask you not to return to Newgate, Miss Langham. But remember, the fever is highly contagious and in most cases deadly. It cares nothing about the distinction between prisoner and visitor!"

"You didn't tell my aunt about—no, of course not," Penelope muttered when she encountered his indignant scowl. "Please tell me about your visit with my aunt. Do you feel—Oh!" she exclaimed in frustration. "There's your carriage, Dr. Ludlow."

The physician merely waved Jessup on. "Let us take a short stroll beneath the trees, Miss Langham," he suggested. "It'll be more pleasant than standing on your doorstep in this devilishly warm sun."

"I hadn't noticed the heat," Penelope said apologetically as they crossed the cobbled street to the footpath circling the enclosed garden in the center of the square.

Peter Ludlow nodded. "Quite understandable, my dear. I

never do after a visit at one of the prisons. Can't get enough of light and sunshine then. Now to Lady Belmont.''

"Yes?"

"First of all let me assure you that the situation is not as grave as it might have been. That grumpy maid of your aunt—''

"Sweetings."

"Hmph! A more inappropriate name I've never heard! But the woman's got a head on her shoulders. Unless Lady Belmont was in actual physical distress, Sweetings poured a spoonful or two of laudanum into the chamber pot, then gave your aunt a small measure of brandy in hot, sweet barley water. That way the medicine bottle gradually emptied, and your aunt felt content."

Penelope's mind was awhirl. "But why didn't Sweetings tell me? I could have—''

Dr. Ludlow interrupted. "That doesn't mean, Miss Langham, that Lady Belmont is not taking frequent doses of laudanum. Too frequent. You must be aware that quite often your aunt suffers from blinding headaches."

Penelope stopped in the shade of a wide-branched plane tree. "Yes, indeed. Poor Aunt Sophy! The only remedy for her headaches is a long rest in a darkened room."

"And laudanum. Sweetings never denied your aunt the opiate when she was in pain. The headaches started after the death of her husband. It is not unusual for a bereaved woman to have physical symptoms of some kind or another, but it is unusual that they persist for ten years."

"My aunt and uncle were deeply attached to each other, I believe." Placing her hand on Dr. Ludlow's invitingly proffered arm, Penelope walked in silence while she thought.

Sweetings's actions, admirable though they were, puzzled her. Why hadn't the dresser confided in her? Did Sweetings believe Penelope wouldn't support her in her effort to keep Sophy away from the laudanum?

As they came abreast with Gunter's, the well-known confectioner across the square from Belmont House, Dr. Ludlow slowed his steps. "Would you care to eat an ice, Miss Langham?"

Penelope's eyes lit up, but she shook her head. "Much

as I would enjoy it, Dr. Ludlow, I mustn't. Aunt Sophy will worry if I don't return to her now. And besides, I'm anxious to have a word with Sweetings.''

"Some other time, then. I shall be seeing Lady Belmont daily until, somehow or other, we have defeated the head-aches without the use of laudanum.''

Dr. Ludlow's phaeton was waiting when they reached Belmont House again. The physician climbed in, told Jessup to ''shake a leg,'' and drove off without another word to Penelope. Belatedly, as she was about to enter the house, Dr. Ludlow seemed to recall his manners—or the dependable Jessup had reminded him, Penelope thought with a smile as the physician half turned in the seat and doffed his hat to her.

Still smiling, Penelope stepped into the foyer. She re-moved her hat and set it own on the Boulle table below the wide, gilt-framed mirror. Her short curls, she noted, were sadly flattened, but a rake-through with her fingers soon had them bouncing again.

"Where is my aunt, Dawson?'' she asked the butler, who, alerted by the closing of the front door, came shuffling through the braize curtains.

"After Dr. Ludlow's visit her ladyship retired to her room, Miss Penelope.''

"And Sweetings?''

"With her ladyship. If I may say so, Miss Penelope, her ladyship appeared in fairly good spirits when the doctor left.''

"Thank you, Dawson.'' Under the butler's indulgent eye, Penelope ran up the stairs and did not slow until she stood before the door leading into Lady Belmont's sitting room. She knocked softly and entered.

Sweetings emerged from the adjoining bedroom. "Her ladyship is resting, miss,'' she said with a repressive frown.

"I shan't stay long, Sweetings.'' Penelope flashed a smile and swept past the scowling woman.

"Auntie,'' she said when she perceived Sophy reclining on the daybed and reading one of the latest novels from the Minerva Press. "I am sorry if I worried you. I returned just as soon as I could, but then I met Dr. Ludlow—''

"Penelope," interrupted Lady Belmont. "Did you go abroad without a hat?"

"No, dearest. Please tell me about the doctor's visit."

Sophy motioned Penelope to the foot end of the daybed. "Dr. Ludlow seems competent enough, but why is your hair so disordered, Penelope?"

Penelope's hands flew to her curls, creating even more havoc than they had done in the foyer. "Is that better? Don't keep me on tenterhooks, Aunt Sophy! What did you and Dr. Ludlow decide?"

"No more laudanum," Sophy said curtly. She placed a marker between the pages of her book and closed it with a snap. "Where is Mr. Rutherford?" she asked, peering shortsightedly toward her sitting room as though expecting him to have come upstairs with Penelope. "And what about Maria? How is she? What does she say?"

"Too many questions, Auntie." Penelope attempted a smile but failed. " 'Twas horrid, Aunt Sophy! Simply awful! And frightening!"

Sophy pulled herself into a more upright position. "What happened?" She reached for Penelope's hand and held it tightly. "Did they mistreat poor Maria?"

"No. Oh, I don't know, Aunt Sophy! You see, Maria hardly spoke to me. She was pleased at first, but then she asked me to leave. She did not respond to my questions nor to Mr. Rutherford's."

When Sophy was silent, Penelope added, "Ju—Mr. Rutherford has gone to Bow Street. He'll find out from Mr. Dare or from Sir Nathaniel Conant on what grounds they have arrested Maria."

After another moment of silence, Sophy said, "Be a dear, Penelope. Write a note to Throckmorton. Ask him to wait on me in an hour—no, in two hours. I must rest. I can't afford a headache now!"

"I'll gladly write the note, Aunt Sophy, but why do you need your solicitor?"

"To have Maria transferred to the master's side. Elizabeth Howe won't lift a finger for her companion. It's up to us to see to the poor girl's comfort."

"Julian already arranged for Maria's transfer, Auntie."

Sophy's penciled brows climbed a fraction. So it was Julian now, was it! She must make an effort to pay more attention to Penelope. Mr. Rutherford was a handsome devil. *Oh, dear!* she thought. *All these complications come at a most awkward time! If only I could have—*

Resolutely Sophy pushed the forbidden thought aside. "We must reimburse Mr. Rutherford for any sums he expended on Maria's behalf," she said briskly. "A reporter can ill afford to give away a large sum of money."

"I didn't think of that! I'll repay him in the morning. First thing! But, do you know, Auntie, when I am with Ju—Mr. Rutherford, I forget that he is a reporter. He—"

"He speaks, dresses, and behaves as befits a gentleman. I know, dear. And it is, after all, quite possible that he has other income besides his wages from the newspaper."

Penelope, thinking of his curricle and the bays and recalling Lady Margaret's words about his childhood near her estate, nodded. If Julian's father was a rector or a vicar with a generous stipend, he could easily give an allowance to his son. Still, it was unthinkable to be beholden to Julian.

A small sigh from Sophy reminded Penelope that the older woman was in need of rest. She bent and kissed her aunt's cheek. "Shall we stay at home tonight? We might finish reading Miss Austen's *Emma* if we sat down right after dinner."

"It sounds delightful, dearest, but I promised Gertrude to attend her musicale."

"And we mustn't disappoint Mrs. Welby."

"No, indeed, Penelope. You know that Gertrude is very sensitive. Since she married that city merchant—rich, I grant you, but so vulgar!—she does not have many friends she can count on."

"But Mr. Welby has been dead these fifteen years or more!"

"The taint of the shop never wears off, Penelope. When a woman of quality marries beneath her, she must bear the consequences." Her aunt paused significantly. "But you need not come if you'd rather have a quiet evening at home. I shall do splendidly on my own."

Penelope rose. A quiet evening was not at all what she

wished. There had been too many already during the past six years, and a soirée at Gertrude Welby's home would not exactly be a frolic either. But Sophy had come to depend on Penelope's company.

"I'll go with you, Aunt Sophy. I believe Miss Stephens and Mr. Braham are to sing, and that at least will be a treat. And Auntie . . . if you don't require Sweetings at the moment, I should like a word with her."

"About the laudanum?" Sophy snuggled back against the cushions and pulled the lacy rug covering her legs a little higher. "Go ahead, Penelope," she said with resignation. "I'd rather you interrogate Sweetings than me."

The dresser, when asked by Penelope to accompany her, was less acquiescent. "I couldn't possibly spare a moment, miss. Her ladyship's lavender silk needs pressing."

"Go along, Sweetings," Lady Belmont called from her bedroom. "I'll wear my black taffeta and my new lavender turban."

Sweetings gave in with poor grace. Muttering under her breath, she followed Penelope along the corridor and, when they arrived in Penelope's room, refused to sit down.

"I wish I knew why you're so crabby, Sweetings!" Penelope said in exasperation. Unwilling to sit while the maid towered above her, she paced restlessly. "I merely wish to thank you for looking after my aunt so well. Dr. Ludlow has explained to me that you tried in your own way to protect Lady Belmont from the ill-effects of Dr. Wise's elixir."

"I didn't know what else to do, miss," the woman said stiffly.

"But why didn't you tell me, Sweetings?" Penelope swung around to face her. "Even this morning when I handed you the laudanum, you didn't say a word."

"What could I say, miss? If her laydship had been laid low with one of her headaches, I would have given it to her, day or night."

"Dr. Ludlow said he planned to cure the headaches without laudanum. Do you know how?"

"Yes, miss." Animation crept into Sweetings's voice, and her stern features relaxed. "He showed me how to rub her ladyship's neck and temples. And it works, miss! Leastways it did this afternoon. But the pain was just starting. It weren't as though her ladyship was laid low with those fierce, blinding stabs of pain that attack her many a day.''

"I have given orders that Dr. Wise is not to be admitted again, Sweetings.''

"Her ladyship won't be needing him anymore. Not if I can help it,'' Sophy's dresser said fiercely. "If that be all, Miss Langham?''

"Yes. You may go, Sweetings.''

After sketching a curtsy, the dresser stalked to the door. "That Dr. Ludlow,'' she said, stopping but not turning to look at Penelope, "seems to know what he's about. Even though he's young enough to be her ladyship's son.'' Then she left, shutting the door firmly behind her.

When the carriage came around after dinner to convey the two ladies to Mrs. Welby's house in Bruton Street, Sophronia, Lady Belmont, descended the stairs resplendently arrayed in black taffeta and lace. Four strings of exquisite pearls were draped around her neck, and her silver-blond hair was topped with a turban of lavender silk. A pearl brooch was strategically placed on the turban, just left of center, below a silver plume, and a pair of pearl drops dangled from her earlobes.

"Magnificent, Auntie.'' Penelope smiled. "I dare Lady Spatterton to best you on this occasion.''

"She won't,'' Sophy said complacently, drawing on her long, lavender silk gloves. "Lillian . . . Lilibeth—oh, you know, that clever girl at Balena's—swore on her mother's grave that no one would have a turban in the least bit like mine. Besides,'' she added with a look of pride mingled with embarrassment, "I myself designed the structure of this headdress.''

"Aunt Sophy! How absolutely marvelous! I shall ask you to design a hat for me, something to go with my new sprigged muslin.''

"You'll want a bonnet, then. What lovely bonnets and hats Helena Twittering and I made when we were young . . .''

A reminiscing glow came into Sophy's eyes. "We were always dreaming to set up as milliners, and, naturally, two handsome dukes or princes were expected to ride up to our little shop and marry us."

Penelope looked at her aunt with wide-eyed disbelief. "You? A milliner? Surely you're bamming me, Auntie."

Sophy fussed with the hemline of her gown. "Is this straight, Penelope? It seems to be dragging at the back."

"If you leave it alone, it'll be just perfect. Are you trying to evade my question, Aunt Sophy?"

"Fustian! Why should I? It is a well-known fact that during the days of my girlhood the Langhams as well as the Twitterings were very poor. My grandfather, your great-grandfather, lost all his money in the South Sea Bubble, and it was not until your father made some wise investments on the exchange that the Langham fortune was restored. I, of course, married my dear Henry, and only Helena and Barbara Twittering remain poor as church mice. But enough of that. We mustn't keep the horses standing."

"And, no doubt, you're eager to show off your lovely turban. It looks extremely well with your black gown."

"I'd gladly give up the turban if I could have my opals instead," Sophy said wistfully. "The black would offset them to perfection."

"True. The pearls, however, add a touch of elegance that no stone could rival."

"Speaking of elegence, my dear!" Glad to give her thoughts a different direction, Lady Belmont cast a look of pride over her niece. "I must admit to some fears when you purchased that deep blue silk, but it made up well. And the gold border is stunning! I only wish you had come to Balena's with me, Penelope. I'm certain you'd have found something more elegant than a velvet ribbon for your hair."

"Ah, but do you not see how cunningly Nancy threaded the ribbon through my curls, and that she sewed rhinestones onto the velvet?"

Lady Belmont took a step closer. "Indeed. For once you look as though you had long hair piled atop your head. Oh, how I wish you had never heard of Caroline Lamb and her shorn locks!''

Penelope smiled a thank-you at Ben, who helped her into her evening cloak while Dawson assisted the dowager count- ess. ''That was ages ago, Auntie,'' she said protestingly. ''In my salad days! I don't care as much about my looks now as about the comfort and simplicity of my hairstyle.''

''And more's the pity,'' muttered Sophy as she stepped through the front door. ''Most likely that's something else I must watch out for.''

Dawson, extending his arm to assist Lady Belmont down the well-lit front steps, allowed himself a tiny smirk. Lucky for her ladyship that Miss Penelope was too far behind to hear her words, but, he admitted to himself, 'twas time her ladyship took notice of Miss Penelope. High time to get the headstrong young lady married before she turned into an old maid, or—heaven forbid!—before she grew so desperate that she might look with favor on a rakish journalist!

After carefully handing Lady Belmont into the coach, Dawson performed the same service for Penelope. He put up the steps, shut the door, and before Penelope had quite settled herself, they were off. They arrived in Bruton Street just in time to hear the timid finale of a bashful young lady's performance on the harp before their hostess descended upon them.

''Dearest Sophy!'' exclaimed Mrs. Welby, a thin, nervous lady attired becomingly in forest-green watered silk. ''I had all but given you up. How wonderful that you are here after all. And dearest Penelope, too.''

Sophy returned Gertrude Welby's embrace affectionately. ''Wouldn't miss it for anything, Gertrude. I said I'd come, didn't I? Now where shall we sit? Mustn't disrupt your program with our tardiness.'' Her gaze swept over the assembled company. ''Is that Henrietta waving to us? With those awful carrot tops nodding on her hat?''

Sophy purposefully made her way to the front row of chairs placed in a semicircle around the pianoforte and the harp. Penelope followed slowly, noting with some dismay that Lady Spatterton was accompanied by her grandson.

Gilbert Bromfield rose to his feet and made quite a show

of settling Lady Belmont in his own chair beside Lady Spatterton. Beaming, he then turned to Penelope. "My dear," he said, carrying her hand to his lips before seating her. "I am glad you've come tonight. There's something I most particularly wished to say to you."

"Pray sit down, Gilbert," Penelope whispered. "I believe the program is about to continue."

Mr. Bromfield depositied his portly figure on the delicate Hepplewhite chair to her left. "There's time yet," he said after a glance at the pianoforte, where a young man was leafing through some sheets of music. "He's only Miss Stephens's accompanist."

With a sigh Penelope resigned herself to her fate. She had discovered long ago that nothing would stop Gilbert once he embarked on one of his monologues. Not even, she feared, Miss Stephens's performance.

"You may recall, my dear Penelope," Gilbert began in his ponderous way, "that I have often warned you about your connection with Miss Hilbert."

Drawing herself up, Penelope shot him a withering look.

"That, in fact," he continued placidly, "I have quite frequently voiced my disapproval of your intimacy with a menial."

"Indeed you have," she said under her breath.

Unmindful of the wrath gathering in Penelope's eyes, Gilbert leaned closer. The reek of garlic and cloves on his breath enveloped her.

"Alas, you did not heed me, Penelope! My worst fears have come to pass. After you hear what I have to say, you will acknowledge my superior judgment in matters where your womanly instincts may lead you astray. You will bow to my superior wisdom."

Applause heralded the arrival of the opera singer. Miss Stephens acknowledged the tribute with a slight smile and a bow of her head, then took her place beside the pianoforte.

Balked of further opportunity to speak to Penelope, Gilbert hissed angrily, just as the pianist struck the first chords of Miss Stephens's song, "You must listen to me, Penelope! Miss Hilbert is a thief!"

chapter
SEVEN

Penelope's hand shot out, clamping around Gilbert's heavy wrist. "Don't you ever say that again, Gilbert Bromfield. I swear I'll box your ears if you dare repeat such slander!"

Demands for silence from the audience made further speech impossible, but throughout the singer's performance Penelope sat seething with wrath. She hardly heard the arias rendered in Miss Stephens's clear voice.

How dare he call Maria a thief!

Responding like an automaton whenever those around her broke into applause, Penelope was startled, after an especially long interval of clapping, to hear Mrs. Welby's invitation to partake of refreshments in the adjoining drawing room.

Waiting only until Gilbert was occupied assisting his grandmother and Sophy to their feet, Penelope slipped out into the corridor. Maria's plight had overset her. If she remained in Gilbert's company, she would surely come to blows with him!

She heard a deep, resonant voice behind her, asking if she would care to go in to supper. Instantly her fertile mind conjured a tall, muscular man whose dark hair tumbled onto his forehead, a pair of gleaming gray-green eyes, a mouth curved into a teasing grin.

She realized then that it was more than Maria's arrest that had undermined her common sense and made her flare up at Gilbert Bromfield with more heat than the occasion warranted. After all, she had heard and laughed off his pompous and often offensive pronouncements for five years.

Hearing the invitation to supper patiently repeated, Penelope summoned a smile to her lips and turned. "I'd be delighted, Mr. Rugby."

The man before her was about thirty-five years of age, a trifle on the short side, but well proportioned, although some might call him stocky. Full brown hair was neatly brushed, and a pair of dark blue eyes looked at her with some concern.

"For a moment I feared you might be unwell, Miss Langham," Benjamin Rugby said, extending his arm and starting to lead her to the drawing room.

"Woolgathering, I'm afraid. I hope you'll forgive me, Mr. Rugby."

"Don't apologize. There are times when I find myself doing the same. And most agreeable times those are," he added softly, as though to himself.

Penelope glanced at him curiously. Mrs. Welby's competent agent? Daydreaming? It had to be a woman!

Pshaw! she told herself scornfully. *Just because you're thinking of a man doesn't mean Mr. Rugby is dreaming of a woman. He might be dreaming of owning a bank, or a mansion in Bloomsbury!*

Threading her way to a table laden with meats, fruit, cakes, and jellies, Penelope noted that Gilbert was on his way to the refreshments as well, just a few steps ahead of her. She took the plate offered by one of Mrs. Welby's six-foot-tall footmen and helped herself to asparagus and ham while considering an apology to Gilbert. Finding herself in front of a platter of lobster patties, a great favorite of hers, she stopped and allowed Benjamin Rugby to serve her several.

Just then Gilbert turned toward her, his protuberant eyes threatening to pop out of their sockets. "Surely you don't propose to eat four lobster patties at this hour of the night, Penelope! They'll upset your stomach, and you'll never be able to go to sleep! Here, take my plate. You'll be much happier with jellies and aspics, y'know."

Penelope's barely soothed anger flared again, and she decided on the spot that it was she who deserved an apology, not Gilbert. "Mr. Bromfield!" she said with awful calm. "I wouldn't dream of eating your jellies, and if you want lobster patties, you must get them yourself. I shan't let you have mine! And now, if you will excuse me?''

She turned on her heel and carried her plate to one of the small tripod tables set out along the walls. Instantly a footman stood at her elbow, offering wine, champagne, and Italian ices.

"Champagne!" Rather more hastily than was wise, she drank the bubbly wine, then took another glass. "Champagne, Mr. Rugby?'' she asked with forced gaiety when that gentleman joined her.

"Don't mind if I do, Miss Langham. I pride myself not a little on the selection of wines for tonight.''

Penelope raised her glass. "Not to forget Miss Stephens's presence. I feel certain that it was you who thought of it. Generally Mrs. Welby has only some very poor amateurs to perform at her musicales.''

Penelope spent a fairly enjoyable ten minutes or so chatting with Benjamin Rugby, sipping her drink, and nibbling the delicious lobster patties while she observed her fellow guests.

The majority of Mrs. Welby's company consisted of what Aunt Sophy would stigmatize as the hangers-on, the toad-eaters, and the spongers. However, the wealthy widow had also drawn three Members of Parliament whom Penelope recognized, one minor official from the Russian Embassy, two bankers, and her special friends Lady Spatterton, Lady Arbuthnot, Lady Margaret Cleve-Abbots, and Lady Elizabeth Howe.

Penelope felt a hard lump forming in her chest. Maria should be with Lady Elizabeth! Maria should be eating lobster patties and drinking champagne—not languishing in Newgate prison!

The delicacies suddenly tasted sour, and Penelope pushed her plate away. Blinking rapidly, she fixed her tear-blurred eyes on Miss Barbara and Miss Helena Twittering, who, late as always, were bowed into the room by Mrs. Welby's butler. Miss Helena, the younger of the elderly spinsters, fluttered up to the hostess, making her apologies in a high, excited voice. Miss Barbara, tall and bony, followed at a decorous pace.

Miss Barbara was worth a glance, and a second one as well. She wore black like Lady Belmont, but Miss Barbara's gown was fashioned of velvet and cut in such cunning fashion that it disguised her angular frame and flattered her very plain features. Penelope instantly recognized the expert touch of Mademoiselle Solange, a very exclusive French dressmaker in Bond Street. Atop Miss Barbara's crimped gray curls rested a black velvet cap trimmed with one perfect, white silk rose. It was so simple and beautiful, it had to come from Balena's.

Or be of Aunt Sophy's design, she thought, relaxing a little.

As she watched her aunt, Mrs. Welby, Lady Elizabeth, and the Misses Twittering converse in a lively manner, Penelope wondered how Miss Barbara, "poor as a church mouse," according to Sophy, could afford the most expensive dressmaker in town and the most fashionable milliner. So engrossed was Penelope in some highly improbable speculations that Benjamin's low voice startled her.

"Woolgathering again, Miss Langham?"

She smiled at Mrs. Welby's agent. "I'm afraid so. You must think me awfully rude."

"I haven't been very good company either." Benjamin turned serious, intensely blue eyes on Penelope. "Miss Langham, I wonder if I might ask you a question. About Miss Hilbert. I know you are her friend, and I haven't seen her for several days. I—I wonder if she might be ill?"

Penelope's smile faded. "Not ill, Mr. Rugby." She faltered under his worried gaze. She had never seen the calm, efficient man so tense. *My goodness!* she thought. *He's in love with Maria! Why haven't I noticed before? And how on earth am I going to tell him?*

Before Penelope could say anything at all, Lady Elizabeth Howe's strident voice carried across to them from the neighboring table.

"I tell you, Sophy," Lady Elizabeth said, "I have a good mind not to take Maria Hilbert back even if she were released from prison tomorrow! A breath of scandal must always be attached to the girl, be she innocent or guilty."

A chair scraped loudly on the polished parquet floor, and

Penelope realized with a start that it was Mr. Rugby's chair.
He stood for a moment, white-faced, staring at Lady Elizabeth
with an expression of helpless fury in his blue eyes.

"Mr. Rugby." Penelope gently touched his arm.

He drew a deep, shuddering breath and with some difficulty focused on Penelope. "Where's Maria?" he asked
hoarsely.

"Maria is in Newgate Prison, Mr. Rugby." Penelope
cringed at the pain she saw in his eyes, but she continued in
a quiet voice. "She was arrested for theft."

"My God!" Benjamin spun on his heel and stormed from
the room.

Penelope remembered Maria in her prison cell, first
radiant with joy, then blushing and turning away. Benjamin
Rugby's "My God!" echoed in her ears. Anguish had
forced that cry from his lips, not, as she would have
expected, incredulity. And Mr. Rugby had asked no questions.

Several of those present in the drawing room had heard
the cry and sent curious glances after Mr. Rugby. Gertrude
Welby went so far as to start after her employee but was
detained by one of her guests, and shortly afterward it was
time to return to the music room.

Penelope could find no pleasure in the duets sung by Miss
Stephens and Mr. Braham. Her mind was too preoccupied
with the puzzle of Maria's behavior and Benjamin Rugby's
strange reaction.

When the musicale came to an end shortly after midnight,
Penelope felt nothing but relief. Her mind was spinning with
confusing thoughts. She wanted to go home, pull the bed
covers over her head, and not be aware of anything until
morning—when she'd be able to talk to Julian.

As the guests filed into the drawing room to wet their dry
throats with another glass of champagne, their hostess
approached Penelope and her aunt.

"I don't know what to do, Sophy," said Gertrude Welby,
looking anxiously about the music room. Her thin fingers
flew to her hair, then to the lace ruffle at her wrists, tugging
and pulling at everything they touched. "I sent a footman to
Benjamin's room and also to the study where he spends
most of his time. But he isn't there!"

"Calm yourself, Gertrude," Sophy said sternly. "If Mr. Rugby was upset by Elizabeth's ill-considered remark, he probably went out to have a drink at some horrid gin shop or other. I've always suspected he had a soft spot for Maria Hilbert, and learning of her arrest in this fashion must have been quite upsetting."

"But Benjamin *never* visits those awful places! What if he comes to harm?"

"You're a pea-goose, Gertrude! You'd think Mr. Rugby were a mere fledgling the way you fret over the man. Gracious! If I had worried each time my son and his friends went on a spree in the less savory public houses, I'd be in my grave now."

Mrs. Welby looked unconvinced. "Your Henry was never alone."

"Mr. Rugby will be just fine," Penelope interposed. "He is a man of sense and, I suspect, despite his lack of inches, a man of considerable physical prowess. He once told Maria and me that he regularly visits Gentleman Jackson's Boxing Saloon."

"Oh, indeed! Dear Penelope!" Gertrude Welby's hands fluttered to Penelope's cheeks in a brief caress. With a tremulous smile she said, "I shan't worry any longer, my dears, but now I must rush. My guests are waiting to take their leave."

As Penelope followed her aunt into their coach, the thought crossed her mind that if Mr. Rugby could visit Gentleman Jackson, so, perhaps, could Mr. Rutherford. Julian's muscular frame strongly suggested regular participation in some form of sport or other, and, she felt, pugilism would greatly appeal to him.

"Gertrude should have had children," muttered Sophy as the carriage started to roll. "She would have learned long ago that fretting only aggravates a bad situation. My Dorothea— even more so than Henry—has taught me that."

With some difficulty Penelope recalled her thoughts from Mr. Rutherford and the manly art of sparring. "Dorothea would have enjoyed travel with my parents and me," she said.

Sophy nodded. "Oh, she was an adventurous soul. In and

out of scrapes ever since she started to walk! Only now, after fourteen years of marriage and three children, is she showing any sense at all. Still rides neck-or-nothing fashion, though,'' she added as an afterthought. ''Which reminds me, Penelope. You haven't taken your mare out for several days. Not ailing, are you?''

''Of course not, Auntie.'' How could she suggest a ride, Penelope reflected wryly, when Julian invited her to a drive? He might not own a mount, and the bays, she suspected, would not tolerate a saddle on their backs.

''You must make friends among the younger set, Penelope. No doubt it's a bore to have no one but a groom to accompany you on horseback. We must make an effort to attend livelier parties. Balls and Venetian breakfasts where you'll meet *young* people!''

''Oh, fiddle, Aunt Sophy! Would you have me compete with seventeen-year-old debutantes for their equally young swains?''

''You've clung to my apron strings far too long,'' said Lady Belmont, blithely ignoring Penelope's protest. ''And I've been remiss in my duty to you. I should have insisted you have a come-out! Only at the time I was—''

Sophy broke off, guiltily aware that five years ago, when Penelope should have made her official curtsy to society, she herself had been moping in her rooms, more often than not pretending a headache in order to wrest a spoonful of laudanum from Sweetings.

But now she need never again have recourse to such measures. Dr. Ludlow with his understanding, his warm, compassionate manner, had promised to help her. Had helped already. The past few days had been quite bearable; only the long nights. . . . Resolutely, Sophy banished the thought.

''I shall speak to Dorothea Lieven about a voucher for Almack's,'' Sophy said firmly. She darted a look at Penelope, but the street lamps did not spread sufficient light to illuminate the interior of the carriage. Penelope's face was but a pale blur, and only the rhinestones in her velvet hair ribbon were clearly visible.

It worried her that Penelope remained silent. Something

must be bothering the child, but, she decided with a faint shrug, this was not the right time to inquire. Tomorrow, Sophy told herself, tomorrow she'd start being a conscientious aunt.

Penelope rose early despite having been kept awake half the night by disquieting thoughts about Maria and Benjamin. She had for some time been aware that a bond of friendship existed between the two, but had put this down to the fact that they both belonged to that unenviable group of persons who fitted neither into the servants' hall nor the dining salon. Until the previous night, however, Penelope had not seen any signs of Mr. Rugby's warmer feelings for her friend.

Perhaps that was not surprising, Penelope reflected as she descended to the library just a few minutes past eight o'clock. Maria had been in Lady Elizabeth's employ for ten years or more, and Lady Elizabeth would not relish losing such a selfless and untiring worker. She would nip in the bud any but the most casual acquaintance between her companion and Gertrude Welby's agent. Maria and Mr. Rugby would, therefore, be at pains to conceal their affection.

And yet—mayhap she had merely been blind. Aunt Sophy, apparently, had not had any trouble recognizing Mr. Rugby's feelings for Maria.

Briskly Penelope pushed open the library door. She should be pouring her energy into the household accounts instead of wasting precious time in speculation about Benjamin Rugby!

Slipping into her chair behind the desk, Penelope opened a ledger with the best of intentions. She found, however, that the neat columns danced before her eyes, and that Mr. Rugby's anguished face superimposed itself on such items as five lengths of shot satin and three dozen bottles of claret purchased in April.

Theft is a hanging offense . . . or, at best, punishable by transportation!

Although Penelope added a row of figures three times, each time she ended up with a different sum. She threw her pen down in vexation.

Was it possible that Mrs. Welby's trusted agent had
something to do with the thefts? Or that he and Maria were
in league? Benjamin Rugby had not been surprised by the
news of Maria's arrest. Only very upset.

Instantly, she was ashamed of her traitorous thoughts.
Maria would *never* steal.

But what about Benjamin Rugby?

Stretching, Penelope leaned against the padded backrest
of her chair. Her eyes strayed to the bookshelves—and
widened. Where once had stood a volume of Dr. Johnson's
dictionary, a gap yawned conspicuously.

She examined the shelves more closely and discovered
that several books had been taken down, but the neighboring
volumes had been cunningly shifted so that a casual glance
would show nothing amiss.

Her hands smacked onto the desktop. She hardly felt the
smarting impact as she flew out of her chair and to the
shelves. *Seven . . . nine . . . Lud! A dozen volumes, or more,
missing!*

Another theft.

Penelope reached for the bell pull behind her desk,
tugging it sharply. When her summons was answered a short
while later, she was once again seated behind the desk
and, apparently, absorbed in the household accounts.

"I reckoned ye would ring soon for yer tea and toast,"
Rachel said cheerfully as she deposited a heavy tray on a
corner of the desk. "It's promisin' to be a right lovely
day. Ye should be out in the park with yer mare, Miss
Penelope."

Penelope wiped her dry pen and laid it on the blotter.
"No doubt you're right, Rachel, but I'll be going for a drive
shortly."

"With that handsome Mr. Rutherford." The upstairs
maid nodded knowingly. "Aye, an' he'll see that ye have
some real good times. Unlike *some* gentleman, who comes
around an' can do nothin' but spout off nonsense about his
'delicate constitution.' "

Penelope frowned repressively. "Rachel," she said, busy-
ing herself with the teapot, "when you were dusting, did
you notice anything amiss with the books?"

Stepping closer to the shelves, Rachel peered at the leather-bound volumes. "Didn't I do right, Miss Penelope? There was so many books gone all of a sudden, I thought I'd better push t' others closer together. I didn't like to see all them gaping spaces. Made everything look untidy, it did. But if ye want gaps—" She reached out, prepared to make amends.

"No, leave it!" Penelope said hastily. "It's fine. Only tell me, when did you first notice the, ah, gaps."

"Two, maybe three weeks ago." Rachel's rosy face fell as Penelope's question sank in. "Didn't ye," she said haltingly, "didn't *you* take them books, Miss Penelope?"

Hiding her dismay behind a smile, Penelope said calmly, "I daresay I did. In the future, Rachel, please do not move the remaining volumes. You see, it's simpler to replace a book on the shelves if you leave the appropriate space open."

"Yes, miss. If that be all, miss?"

"Thank you. You may go, Rachel."

Curtsying and murmuring apologies, Rachel backed out of the library while Penelope absently spread strawberry preserves on a slice of toast.

The opals—and several missing books.

With a sigh, Penelope stared at her ledger. She ought to be getting to work or she'd never be done before her drive with Mr. Rutherford.

Julian. He'll have news from Bow Street.

For a couple of hours, Penelope immersed herself in her aunt's accounts, a task that had not before seemed onerous to her. This morning, however, she was plagued by a very elusive six and four pence that kept evading her. Her temper, already thrown out of kilter by the missing books, mounted steadily.

When Ben came to inform her that Mr. Rutherford was outside, asking if she were ready for a drive, she said crossly, "Tell him I'm not. Ask Mr. Rutherford to step inside, but, for goodness' sake, don't let him come up here or I'll never find it!"

Ben tried to hide his bewilderment behind a mask of imperturbability. "Beggin' your pardon, Miss Penelope," he said in a fair imitation of Dawson's bland voice. "Mr. Rutherford asked that you excuse his not comin' inside. The bays be very fresh this mornin'. He daren't trust one of them urchins to hold them."

"Exasperating man!" She slammed the ledger shut and rose to her feet. "Tell him—no, don't tell him anything. I'll do it myself," she said, following Ben from the room.

"You might want your wrap, Miss Penelope," the footman suggested after a glance at her short, puffed sleeves. "It's still cool out."

"Oh, very well. Assure Mr. Rutherford that I'll be down in five minutes."

In her bedchamber Penelope hastily pulled a spencer over her cream-and-chocolate-striped gown. A chip-straw hat tied with emerald ribbons, the exact shade of her spencer, and a pair of brown kid gloves completed her outfit.

Still feeling rather disgruntled, Penelope hurried downstairs, but when she stepped through the front door, opened by a grinning Ben, the feeling of ill-usage lifted. The sight of Julian dressed in a bottle-green coat of excellent tailoring, tan breeches, gleaming Hessians, and effortlessly holding the prancing bays in check, caused a sensation of breathlessness that she could attribute only to her anticipation of an outing. Surely the smile lighting up his face and eyes could have nothing to do with it!

"No, pray don't get down," she called, tripping down the wide marble steps when she saw Julian prepare to descend from the curricle. "The bays might take off and leave us behind."

"That would be a shame." Laughing, he reached down to pull her up beside him. "Where to, Penny, my love?"

"Anywhere," she said recklessly, making up her mind that instant that she quite enjoyed his improper way of addressing her. During the short time they would have in each other's company looking for her aunt's opals, she would not mar their friendship by insisting on a formality that was obviously alien to his nature.

Julian steered the bays south, toward Green Park, and for a while Penelope remained silent, quite content to relax against the squabs. She watched mobcapped maids and gangly delivery boys darting around elegant ladies and gentlemen as they strolled past the shops or stood about, exchanging pleasantries and gossip.

The day was overcast, but the clouds hiding the sun were white and fluffy, carrying no threat of rain. A breeze tugged at the bow under her ear and fanned it gently against her cheek. Pleasure and a sense of freedom slowly spread through Penelope, and yet her troublesome thoughts refused to be completely banished.

"What is it, Penny?" Julian asked quietly as they turned into the park.

For an instant she was tempted to tell him about her discovery in the library, but she dismissed the notion. A few books were unimportant when Maria's life might be at stake. Besides, she had yet to tell Julian about Benjamin Rugby. A daunting prospect, for she did not wish to prejudice Julian with her suspicions. She must relate the facts only. Unfortunately, her feelings and impressions were difficult to separate from the facts.

"Will you think me selfish and utterly base if I said I'd like to drive for a very little while without speaking of the thefts?" she asked.

He glanced at her sharply. He had not been mistaken. Something *was* bothering her. "I'll think nothing of the kind. It's a wonderful notion," he assured her warmly.

Although Penelope responded with a smile, the troubled look did not leave her expressive eyes. As Julian guided the horses out of Green Park and into The Mall, he could not help but wish that she would trust him implicitly and speak her mind without mincing words.

A most irrational wish, he conceded, but there it was! What had started as a ruse to see Penelope again had turned into a legitimate quest. He wanted to help her!

Absently he gazed at the huge chestnut trees lining The Mall. Their wide branches formed a dome over the carriage, and their blooms, like fat, white and pink candles, stood proudly among the dark green foliage. Simply having Penelope at his side turned springtime into a wondrous experience— but she wasn't seeing the lush colors or feeling the mellow air. She looked more troubled than before.

"Penny, my love," he said with an attempt at lightness, "if you persist in ignoring both me and Mother Nature, we may as well discuss what's so obviously on your mind. Do you want to tell me about it, or do you first wish to hear what I learned in Bow Street this afternoon?"

Startled, Penelope raised her eyes to his face. Could he read her mind? She had just been thinking of his visit to Bow Street.

"Yes, tell me, Julian." Eagerly she leaned toward him. Julian might have learned something that would set all her fears about Maria and Benjamin to rest. "Did you speak with the magistrate, Julian? What did he say?"

"I spoke with Sir Nathaniel Conant and with Theobald Dare." Julian slowed the horses to a walk, then turned to face Penelope. He felt like a traitor when he saw the expression of hope mingled with anxiety in her wide, brown eyes.

"What did they say?"

"Penny," he said gently, wishing he had the power to shield her from hurt. "Maria will not be released. The evidence Theobald Dare collected against her is overwhelming."

chapter EIGHT

Penelope listened in stunned silence to Julian's disclosures. Theobald Dare had painstakingly interrogated the servants of Lady Belmont's friends, including the staff of Lady Elizabeth Howe. From one of Lady Elizabeth's maids, whose brother was employed as a junior clerk at a bank, the Bow Street runner had learned that Maria was sending money to Switzerland on the twentieth of each month.

"And since the valuables were taken each month just prior to the twentieth," said Julian, "Theobald had no trouble convincing Sir Nathaniel that the bank's records should be examined."

Penelope shook her head. "It's all a misunderstanding. I know it is!"

Julian could feel her trembling. He cast a quick glance at the passersby, then slipped an arm around her waist. *To hell with the gapers!*

"No mistake, I'm afraid, Penny. Every month Maria transferred eight guineas to Geneva. To the account of 'Susannah Maria Hilbert, a minor.'"

"That's no crime! Aunt Sophy sends a monthly draft to her grandson in Venice."

"Maria's account at the bank shows a balance of fifteen shillings and eight pence. Has shown it since December of last year, Penny. Maria's quarterly salary from Lady Elizabeth is only nine pounds."

Penelope blanched. "Take me to Newgate Prison," she demanded. "I must speak with Maria."

Julian nodded. She was a pluck one, his little Penny. Displayed none of the missishness he would have expected from a gently bred young lady.

Twice Penelope and Julian drove to Newgate Prison. Twice they were turned away. Miss Hilbert was not allowed visitors, the warden said importantly. No, he could not give a reason. Orders were orders, and he must abide by them! He could only say that after a late-night visitor had left on the previous day, word had come from Sir Nathaniel Conant not to let anyone else see Miss Hilbert.

Not even a bribe offered to the matron, a bribe which, Julian assured Penelope, would open the gates of hell, produced as much as a tiny crack in the prison gate.

On the following day, after a third abortive attempt to see Maria, they stopped in Bow Street demanding to see the chief magistrate. Sir Nathaniel, they were told by his clerk Mr. Butterwick, was not available. Neither was Mr. Dare.

The evidence against Maria is overwhelming! For several days, Penelope was haunted by these words. Stubbornly she fought against them, yet again and again she'd recall the dull red flush spreading across Maria's face, the stricken expression in her eyes, and her sudden turning away.

She remembered Benjamin Rugby's reaction when he heard of Maria's arrest for theft; and from Mrs. Welby, who called daily in Berkeley Square seeking comfort and advice from Sophy, Penelope learned that Benjamin was still missing.

Penelope appropriated the small parlor on the ground floor as her own. When she wasn't out with Julian, this was where she stayed, tensing each time she heard a carriage enter Berkeley Square, then sighing with frustration when it passed or when it stopped to disgorge one of Sophy's numerous friends instead of Julian bringing welcome news.

On the fourth day, having worn a path on her aunt's Axminster carpet with her ceaseless pacing, Penelope gave in to her protesting feet and sat down on one of the brocaded chaise longues in the front parlor. She picked up her needlepoint, worked a few stitches, then flung it across the room, where it lay atop a tangled mass of wool floss that had suffered the same fate an hour earlier.

Penelope looked at the clock in its tall marquetry case, standing between the two bow-fronted windows. Not quite three o'clock yet. Julian would be at the office of *The Times*. Later in the evening he would be making the rounds in Covent Garden, visiting those ale and chop houses he knew to be favorite trysting places of the Bow Street runners. He planned to ply Mr. Dare with food, wine, and questions to find out why they could see neither the magistrate nor Maria.

Deep, rumbling noises inside the clock case alerted Penelope to the approaching full hour. In the ensuing deep-sounding booms, followed by loud, answering bongs from the clock in the hall, she all but missed the rapping of the knocker against the brass plate on the front door. The caller, however, persisted with his wild tattoo just a little longer than the clocks.

Penelope sprang to her feet. She hadn't even heard a carriage, and yet here was Julian! In a hurry! Flying out into the foyer, she saw Dawson approach from behind the green baize curtain, but she did not wait for him to perform his duties at the door. She flung the heavy front door open, then, expecting to see Julian, stood as though turned to stone.

The pale young woman outside looked pleadingly at Penelope. When Penelope did not speak, a dull flush of embarrassment spread over her face, and after a moment she slowly turned away.

Penelope regained control over her voice and limbs. "Maria!" she shouted as she rushed after her friend, catching her shoulders and drawing her into a wild hug. "Maria! You're free! How—when were you released? Oh, what the dickens are we doing out on the steps?" she added, half laughing, half crying. "Come inside!"

Maria, however, had second thoughts. Having run all the way from Lady Elizabeth's house in Brook Street with the sole intention of unburdening herself to her dear friend Penelope, she now drew back.

"I should never have come! It was wrong of me. I mustn't drag you into this. I am dreadfully sorry, Penelope!"

"Well, that's a speech of which I can neither make heads nor tails, my dear," Penelope said. "So you had best step into the parlor and explain it to me."

She might still have had a difficult time coaxing Maria up the stairs, but Dawson, observing the two young ladies in what looked suspiciously like a tussle, bore down on them. Taking one of Maria's elbows in a firm grip and nodding to Penelope to take the other, he said coaxingly, "Go ahead and lean on me, Miss Hilbert. I'm not too old yet to give support to a pretty young lady. Come on in now. Mind your step."

They deposited Maria on a chaise longue, and while Penelope raised Maria's feet and covered them with a rug, Dawson executed a stately bow, saying, "I'm that pleased to see you've returned, Miss Hilbert. All of us belowstairs were praying for you." Starting for the door he added, "I'll see that Maurice sets a tray with some of his pastries, and Mrs. Dawson will make you a nice cup of tea. There's nothing a cup of tea won't set to rights, she always says. And I've found her to be quite correct."

The two young women looked at each other. Maria was very pale with dark smudges ringing her eyes, telling of the sleepless nights she had spent in prison. Her light blond hair was drawn into an immaculate chignon at the nape of her neck, and she wore a crisp gown of pale gray bombazine.

Drawing a stool close to the chaise, Penelope sat down beside her friend. "You've seen Lady Elizabeth," she stated.

Tears welled up again in Maria's gray eyes, but she blinked them away. "Lady Elizabeth is looking for a new companion. She asked me to remove my things by tonight."

"I'll send Arthur to get your trunk. You'll stay with me until you can decide what to do next."

A moan escaped Maria. She threw her hands up, covering her face. "No, Penelope!" she cried in a muffled voice. "You won't wish to ask me when you learn what I've done!"

Gently but firmly Penelope uncovered her friend's face. "As soon as Dawson has brought the tea, you shall tell me everything, but now let me look at you, Maria. Are you all right? You didn't catch the fever, did you?" she asked anxiously.

"Physically I am fine. A little tired. That's all."

"I was so worried!" Penelope squeezed the cold hands resting in her own. "I tried to see you again. Twice."

Maria's eyes widened. "You did? I was afraid I had completely lost your friendship that first time."

"They wouldn't let me in."

Dawson, assisted by Rachel, entered just then with laden trays and set out the teapot, cups, and plates within Penelope's reach.

"Dawson," said Penelope, "would you please send Hunter and Arthur to Lady Elizabeth's house to fetch Miss Hilbert's trunk? And ask Mrs. Dawson to prepare the chamber next to mine."

Maria wanted to protest, but decided against it. Penelope could be so stubborn, and it would be just as easy later on to load her few belongings into a hackney here as in Brook Street.

Pouring tea and adding sugar and cream, Penelope asked, "When were you released, Maria?"

"At noon." Maria accepted her cup and sipped gratefully.

Although her meals had improved with her transfer to the master's side, they had never been very good, and the tea she'd been sent had always arrived cold. "I must thank you, Penelope, for having arranged my move," she said awkwardly.

"Oh!" Penelope recalled that she had not yet reimbursed Julian. "Don't thank me. It was Mr. Rutherford who thought of it. Do you remember? He was with me when . . ." Her voice trailed off. How horrid this conversation was! Horrid and awkward!

Drawing herself up a bit straighter, Penelope said, "Maria, I know that you were arrested because of the money you sent to Switzerland. But why have you been released? Did they—tell me, did they catch the thief?" she asked excitedly.

"No." Maria pressed shaking fingers against her cheeks. "They arrested Benjamin."

"Mr. Rugby?"

Maria's gray eyes swam with tears. "He's not a thief, Penelope! He came to see me. Came straight from Mrs. Welby's musicale when you told him of my arrest."

"So he's the mysterious late-night visitor the warden told us about."

"He . . . he promised to have me released. I didn't know then what he planned to do. I swear I didn't. I would never have accepted his sacrifice."

"I was right. He *is* in love with you," Penelope said softly.

A blush stole across Maria's face. "Yes," she murmured, then, her voice growing harsh, she said, "And now Benjamin is in that horrible place! In Newgate Prison!"

Penelope was beginning to understand. "He went to Bow Street and confessed that he committed the thefts, didn't he?"

"Yes!" Maria cried. "But only to save me! Benjamin is no thief. *I* stole Lady Spatterton's necklace and sold it! It was I, not Benjamin!"

Cold shivers spread all over Penelope's body. The roof of her mouth felt dry, and she knew that, even if she found the necessary words, her voice would not obey her.

Maria a thief!

Penelope rose and stepped over to the what-not in the

corner by the fireplace. A diligent search of its contents finally disclosed an almost full bottle of brandy. After pouring generous measures into two glasses and fortifying herself with a large sip, she returned to the chaise longue.

"Here," she said, and her voice was just a bit unsteady. "Drink some of this, Maria. You'll need it, for I won't give you any peace until you've told me everything."

"You do not turn from me in disgust? You don't even ask me if I have stolen all those other items as well? If I remember correctly, the Bow Street magistrate charged me with five burglaries, including the theft of your aunt's opals!"

"Fiddle!" Penelope said impatiently. "As though you would!"

"Then you'll help me clear Benjamin's name?"

"I'll help you, Maria, but first we must make certain that you won't have to go back to prison. Can we buy Lady Spatterton's pearls back?"

Maria's head drooped. "I fear not. I went back to that horrible man the very next day, and he told me they were sold."

"What horrible man? Didn't you go to a jeweler?"

A strand of pale blond hair escaped from the chignon as Maria shook her head. "I dared not. I was afraid the pearls would be recognized."

Penelope had only seen them once, three long ropes fastening around the wearer's neck with a large diamond clasp, and she doubted not that Maria was right. Any self-respecting jeweler would have immediately made inquiries. "Where, then, did you sell the necklace?"

"In Fetter Lane. I remembered one of the footmen telling us in the servants' hall that Fetter Lane boasts more pawnbrokers and fences than honest shopkeepers."

With a shudder of revulsion Maria remembered the dark, dusty shop and the old man who had fondled the pearls in his grimy hands. She heard again the clacking sound made by his long, black-rimmed fingernails as he drew the strands through his fingers, counting the pearls.

And the following day, when she had asked, then demanded to be allowed to buy the necklace back, he had cackled with laughter and told her she had more hair than wits if she believed that he still had the pearls.

"How much did he give you for the necklace?" asked Penelope.

"Twenty pounds."

"What!" A drop of brandy spilled onto Penelope's gown as she sat up indignantly. "It must be worth ten times that!"

"I know, but Sprott is 'a businessman not a charitable institution,' as he himself informed me. And I really don't want the money now, Penelope! I'd gladly give him twice the amount if only I could return the pearls to Lady Spatterton!"

"Don't upset yourself." Penelope handed over her handkerchief when she saw Maria fumble blindly with the clasp of her reticule. "Julian and I will see to everything for you. If you still have the twenty pounds from—what's his name? Sprott? How did you get the money you sent to Geneva every month? And why in heaven's name didn't you come to me if you needed funds?"

Maria blushed a fiery red, then paled again. "How could I ask you? I cannot accept money from my best friend when I have no means to repay you!" She looked down at her nervously clutching hands. "But I had to tell someone," she whispered. "And so I went to Benjamin."

"Mrs. Welby obviously pays him a better salary than Lady Elizabeth pays you."

"Yes," Maria said simply. "A very generous salary. Benjamin has money saved so that we can buy a small house when . . . when we marry. And he offered to pay all expenses for—" She broke off. In an effort to maintain her composure, she picked up her glass and drank.

"For Susannah?" Penelope asked gently.

Maria choked. "Yes," she sputtered. "My daughter Susannah Maria. She is twelve years old."

Penelope's eyes widened. Maria was eight-and-twenty. She had been a child herself when Susannah was born! "Will you tell me about her?"

Maria set down her glass, flung the rug off her legs, and rose. "Let's go sit by the window."

The two comfortable armchairs facing each other in the

bow window had ever been their favorites, Maria always choosing the one on the right, Penelope the slightly smaller one on the left. And thus it was again on this day.

"I don't know where to begin," Maria said helplessly.

"The beginning?" Penelope suggested and knew a moment of satisfaction when a spark of her old humor briefly lit up Maria's eyes.

Leaning her head against the back of her chair and turning toward the window, Maria seemed to be addressing someone beyond the glass panes. "I was sixteen," she began in a hesitant voice. "Well, almost sixteen..."

Slowly her voice gained confidence, and while nursery maids took their charges for an airing in the enclosure out in the square, while ladies and gentlemen rolled by in their open carriages on their way to Hyde Park, Maria told of her brief, passionate love affair with a young ensign on leave from Sir John Moore's troops.

Maria's father had been the rector of a small but prosperous parish in Sussex, and Maria was brought up very strictly. Yet all her father's strictures, all her mother's warnings, were forgotten when the handsome young man in his red tunic and gold braids told her he loved her.

"He promised to marry me, Penelope, before he returned to Portugal. Then he announced his betrothal to the daughter of an earl while I gave birth to our daughter."

"Oh, my dear!" Penelope cried out. "How you must have suffered!"

A sad smile flitted across Maria's face. "It was nothing compared to the pain and fear I suffer for Benjamin. With my parents' help I recovered from the shock. But then Susannah began to ail. Our doctor diagnosed consumption."

"Maria, I am sorry." Reaching out, Penelope took Maria's hand and squeezed it gently. "Now I understand why Susannah is in Switzerland. I read about the hospitals among the pine trees, where the air is beneficial to the patients."

"I took Susannah to Switzerland in the fall of 1808. She wasn't two years old yet. It was the last time I saw her."

As though Maria wished to prevent an expression of sympathy from Penelope, she rushed on to say, "I started to work for Lady Elizabeth as soon as I returned. Even so, I would not have been able to pay for Susannah's stay in the sanatorium, had my father not helped.''

''Your father died eighteen months ago,'' Penelope said. ''Your brother now holds his living. Could he not help you?''

Maria was silent for a long time, then sat up and looked fully at Penelope. ''My brother refused to pay for my 'bastard brat' as he calls her,'' she said in a harsh, bitter voice. ''In December, I sent the last of my savings to Switzerland, and in January, two days before the next payment was due to be sent— Oh, Penelope,'' she cried. ''The pearls were in the chamber where we left our cloaks that night! Just lying there on top of the small rosewood table! And I kept thinking, what if a servant saw them and took them?''

Penelope sat motionless, staring out into the square where the shadows were lengthening and the nursemaids collected their charges to take them home before the evening air would turn cool.

What utter confusion, Penelope thought numbly. *What a terrible mull!* Maria seemed to believe that Benjamin would be released as soon as his innocence was established. But how—if he himself insisted that he was the thief?

And if the Bow Street runners did indeed find that he could not have stolen the articles because, perhaps, he was somewhere else at the time, wouldn't they simply come for Maria again?

''I must go back to Bow Street,'' Maria said. ''I cannot let Benjamin take the blame for what I did.''

''No!'' Penelope jumped up. She laid her hands on Maria's shoulders, pressing her back into the chair. ''You can't do that. Think of Susannah!''

''They don't often hang people anymore,'' Maria said tonelessly. ''Not for stealing. If I'm transported—*you* would look after Susannah, wouldn't you, Penelope? It wouldn't be too great a financial burden?''

''Of course I'd look after Susannah!''

With a feeling of shame, Penelope remembered the large amount of money at her disposal. She doubted not that she had sufficient funds in her account at Hoare's Bank to pay for Susannah's care for several years. And she had her investments.

If only Maria hadn't been too proud to ask for help sooner! "I shan't let you be transported, Maria! Just give me a moment to think."

Two gentlemen strolled into view below the window. Penelope recognized old Colonel Wringer and his nephew, who lived in the tall brick building at the corner of Berkeley Square and Charles Street. Colonel Wringer, dressed in one of his old-fashioned frock coats, carried a folded newspaper under his arm.

Penelope stared at the newspaper. "Excuse me for a moment, Maria," she said. "I must write a note to Mr. Rutherford. He knows the Bow Street runners well, you see, and also Sir Nathaniel Conant."

Penelope hurried to the study where she quickly penned a note. As she returned to the parlor, Arthur came through the hall and said, "We've brung Miss 'Ilbert's trunks, Miss Penelope."

"Thank you, Arthur. And now, would you please take this note to Mr. Rutherford? He should be at the offices of *The Times*. Do you know where they are located?"

"Yes, Miss Penelope. H'in—" Arthur broke off, waiting for the two clocks to announce to all and sundry that the hour was four o'clock. "H'in Printing 'Ouse Square, Miss Penelope."

Penelope carefully folded the note. Handing it to the footman, she said, "Be sure to ask for the address of Mr. Rutherford's boardinghouse if he is not there."

"H'of course, miss." Looking affronted, Arthur bowed, then stalked off.

Penelope had barely rejoined her friend when Lady Belmont followed by two long, trailing scarves rushed into the parlor. "Dearest Maria! No one told me you were here until I asked about the commotion on the stairs and in the corridor. Your trunks, you know!" she cried, enveloping Maria in a hug from which that young lady found it rather difficult to extricate herself since one of the scarves had wrapped itself around her arm.

"You don't mind, then, that Penelope invited me to stay?" Maria asked shyly. She took the scarves from Sophy's fluttering hands, folded them neatly, and draped them over the arm of a chair. "Lady Elizabeth dismissed me," she added in a low voice.

"I shall have to have a talk with Elizabeth. She's getting too top-lofty by half. Don't you worry, Maria. She'll have you back!" Sophy laughed. "Elizabeth can't live without a companion, and I doubt she'll find anyone willing to do all those millions of tasks you perform daily. She'll beg you to return to her!"

"I hope Lady Elizabeth will find a new companion," Maria said quietly, "for I intend to marry Mr. Rugby. Until then, if Lady Elizabeth needs me, I'll be happy to help out."

Sophy exclaimed at the news, and while they sipped champagne from the well-stocked Belmont cellars, Penelope explained why Benjamin Rugby was now imprisoned instead of Maria. She carefully refrained from mentioning Lady Spatterton's pearl necklace and, when Maria would have done so, shook her head at her friend and deftly changed the subject to Dr. Ludlow.

"Oh, I wish he'd come!" cried Sophy. "If only he didn't have so many patients!" Her hands flew to her head, rubbing against her temples and neck. "I'm afraid a headache may be coming on, and I have sent Sweetings to Grafton House for new ribbons for my nightcaps. I am tired of pink," she said plaintively.

"Let me massage your neck, Auntie." Penelope rose to stand behind Sophy's chair, but after a few minutes had to admit defeat. She could not relax the tense spots she felt under her fingertips, and her aunt squirmed and fidgeted so much that she found it difficult to concentrate on the massage.

"Why don't I take you upstairs, Lady Belmont," suggested Maria. "If you loosen your stays and lie down on your bed, I'll rub your neck and shoulders. I've often done the same for Lady Elizabeth."

Sophy agreed to the scheme and after some fussing with the shawls, which had to be draped just so, left with Maria.

A sigh escaped Penelope when the door closed behind them. Slowly she walked over to the window. Leaning her forehead against the cool glass, she reflected wryly that, before the day was out, she would most likely suffer from a worse headache than her aunt had ever known.

If only Maria had not taken the necklace! But she had, and having been informed of the circumstances, Penelope could not blame her. Instead, she directed her anger toward Lady Elizabeth, who did not pay Maria half enough for her untiring services. Maria had been with the widow for ten years; surely a sign of fortitude and great character strength when Lady Elizabeth's servants generally stayed no longer than ten weeks!

Poor Maria. It must be simply awful to have a child and not be able to see her. And Maria was not safe yet! If it should become known that one of the thefts must indeed be laid at her door . . . ! And even if they could prove that she tried to retrieve the necklace, it would not help her then.

The necklace! Closing her eyes, Penelope envisioned the luminous strands hidden away in a filthy drawer in Fetter Lane. Who in his right mind would go to Fetter Lane looking for valuable pearls? No one!

Sprott must have lied to Maria. He could not possibly have found a buyer from one day to the next.

The clip-clop of horses' hooves on the cobbles and the rattle of carriage wheels rang loud in her ears. Her eyes flew open just as Julian pulled his curricle to a halt in front of the house. She saw Arthur leap down and run to the horses' heads, then Julian descended in a more leisurely fashion.

A feeling of warmth washed over Penelope as Julian walked up the steps to the front door. Not until this moment did she realize how much she had looked forward to his coming, how much she depended on his strength and his confidence.

Pushing away from the window, Penelope rushed out into the entrance hall just as the knocker fell against the brass plate. Breathlessly, she flung the heavy door open.

"Julian! I can't tell you how glad I am to see you! No, don't take your gloves off. We must drive to Fetter Lane this instant!"

Without undue haste Julian reached out, halting her mad dash down the steps with a firm grip on her upper arm.

"Not if you twist your ankle or break your neck, my dear," he drawled, noting the high color in her cheeks, the bright sparkle in her eyes. "You wrote that Maria has been released from prison. So what's the great hurry? Surely I'm entitled to a better explanation than your illegible scribble."

For an instant her eyes flared with impatience, then the flame died. "I shan't rip up at you, Julian," she said in a voice heavy with reproach. "I'll save my anger for Sprott. Only let's not dawdle, I beg you. There's not a moment to be lost if we want to recover Lady Spatterton's necklace!"

He bowed. "Very well, Penny. You may explain on the way to—Fetter Lane, you said?"

"Yes. Only come now, Julian," she said, pulling him toward the curricle.

And you believed she was excited to see you, Julian chided himself. *Because it's been twenty-seven-and-a-half interminable hours! You bloody fool!*

chapter
NINE

"**Y**ou'll not credit what Maria disclosed to me, Julian!" Penelope stepped into the curricle, in her haste displaying rather more ankle and calf than was seemly.

She thought she heard a whistle behind her, such as she had heard from the boys and men outside Newgate Prison when Julian kissed her. She looked, but there was only Julian, waiting patiently until she had arranged the folds of her gown about her feet before climbing in beside her.

"I shan't even venture a guess," he said, "but I warrant it's something quite out of the ordinary to make you dash off without your hat and gloves, or,'' he added, glancing at the short, puffed sleeves of Penelope's muslin gown, ''a wrap.''

''The sun's still out,'' she said dismissively.

Julian took up the reins, nodded to Arthur to let go of the bays' heads, and off they went at a brisk pace. ''But for how long, Penny, my love? It must be close to six o'clock, and it'll turn cool very soon.''

Her bosom swelled. ''If you mean to scold me, Julian—''

''Not at all. I'm merely concerned that I shall lose my coat before long. And a man's lawn shirt is not much better than a lady's muslin, don't you know?''

''Of all the odious—'' She broke off, looking at him with suspicion. There was a definite twinkle in his gray-green eyes, and his mouth twitched suspiciously. ''I *am* a gullible flat. You're bamming me, Julian. How can you, at a time like this?''

''You're just not up to snuff, Penny.''

''I asked you not to call me that!''

''Did you, my love? Let me assure you, though,'' Julian said while shrugging out of his coat, ''that I've been waiting for just such an occasion to show you how very gentlemanly I can behave.'' Holding the reins in one hand, he started to drape his coat across her shoulders.

''Th-thank you.'' His body's warmth still lingered in the material, caressing her bare arms and penetrating the thin muslin of her gown. ''But there was no call for you to do this, Julian. I was quite comfortable.''

''It was very necessary,'' he said. ''Now, when the hours till I see you again drag too long, I shall wear this coat, and the essence of you will be with me.''

Her eyes flew to his face. Surely he was teasing again. But his expression held none of the mischief she expected, and the smile he bestowed on her was open, holding not a particle of guile.

Disconcerted, Penelope looked down at her hands, telling herself not to be a wet-goose; it was quite absurd to suspect that Julian had conceived a *tendre* for her. Why, she was almost an old maid. Almost on the shelf. Besides, he would know that nothing could come of an attachment between a lady of quality and a reporter.

Wouldn't he?

It took her a few moments to recover her composure, but finally, realizing that her prolonged silence might give him the notion that she was affected by his words and that, moreover, they were fast approaching their destination, Penelope roused herself sufficiently to inform Julian of the fate of the Spatterton necklace and of Benjamin Rugby's arrest.

"So that's what was in the wind," he said. "I felt certain Theobald wasn't telling me all of it when he enumerated the evidence against Miss Hilbert. But that's bad news!"

"Why? Surely, if Mr. Rugby is innocent, we'll be able to prove it!"

"We? Are we to save the whole world, Penny?"

"Only Maria, and Benjamin Rugby. And then, of course, it would be awfully nice if we could recover Aunt Sophy's opals."

"Of course. But I must warn you that Theobald Dare most certainly discovered something against your Mr. Rugby. Why else would Sir Nathaniel have kept him—and Miss Hilbert—for three days? And then, suddenly, Miss Hilbert is free to go, and Rugby stays!"

"I daresay you're right." Penelope thought for a moment, then, brightening, said, "There's only one thing to be done. We must find out *what* the Bow Street runner found against Benjamin Rugby and prove that it isn't so!"

"I was afraid you'd say that."

"No, you weren't, Julian. You were hoping I wouldn't give up. Remember, it was *your* notion to write an article, 'Lady and Reporter Solve Mysterious Thefts.'"

"Ah, yes. A reporter's obligations. What a settler, Penny! Did you have to remind me of my position?"

Their eyes met. Penelope felt a flush warm her face. She shook her head, denying his accusation, but she could not form the words to reassure him. Had it, indeed, been her intention? Had she planned to remind him of the disparity of their stations?

"Well, here we are," said Julian, turning his bays from Fleet Street into Fetter Lane. "What did you say the name of the fence is?"

"I don't know for certain that he is a fence. He might be a pawnbroker or a moneylender, but I believe Maria called him Sprott."

"He may have spoken the truth when he told Maria that he sold the pearls. You realize that, don't you, Penny?"

Penelope stared at the malodorous refuse littering the street, the peeling storefronts, the broken doors and windows. The women and children scurrying out of the curricle's path were ragged and unkempt, their faces sharp and unsmiling.

Who'd come to buy pearls in this neighborhood?

Few men were about, but those few, gaudily dressed in imitation of the Bond Street dandies and lolling against the door posts of some gin or ale house, stared boldly at Penelope. Despite Julian's presence—his broad shoulders not inches from her—she felt vulnerable under their insolent looks.

And Maria had come here on her own!

"We're looking for a man named Sprott," Julian called out to a boy, taller and huskier than the band of urchins surrounding him. Fetter Lane boasted no sidewalk, and the children were playing some game with pebbles and small rocks in the gutter. "Do you know where Sprott lives?"

The boy jerked his dirt-streaked chin northward. Barefoot, dressed in a pair of torn breeches and an oversized coat, he started to walk alongside the curricle. About a dozen urchins detached themselves from the knot of ragged children and followed him at a respectful distance. The silent procession continued for the space of six or seven buildings, then the boy stopped before a house that looked, if possible, meaner than its neighbors.

Julian brought the curricle to a halt. "This is where Sprott lives?" he asked, eyeing the doorless entrance with some doubt. Surely no pawnbroker or fence would have his place of business in this tumbledown house.

"Second floor," the boy said gruffly. "An' ye better let me an' the boys take care of yer 'orses."

Julian nodded. He reached into his pocket, selecting a coin. Tossing it to the boy, he said, "When I come back, you'll get another shilling and the members of your band sixpence each.''

Penelope gave a start. She hadn't brought a purse or a reticule, and here Julian was spending money on her behalf again. How in heaven's name was she to buy Lady Spatterton's necklace?

"Julian," she said urgently. "I just remembered—Sprott paid Maria twenty pounds. But I didn't bring any money."

"Don't fret." He sprang lightly from the curricle, then came around to help her down. "I have enough to pay him twice that amount. Come along now. We don't want to leave the horses too long. Someone," he said with a speaking glance at two men lounging in the doorway of a gin shop across the road, "may take it into his head to drive off in a curricle-and-pair."

As they approached Sprott's place of business, Julian's frown became forbidding. He eyed with disgust the filthy, crumbling stone steps leading straight from the street to the entryway. "I hate to have to take you inside with me, Penny, but I can't very well leave you outside either. I suppose I should never have allowed you to come along."

"But then you wouldn't be here either," she pointed out, "for I wouldn't have told you about it."

"You would, no doubt," he said with a smile, "have taken Dawson to lend you countenance. Mind your step, Penny!"

Penelope stared at the narrow stairs winding steeply to the upper floors. Grease, filth, and refuse littered the steps. On one or two that she could see in the increasing gloom, the wood had splintered, and great, jagged edges stuck out, threatening to trip the unwary. And the smell drifting in a palpable cloud from above, why, it was first cousin to the stink of Newgate Prison!

Clamping one hand over her mouth and nose and with the other lifting the hem of her skirts as far as she dared, Penelope picked her way carefully to the next story. Julian's hand on her elbow did much to hearten her, yet she did not quite lose her fear of slipping on spilled grease, or something even worse, and tumbling headlong down the filthy stairs.

When they reached the second floor, Julian stopped before a stout oak door blocking off the stairwell and landing from Sprott's flat. In contrast to the rest of the house, the door was fairly new and boasted solid iron hinges and a lock.

"I didn't think too highly of Sprott when the boy pointed out this building," he said, "but I own I was mistaken in him. Sprott does have some sense."

Julian tried the door but found it locked. Raising a fist, he hammered on the panels.

Standing a little farther back than he, Penelope saw an eye appear at a small knot hole in the door, at about the same height as Julian's shoulder. She tugged on Julian's sleeve and, when she caught his attention, pointed silently to the observer.

"Sprott! If you're open for business, let us in," Julian demanded. "If you're closed, we'll go elsewhere, but don't expect me to stand kicking my heels out here!"

Instantly the eye disappeared and a piece of cloth was stuffed into the hole. A key turned smoothly, betraying its action only by a soft click as the lock snapped back. The door swung open on well-oiled hinges.

"Pardon me," Julian murmured, taking Penelope's hand and entering the dark corridor just ahead of her.

"Good evenin', m'lady, m'lord."

Penelope could not see the man, but the servile tone of his grating voice awoke instant distrust in her breast, and when she heard the door close behind her, pitching them into stygian darkness, she could not quite suppress a shiver of fear. Tightening her fingers around Julian's warm hand, she stood stock-still.

"Let's have some light, Sprott!" Julian said sharply. "Have your wits gone abegging, man? You must have seen the lady with me. Do you wish her to take a fall?"

"Patience, patience, m'lord. I'm a poor man. Must practice economy."

The meager flame of a taper flickered, briefly illuminating a scraggly, gray beard and a nose that must have been broken at least twice to acquire its crooked and at the same time flattened appearance.

The wick in an old-fashioned oil lamp caught on the burning taper, and as Sprott turned up the light, the man and his abode were revealed in all their dirty splendor.

He was a small, hunched man with raisin eyes and hands like bony claws. Four rooms, two on each side, led off the narrow hallway. The doors stood open, exposing a jungle of clothing on racks, hooks, and spilling from barrels; there were weapons of all kinds and description, silverware, china, books, paintings, and bric-a-brac.

Penelope could see now why the place had been so dark: heavy planks were nailed across the window in each room, denying entry to light and, she supposed, possible intruders.

"Come, m'lady. Come an' have a seat." Bowing and scraping, Sprott waved her into the last room on the right. Then, seeing her hesitate, he scuttled ahead to dust off a chair with the flick of one of his long coattails. "There now, that's better, ain't it?"

His coat, his whole person, were no cleaner than anything in the room, and Penelope declined his offer of the chair. "I've come to see some jewelry," she said. "Pearls."

Sprott's small, dark eyes flicked from her to Julian. He chuckled, and the sound grated in Penelope's ear as much as his voice did.

"Well now," said Sprott, setting the lamp on the heavy pedestal table in the center of the room and seating himself behind it. "Well now. In the gen'ral way of things, when a lady comes to me humble establishment, she's wishful of sellin' me something. To tide her over until quarter day so to speak. An' if she's wishful of buyin', she hares off to them fancy Rundell and Bridge's."

"I want to buy from you," Penelope said stubbornly.

"Pearls." Sprott's eyes held a faintly menacing gleam. "Yes."

"Ye wouldn't have anything of a partic'lar nature in mind, would ye, m'lady?"

Julian, who had so far stood by as though he were no more than a mere footman, took a step closer. "Something very particular, Sprott. We want to buy the pearls sold to you in January. And don't say you can't remember, for I doubt you've ever been offered a necklace of similar value before.''

Sprott didn't try to hide behind the facade of well-meaning shopkeeper any longer. ''Then I won't say it.'' He sneered. ''And what's more, ye can't buy 'em.''

Penelope put a tight rein on her rising temper. ''Mr. Sprott, you paid twenty pounds for the pearls. We're prepared to buy them back for twice as much.''

He smirked. ''Forty sovereigns? When they're worth close to three hundred?''

''How much do you want?'' asked Julian.

''That being a moot question, I won't try ter answer, m'lord.''

Julian took another step toward the table. He was so close now that Sprott, even if he were half blind, could not mistake the threat in the gray-green eyes or ignore the powerful muscles of arms and shoulders displayed beneath the lawn shirt.

''I want that necklace,'' Julian said softly. ''If I have to turn this place inside out—''

''Nay!'' Sprott thrust back his chair and jumped to his feet. '' 'Twouldn't be no use, m'lord! I don't have the pearls!''

''Where are they?'' In a few quick strides, Julian rounded the table. His hands shot out, fastening on the lapels of Sprott's coat. Slowly he raised the man off the ground. ''Where?''

Sprott let out a squeak. ''Sold!''

''Liar!'' Despite her repugnance for his person, Penelope stepped closer. ''You said yourself that anyone wishing to *buy* jewelry would go to Rundell and Bridge's.''

''Set me down!'' shrieked Sprott. ''I'll explain, only set me down!''

''Don't,'' said Penelope, but Julian slowly let the sweating man down.

Brushing a sleeve across his forehead, Sprott fell into his chair. ''I have connections in Italy,'' he choked out. ''An' on the mornin' when Miss Hilbert wanted to take the necklace back, me buyer had just left—with the pearls an' several other items too, ah—''

"Too hot for you to sell in England," said Julian scathingly. "That I can well believe."

"He"—Penelope pointed a shaky finger at Sprott—"he said 'Miss Hilbert'!"

"So he did." Fighting his desire to throttle the old muckworm, Julian moved himself and his itching hands behind the solid barrier of the pedestal table. "Surely the young lady didn't volunteer her name. How did you weasel it out of her?"

"Can't be too careful," Sprott whined. "I had her followed. Only to protect meself, you understand! Well, 'twas Lombard Street to a China orange that she had nabbed the goods from some well-heeled old dame!"

Julian advanced again. "You filthy, stinking sewer rat!" he said in a voice that was barely audible but made the hair at the back of Sprott's neck stand on edge.

"Ah, but 'twas a good thing I did, m'lord. Ye won't credit this, but Miss Hilbert threatened me with the Bow Street runners when I said she couldn't buy them baubles back. Threatened *me*, the great Sprott!"

His fingers curled around the knob on the drawer attached below the tabletop. "Had to set her straight, m'lord," he babbled. "Had to point out that Bow Street would be very interested to learn where *she* got them pearls. Very interested! Told her she'd end her days on the nubbin' cheat."

Applying to his ancestors for help in his hour of need, Sprott jerked open the drawer. His fingers closed around the silver-mounted handle of a deadly accurate hairtrigger pistol.

Julian threw himself across the table, one hand going for Sprott's throat, the other for the weapon arm. Sprott struggled valiantly, but he was no match for Julian's superior strength. Julian rammed Sprott's elbow onto the tabletop. Sprott screamed; the gun clattered from his numb fingers, discharging its shot with a deafening bang.

Startled, Penelope dropped the heavy silver teapot she had picked off a shelf to bash against any part of Sprott's anatomy that might offer itself as a target.

"Julian!" she cried.

"I'm quite unharmed."

Julian hauled Sprott to his side of the table. As he turned

to look at Penelope, his eyes fell on a bloodied object on the cluttered shelf behind her. "The unfortunate victim of this altercation," he said in a strangled voice, "lies on that shelf. But don't look! It's not a pretty sight."

Cautiously Penelope took a peek. "A rat!" She blanched and left the vicinity of the shelf rather hastily. "Julian, how can you laugh! And you, sirrah," she said to Sprott, "are a rat as well. Let that be a lesson to you!"

"What else have you found out about Miss Hilbert?" asked Julian, his hand still on Sprott's throat.

"She . . . she works for Lady Elizabeth Howe an' . . ."

"And what?"

"The pearls . . . they was Lady Spatterton's pearls."

"You bastard!" Julian said through his teeth. "You knew that the young lady would come back to redeem the necklace! You must have known it!"

He wanted to drag the man by his scrawny neck all the way to Bow Street. He wanted to— But he must see Penny safe. He tossed Sprott against the table. "Come, Penny. I feel stifled in here."

Penelope would have said more to Sprott but, remembering the dark corridor, hastily availed herself of Julian's proffered hand. The stairwell, too, was now steeped in complete darkness, and when she stepped outside, she was not surprised to see that dusk had fallen, hiding the filth and squalor of Fetter Lane. But no degree of darkness could disguise the awful stench.

While Julian paid off the urchins, she stood for a moment outside Sprott's house, looking up at the second story. Not a sliver of light showed in the boarded-up windows. The whole floor looked deserted.

Penelope turned to join Julian at the curricle. Raising her skirts to step over a pile of refuse, she was caught by surprise when suddenly the basement door behind her burst open. A beam of light fell on the refuse at her feet.

Gasping, Penelope took a step backward. A dog! A big dog, its body so torn and mangled it looked like a mass of blood and bones. And it lay right in front of the curricle.

"Julian," she whispered, but her voice did not reach him, surrounded as he was by the excited mob of young boys. She retreated farther, until the strip of iron railing around the area steps pressed against her hips.

She felt her stomach heave and her head go cold and numb. Quickly she turned around. Clasping the rail, Penelope prayed she wouldn't be sick.

A young girl, wearing a low-cut red taffeta gown, her golden curls arranged artfully atop her head, stood in the open shop door of the basement below. "Erskin!" she called to someone inside the shop. "Are ye comin'?" She giggled, adding, "Or shall I ask Tom Warbler to take me to Vauxhall?"

"I'll 'ave 'is 'ide if 'e casts 'is ogles over ye just one more time!" a man replied threateningly, but the girl only giggled again, then turned to come up the short flight of stone steps.

She was pretty in a bold way, Penelope noted vaguely. Kohl had obviously been applied to her eyes, and paint of a provocative shade of carmine to her lips and cheeks. She stopped when she saw Penelope staring down at her.

The girl's eyes widened, then she hurtled up the last few steps, shrieking, "Best hurry, Erskin, or you'll not get past! The lady looks ready to cast up her accounts!"

A young man stepped out of the basement shop, shot one look at Penelope, then took the stairs two at a time to carry himself and his natty gold and turquoise waistcoat to safety. "Eh, let's see Sprott first, luv," Penelope heard him say.

Then she was very sick indeed.

She was aware of strong hands holding her head, of a deep, soothing voice murmuring words of encouragement. When the worst was over, a large handkerchief smelling faintly of bay rum was pressed into her hands.

"There now, my love," said Julian. "Feeling better?"

Penelope nodded. With shaking fingers she wiped her face. "It was the dog," she said, leaning weakly against him.

In the light streaming from the open basement door Julian saw the freckles on her nose stand out boldly against the pallor of her skin. Tremors shook her slender frame, and her eyes looked too large for her pale face.

Julian swept her up into his arms. "Dog baiting," he said

curtly as he carefully stepped over the mangled animal. "It's still practiced by some folks."

Not until they had left Fetter Lane well behind, did Penelope's mind begin to function again in its customary, precise manner. It told her in no uncertain terms that she had sunk herself below reproach. That she had been sick was bad enough, but that Julian had been there to witness her humiliation was not to be borne!

A wave of shame washed over her, leaving her weaker than before. He had even helped her, had held her head! *Like a father!* But he had called her my love, which didn't sound fatherly at all and made everything so much worse.

"I am sorry, Julian," she murmured. "I don't understand why I turned so missish. I never before—"

"Great Scot!" Julian interrupted in some astonishment. "Missish? If you don't stop apologizing, I'll call you worse than missish! First the rat, then the dog—why, it would turn the stoutest stomach. It did mine, I assure you."

A sound halfway between a sob and a choke of laughter escaped her. "At least you didn't cast up your accounts, Julian."

"That's better," he said approvingly, "but don't let Maria hear that expression. It is not at all the thing for a lady to say."

"No, is it? I learned it from that young lady who came out of the locksmith shop in the basement."

"She was *not* a lady," Julian said sternly.

Penelope fell silent. There had been something remotely familiar about that young girl, but she couldn't quite put her finger on it. She made a mental review of the maids and serving girls she had met in the homes of her aunt's friends. None of them fit the description.

She closed her eyes, trying to recall every feature of the pretty, rouged face, but all she suddenly remembered was a shingle attached to the door frame above the girl's blond locks.

Samuel Abel—Master Locksmith.

The locksmith employed by her aunt whenever a key had been misplaced!

chapter
<u>TEN</u>

There was no reason to feel uneasy, Penelope told herself. No reason why she should think of Samuel Abel and immediately remember that the thief must have had a key or an accomplice inside each house he had robbed . . .

"Spring 'em, Julian!" Penelope demanded imperiously. "There is something I wish to ask Dawson."

"And," Julian pointed out, "we must take another look at that list of suspects we made."

The bays picked up speed, and shortly the curricle rattled at a spanking clip down brightly lit Piccadilly, causing one dowager, whose lozenged carriage they overtook, to lower her window and shout, "Where's the fire?"

Julian chuckled and with barely a check swept around the slower-moving vehicle and into Berkeley Square. He feathered the corner into the square, then pulled up with a flourish before Belmont House. As Julian sprang to the ground, the front door was opened by Arthur. Soft light spilled from the wall sconces in the foyer down the marble steps.

"Please take Mr. Rutherford's curricle into the mews, Arthur," said Penelope, hurrying up the stairs. "Where's Dawson?"

"H'in the dining salon, Miss Penelope. Miriam be takin' 'er first lessons layin' the table." Arthur marched off to take the bays to the stables in the mews.

Penelope stood in the entrance hall, undecided whether to interrupt Dawson in his exacting task or change out of her undoubtedly soiled gown, when the old butler's shuffling steps approached from the rear of the hallway and, at the same time, Julian came running up the front steps.

"Miss Penelope," said Dawson, a martial gleam in his eyes. "You shouldn't have gone out without your pelisse. Her ladyship was that worried when she heard you'd rushed off with Mr. Rutherford and no more than a muslin gown to protect you from the treacherous night air."

"And who was the feather head to tell my aunt?" Penelope said crossly. "As you see for yourself, Mr. Rutherford took excellent care of me."

Slipping Julian's coat off her shoulders, she handed it to the affronted butler. "Have it brushed and pressed, Dawson. And also have a place set for Mr. Rutherford. He will stay to dine."

Julian looked at her in some amusement. "On your high ropes, Penny? But no more will I stay to dine than you planned to invite me. You know very well that I cannot sit down at the dinner table in all my dirt—and boots. Lady Belmont would think me a very loose fish indeed."

Although Penelope suspected that Julian would not at all pay attention to what her aunt, or, for that matter, anyone, might think of him, his refusal had an astonishing effect on Dawson's attitude. The butler mellowed quite visibly.

"Her ladyship is not one to stand on ceremony, Mr. Rutherford," Dawson said in a fatherly manner. "And as to your boots, if you wouldn't mind stepping belowstairs for a minute or two, we'll have them bright and glossy in no time at all. But as for you, Miss Penelope," he continued, casting a baleful look at the hem of her gown, "you had best make haste and change afore her ladyship lays eyes on you."

Torn between annoyance and amusement, Penelope opted for the latter. "Oh, very well," she said on a gurgle of laughter. "But I wish you would stop treating me like a nursling, Dawson."

A responsive glint momentarily brightened the rheumy old eyes. "Be that as it may, Miss Penelope. You know very well that her ladyship would have a spasm if she saw the bloodstain on your gown."

"The rat!" Penelope exclaimed.

Gingerly raising her skirt, she started up the stairs.

"Dawson! If you didn't make me forget the reason I wanted to see you!" She half turned, gazing down at him with an air of suppressed excitement. "How long has my aunt employed the locksmith Samuel Abel?"

Julian instantly looked alert, but Dawson frowned and shook his head. "I don't rightly remember, Miss Penelope. Seems like he's done our keys and locks for as long as we've been in residence here. Leastways I cannot recollect that we've ever employed any other. A most respectable man is Mr. Abel, and great-grandfather to our Miriam."

"Yes," Penelope said softly. "I had forgotten. Is Mr. Abel employed by any of my aunt's friends?"

"Indeed he is. He's been going next door to Lady Margaret's house. I couldn't say about any of the other ladies, though."

"Thank you, Dawson. Show Mr. Rutherford into the library when he's presentable."

Pretending not to see Julian's questioning look, she hurried to her room where she rang rather violently for her maid. Penelope had stripped off her gown and was bathing her arms and face when Nancy entered.

"I need a complete change of clothes, Nancy. And you may burn this gown, the stockings and slippers." Penelope could not quite repress a shiver as she pointed to the pile of clothing beside her dresser.

"Burn 'em, miss?" Nancy asked, startled. "Yer new muslin?"

"You may clean the garments," Penelope amended after a moment, "and keep them for yourself. Only don't wear the gown in the house. I don't want to lay eyes on it again."

"Thank 'ee, Miss Penelope!"

Hurriedly Penelope slipped into a dinner gown of soft crepe, fashioned in the new, full-skirted style, with elbow-length bishop sleeves. The deep rose of the material, according to its designer Madame Céleste, flattered her complexion and in some mysterious way made her hair look more gold than light brown.

Undecided, Penelope stood before her jewelry case. If she chose the single strand of pearls her parents had given her on her fifteenth birthday—only three months before they were carried off by the fever—Julian might believe she was trying for a girlish look, trying to hide her three-and-twenty years.

If, on the other hand, she wore the diamonds, might not he take it as one more reminder of the difference in their stations?

Mayhap no jewelry at all?

Penelope shook her head. Aunt Sophy would be sure to notice and ask awkward questions.

Catching Nancy's wide-eyed stare in the mirror, Penelope snatched up a ruby pendant her father had purchased in India. "Please help me with the clasp, Nancy."

When the catch was fastened, Penelope, carefully avoiding the mirror and the sight of her most ostentatious piece of jewelry, hurried to the closet. Opening the tiny sea chest, she was confronted by Sophy's last bottle of laudanum.

"Fie, Penelope!" she muttered under her breath. "Fie and foul! How could you have forgotten!" Turning to her maid, she called out, "Please empty this into the slop bucket, and dispose of the bottle, Nancy!"

After she had removed the folded list of suspects, Penelope pushed the chest to the back of the closet. The paper barely fit into her tiny, beaded reticule. In fact, the drawstring caught on one corner, but it would have to do.

Out of breath, Penelope arrived outside the library just as the hall clock on the ground floor struck the quarter hour before eight. Only a few minutes to discuss Sprott, Samuel Abel, and the suspects before dinner!

She pushed the door open. "I hope I did not keep you waiting, Julian."

"Not at all."

He rose from his chair before the desk, showing a coat without a wrinkle and Hessians so highly glossed that they could put a mirror to shame. "Dawson clucked over me like a mother hen and only let me go a scant five minutes ago. However, he graciously permitted me to carry up some sherry since your aunt is closeted with Peter and has put off dinner for another hour."

"Oh. Dr. Ludlow came. I'm so glad!" Penelope took her seat behind the desk. "I hope Aunt Sophy asks him to stay to dine with us. He would be company for you.''

Julian poured sherry into Waterford glasses. ''You mean your aunt could not, then, scold you for having invited me.''

Penelope ignored the teasing gleam in his eyes. ''Shall we?'' she said, spreading the list on the blotter and smoothing the folds.

''Yes, Miss Langham.''

Julian pulled his chair closer, seemingly intent on studying the names they had set to paper less than a week ago, but Penelope was not deceived. There was that certain look on his face that told her all too clearly he was still in a teasing mood, and that, before the night was over, he'd resume where of necessity he must leave off for the nonce.

Forcing her mind to the matter at hand, she said, ''Despite your warning I didn't want to believe that the pearls might be sold. How I wish it weren't so!''

Julian looked up. ''Penny, why did you ask Dawson about the locksmith?''

''It's the strangest thing, Julian. I was trying to think why that girl in Fetter Lane looked familiar—or, mayhap, she merely reminded me of someone. In any case, I suddenly recalled the shingle above the door of that basement shop: 'Samuel Abel, Master Locksmith.' And, of course, Samuel Abel of Fetter Lane is the locksmith who replaced our locks after the burglary!''

''And he has been employed before,'' Julian interposed. ''By Lady Belmont and Lady Margaret.''

''A locksmith would have no need to break into a house.''

Julian nodded. '' 'Twould explain why there were no signs of forced entry.'' Absently he took a few sips of sherry. ''We must find out if he has, in the past, been retained at the other homes, Penny.''

''But Mr. Abel is eighty years old if he is a day, Julian. And he is—he looks respectable! I liked him when he came last week. And he is Miriam's great-grandfather!''

Julian smiled. ''And that, in your eyes, exempts him as a suspect. But remember, Penny. It was Miriam who said that she heard nothing on the night of the burglary, even though she was not asleep.''

"You said yourself she couldn't have heard a thing in the attic!"

"*Was* she in her bed? We only have Miriam's word for it, my love."

Penelope drew herself up. "Julian, I wish you would stop flirting with me. It is not at all the thing to call me your love. It is, in fact, quite forward in you, and very distracting!"

Under his gaze, a blush stole into her cheeks and bid fair to rival the color of her gown, or that of the ruby.

"Is it now?" he marveled but said no more, leaving her to wonder to which of her pronouncements he referred.

"Yes! And besides, I'd like to know why you're looking at me like that. You've done it before, you know. Laughing at me with your eyes while you keep your face perfectly serious!"

"But I'm not laughing at you! Smiling perhaps," he conceded, "and that I can hardly help. You are very beautiful, you know. And so," he added wickedly, "is your pendant. Is it not too heavy for your slender neck, though?"

Her blush deepened. "And you have diverted my mind from Miriam long enough, Julian," she said severely. "Mind you, I would normally have scorned any notion that the thief or one of his cohorts might live here in the house, but ever since the matter of the missing books, I have been uneasy. And Miriam was awfully upset when I interviewed her after the burglary."

"What missing books?" Julian asked sharply.

"Take a look at the shelves." Penelope rose. "There," she said, pointing to a section where the books stood widely spaced. "Two illustrated volumes on native plants and herbs should be standing right there. Very valuable! They were handwritten and bound in some monastery more than one hundred and fifty years ago."

She pointed to the shelf above. "And here, *The Country Housewife's Family Companion,* and *Essays Medical, Philosophical, and Experimental*. There must have been three or four volumes of the latter. All in all, I daresay, a dozen books are gone."

Julian poured himself another glass of sherry. "Have you spoken to the servants?"

"I asked Rachel. She does the dusting." Penelope resumed her seat behind the desk. Picking up her glass, she absently twirled the stem between her fingers. "Rachel noticed about three weeks ago that some of the books were missing, but she assumed I had taken them."

"Do you believe that Miriam might have had a hand in it?"

"No. At least I don't wish to believe it. I taught Miriam to read, and my aunt made her a present of all the books Henry and Dorothea had collected in the schoolroom."

"Your Belmont cousins?" he interrupted.

Penelope nodded. "Yes. When Miriam had read the children's books, I made it a point to check out suitable volumes for her at the lending library. So, you see, Miriam need only ask me—" Penelope broke off when Julian removed the dangerously tilting glass from her busy fingers.

"I wish you'd drink it, Penny." Julian looked at her keenly. "What is the matter? Have you grown bored with the burglar hunt?"

Her eyes flew to his face, then dropped before the warm concern in his. "Not bored, Julian. Chickenhearted."

"You? I don't believe it!"

She chuckled softly at his exclamation. "In truth, I expected excitement and adventure when I agreed to your scheme, harebrained though it may have been, but—"

"Surely you won't deny that we had quite a splendid adventure today!"

"I don't deny it. In fact, I wish I could have shot the pistol from Sprott's hand. The gall! He dared pull a weapon on us!"

"Do you know how to shoot?" Julian asked, carefully hiding his relief that there had been no such opportunity for Penelope. She might have hit *him* as he had lunged across the pedestal table, struggling to point that deadly little barking iron away from him and Penelope.

"Well, my papa taught me to shoot while we traveled in India and Turkey. But that was with a gun. He never would permit me to touch his pistols. I daresay there's not much difference, though."

Julian cast his eyes heavenward. "But why, if you feel that way, do I get the suspicion that you wish to hedge off?"

Penelope held up a hand in protest. "You misunderstand, Julian. I do not at all with to . . . hedge off. Since I learned of Maria's predicament, I wish more than anything to find the scoundrel who made it appear as though she had committed a whole series of thefts. Only I cannot help feeling apprehensive. Everything is beginning to point to someone in my aunt's employ."

"What a numbskull I was!" Julian snatched Penelope's list around and studied the dates. "Something you just said," he muttered. A series of thefts . . . By Jupiter! I should have wrung Sprott's neck to get more information from him!"

Penelope drew in her breath. "Do you also suspect that he may have something to do with the other thefts, Julian? I do. But no"—she shook her head, her excitement dying—"he's a receiver, a fence. Not a thief."

"He's a fence all right, and very likely knows more thieves than a parson knows sinners! It may be farfetched, and it all depends on what Maria told him, but if she gave him the notion that there might be a way to sell some valuable stuff across the Channel every month—"

"It does sound farfetched, Julian, but personally I like the notion. If Sprott employs his own flock of thieves, none of the servants need be suspect any longer, nor," she added on a gurgle of laughter, "Miss Barbara Twittering."

Julian raised a brow. "Is she not one of your aunt's friends?" he asked, eyeing the list. "Yes, I thought so. And there's a Miss Helena Twittering as well. What made you think of Miss Barbara as a thief?"

"Merely a flight of fancy. Aunt Sophy generally refers to the sisters as 'poor as church mice.' They won't accept assistance. They call it charity, and would rather sell their meager possessions one by one. Yet I saw Miss Barbara last week attired in a gown and hat that must have cost a small fortune."

"We must, of course, investigate everything, Miss Barbara included, but first I shall speak with Maria. Then I'll pay a visit to the venerable locksmith."

"It might not hurt to ask him about the young lady I saw coming out of his shop," said Penelope.

"Or the young smart! He, after all, suggested a visit to Sprott when he joined his sweetheart in the street."

"His name is Erskin." Seeing Julian's astonishment, Penelope added, "It's what the young woman called him."

The dinner gong brought their discussion to an abrupt halt. As they descended to the small dining salon on the ground floor, Julian said, "I wish you would keep your aunt entertained after dinner, Penny, so that I may speak with Maria."

"Of course." Penelope laid a hand on his arm. "Only promise me to be gentle, Julian. Maria is quite distraught on account of Benjamin Rugby."

He covered her hand with his. "I promise."

Reassured yet strangely unsettled by his touch and the caress of his voice, Penelope entered the dining room. Her aunt was already seated in her customary place at the head of the table. Peter Ludlow sat to Sophy's right.

"Isn't this delightful?" cried Sophy. "Penelope, we shall have two gentlemen to keep us company tonight!"

Beaming, she beckoned to Julian. "Come, Mr. Rutherford. You shall sit to my left. You know Dr. Ludlow? But of course you do. He told me you two know each other from the Peninsular campaign."

"Indeed, Lady Belmont. Many's the time Peter patched me up. I daresay he was quite bored with my company after a while."

Sophy, whose contact with gentlemen of less than sixty years had been extremely limited, looked confused. "Bored, Mr. Rutherford? I should think he must have been quite concerned about your welfare."

"And so I was," said Peter Ludlow, taking pity on her. "And quite relieved when, after a particularly close brush with death, his father ordered him—"

"I don't believe that nine-year-old incidents of a long-gone war will contribute to the ladies' enjoyment of the evening," Julian interrupted. He wasn't generally curt. Definitely not with Peter, one of his oldest friends, who had faithfully stood by him during the scandal five years ago.

In fact, Julian would have felt hard-pressed had he been asked to justify his behavior. He only knew he did not want Peter to disclose that he had held a commission in the Light Bobs. And there was no doubt about it, Peter had been about to say that Julian's father had ordered his only son and heir to sell out.

He felt Penelope's eyes on his face but dismissed the stab of guilt caused by her startled, questioning look.

Peter Ludlow cleared his throat. "Ahem, yes. Daresay you're right, old boy. Lady Belmont"—he smiled ruefully at his hostess—"pray forgive my boorishness, ma'am."

"There's nothing to forgive, dear Dr. Ludlow." A faint glow of color appeared under the delicate layer of Sophy's face powder, and her light blue eyes sparkled in a decidedly militant manner at Julian. "After all, it was not *I* who took offense!"

"Auntie," Penelope interposed hastily. "Where is Maria?"

"Oh, the poor child!" Distracted, Sophy turned to her niece. "She begged me not to insist on her joining us for dinner. Said she couldn't eat a bite as long as Mr. Rugby is languishing in that awful place, but she promised to join us in the drawing room."

"Well, I hope you had a tray sent to her room," Penelope said practically. "It won't help Mr. Rugby one whit if Maria starves herself."

Satisfied that Julian would have his opportunity to question Maria, Penelope addressed herself to the excellent turtle soup Arthur had placed before her. After a few moments, seeing that her aunt had overcome her brief flare of indignation and was conversing amicably with Julian, Penelope smiled at the physician on her left.

"Tell me, Dr. Ludlow," she said softly. "Is my aunt responding to your treatments?"

"Very well indeed, Miss Langham. A slight instability of temper, a certain sharpness of disposition must be expected for a course of several weeks, perhaps months. But I feel certain," he said, looking at her severely from under his bushy brows, "that you will understand and excuse such slight inconveniences."

Penelope unflinchingly met his eyes. "Yes, of course, Dr.

Ludlow. My aunt has always had a somewhat volatile temperament, and I imagine the sudden . . . change in her habits is rather difficult for her to deal with. She won't discuss it with me, you know, but I promise you I shan't take offense if she snaps at me or—oh, whatever! I don't really know what to expect, you see.''

Peter Ludlow laid down his spoon. ''You really have no cause to worry about anything, Miss Langham. I have stressed to your aunt, and she quite perceives the wisdom of my dictum, that she must *never* again take so much as a drop of laudanum. And so I have informed Lady Belmont's dresser as well.''

''Sweetings is devoted to her mistress. If you have won her over, then half the battle is won.''

They could say no more, for Sophy had turned away from Julian. The conversation became general, ranging from the Burlington Arcade, a hundred-ninety-foot shopping arcade under construction along Piccadilly, to Dr. Ludlow's influenza patients and the programs of the Philharmonic Society.

Julian proved himself a charming dinner companion, and if, occasionally, his sallies of dry wit went beyond Sophy's understanding, she could smile on him with tolerant amusement. And when in need of a respite, Sophy only had to turn to Dr. Ludlow, who would instantly be all attention and could be counted on to enter fully into her sentiments on the loss of her precious opals. When it was time for the ladies to withdraw, Sophy was quite in charity with both gentlemen.

Nodding to Penelope, she rose. ''What a delightful dinner this has been! I am very much tempted,'' she said with an arch look at Peter Ludlow, ''to make a habit of it.

''And now, gentlemen, you must promise me not to curtail your enjoyment of the port, which, I am sure, Dawson has selected with great care. 'Can't rush your port,' is what my dear Henry always used to say.'' Sophy frowned. ''Or something to that effect. Come, Penelope. We shall await the gentlemen in the Chinese drawing room.''

Dawson opened the door to allow the ladies to pass into the hall. Penelope turned in the doorway. ''Remember, Julian,'' she said before slipping out, ''I want you to meet Maria.''

The two men resumed their seats. Arthur whisked the cloth off the table, and Dawson set out the decanter of port and a box of Spanish cigars. After assuring himself that Arthur had set out glasses and a bowl of nuts, the butler executed a stately bow, then ushered his underling from the dining salon.

Julian met Peter's eyes above the crystal decanter. One corner of Julian's mouth twisted upward. "I had forgotten the pomp and ceremony involved in dining," he said ruefully.

Peter reached for the wine. Pouring for both of them, he appeared to be directing his attention to the glasses. "How long since you've been home?" he asked casually.

"Two years." Julian sampled the port. "Excellent stuff. Either Dawson is an expert, or the late Lord Belmont himself laid down this bottle."

"Why haven't you been to Steeple since, Julian? Surely your father has gotten over his wrath by now."

"You don't give up, do you, Peter?" Julian regarded his friend lazily over the rim of his glass. "Let's just say that my presence at Steeple does not contribute pleasantly to the atmosphere in the house."

Peter Ludlow raised a bushy brow but said nothing.

"Damn you, Peter," Julian said softly. He tossed down his wine, then reached for the bowl of nuts. "Pater and I made our peace that first year after the scandal. I suspect he's even come to the conclusion that I may not be quite the black sheep he believed me to be. But m'mother . . ."

Selecting a walnut and cracking it with his hands, Julian said in a tight voice, "Now, she's a different kettle of fish. Still bursts into tears every time Melissa's name is mentioned. And Mother mentions it with almost every breath she draws."

"And you? Are you still bitter, Julian?"

"Was I bitter?" Julian drawled, his low voice quite at odds with the hard glint in his eyes.

Peter Ludlow had known Julian for too many years to be deterred by a mere look. "You were very bitter. Admit it, old boy. You were devastated when your betrothed suddenly announced that she'd rather marry the heir to a dukedom than the heir to a viscountcy."

"Leave it be, Peter. It's all water under the bridge."

Peter carefully selected a cigar, nicked the end with the sharp little knife provided with the humidor, and made quite a ceremony of lighting it on one of the candles on the table. "You know," he said when the cigar was lit to his satisfaction, "I'm beginning to suspect something havey-cavey in your relationship with Miss Langham. Does she know who you are? Or Lady Belmont?"

Julian raised a brow. "You've heard them address me, Peter."

"Then why did you rake me down like some damned schoolboy when I mentioned your commission? Are you trying to tell me you did *not* want to hide that you were an officer, the youngest brigade-major, in fact? With quite a few decorations to your name?"

Julian thrust back his chair and rose. "The port has addled your brains, my friend. Come, we'd best not keep the ladies waiting."

But Peter did not move. "Lady Belmont is my patient," he said quietly. "You had better give me a damned good reason why you don't want the ladies to find out that your father is Viscount Steeple. A blind man can see that there is something between you and Miss Langham, but it better be good, Julian!"

"What are you saying, Peter?" Julian's dark brows snapped together. "Do you suspect me of wishing to seduce the young lady?"

"During the year following the affair with Melissa, you made yourself quite a name, old boy! Keeping one mistress after another, squiring the most dashing barques of frailty in the park—at the most fashionable hour!"

"Enough!" Julian said sharply. "I stopped that folly the moment I found something more worthwhile to do." He stepped closer to Peter, regarding him intently. "What the devil did you mean when you said there's something between Miss Langham and me?"

"Cut line, Julian! Do you think I didn't notice the looks

that passed between you? If ever two people were in tune with each other, it's the pair of you.''

Julian sat down heavily on the chair vacated by Penelope a short while ago. ''Damn you again, Peter! You see too much.'' He refilled his glass and drank deeply. ''She's a fetching little thing, my Penny,'' he murmured. ''When I met her, she was all starch and propriety, and I thought 'twould be a lark to flirt with her. To make her come alive.''

''And now you're well and proper hooked,'' Peter said with a wide grin. ''My congratulations, old boy!''

''It's early for that,'' Julian said ruefully. ''I can't just suddenly walk up to her and say, 'Would you marry me? I am really not quite the lowly reporter you believe me to be, Penny, my love. One day I shall sit in the House of Lords—and not to take down the speeches.' ''

''It'll be worse if she learns it from someone else.''

''The thought has occurred to me. And that, my friend, is why I raked you over the coals for talking too much.''

Peter tossed his half-smoked cigar into the brass receptacle. ''Mustn't keep the ladies waiting. Do you know the way to the Chinese drawing room?''

''Indeed I do, but you forget there'll be at least one footman stationed in the hall to show us the way.''

Chuckling, Peter opened the dining-room door. ''Don't let it scare you! Poor, lowly reporter that you are. But—'' He stopped short and, suddenly serious, turned to face Julian. ''Don't let this masquerade go on too long, my friend. There is something about Miss Langham—a look of pride and stubbornness—that should warn you. You may find your hopes dashed if you don't watch out.''

''I know. But in truth, what I fear most at the moment is that she *will* discover who I am and will hear of the old scandal. Someone, no doubt, would very gladly inform her that I've been dubbed the most despicable jilt.''

chapter
ELEVEN

"*I*'ll go and fetch Maria now, Auntie." Penelope hesitated on the threshold of the Chinese drawing room while Sophy tripped toward one of the crimson chairs drawn up in a semicircle before the fireplace. "Shall I bring your shawl? It's rather chilly tonight."

As though to confirm Penelope's words, Sophy hugged her arms to her breast. The filmy overdress of her mauve dinner gown swirled as she turned to look back at her niece.

"Stay, Penelope! Don't—" Sophy broke off on a brittle trill of laughter. "Yes, it is quite cool, isn't it? Should I have had a fire laid, I wonder?"

"There's wood in the grate. I'll just set a taper to it, shall I?" Forgetting Maria and seeing only her aunt's strange mood—so at variance with her gaiety during dinner—Penelope stepped into the room.

"Come and sit right here, Aunt Sophy," she said coaxingly after she had pulled a chair closer to the hearth.

She lit a screw of paper on one of the candles atop the mantel ledge, then thrust it among the kindling in the grate. Within moments, the dry twigs caught fire. Flames started to curl around narrow wedges of split logs atop the kindling wood, then grew and licked like greedy yellow tongues at the heavier, round logs crowning the whole.

"I daresay coal would give more heat," Sophy said, looking gloomily into the crackling fire. "But I do like the smell of burning wood."

Seating herself, Penelope stretched her feet toward the hearth. From the corner of her eye, she studied her aunt's

133

face, the drooping mouth, the faint lines etched into Sophy's forehead and around her eyes. Lines that hadn't been there a week or two ago.

"Can I help, Auntie?"

The silver-blond head came up with a jerk. "I beg your pardon, Penelope. I fear I was woolgathering. Didn't you— oh, never mind. I'm glad we have a few moments to ourselves, my dear."

Penelope smiled encouragingly when Sophy fell silent again. "Yes? What is it, Aunt Sophy?"

"Dearest—" Sophy drew breath, then plunged resolutely ahead. "Is it wise to go jauntering about with Mr. Rutherford the way you do?"

"Jauntering, Aunt Sophy?" Having anticipated that her aunt meant to speak about Dr. Ludlow's treatments, Penelope was caught by surprise and felt, unaccountably, on the defensive. Sophy had not questioned her activities in many a year. Why now?

"I'd hardly call it jauntering, Aunt Sophy, when all our time is spent looking for the thief! I told you that's what we would be doing."

"Yes, so you did. But I still don't understand why you can't leave it to that Bow Street runner. After all, it's his duty to protect innocent citizens from cutthroats and thieves and the like."

"No doubt Mr. Dare would be the first to agree with you as to his 'dooty.' He seems, however, to have the unfortunate knack of nabbing the wrong person."

"Penelope, is that thieves' cant Mr. Rutherford has taught you!" Sophy exclaimed in scandalized accents. With a puzzled frown, she added, "On the other hand, he is perfectly able to discourse intelligently on the various programs of the Philharmonic Society. You'd think he were a regular subscriber to their concerts."

"Mayhap he is, Auntie. We don't attend often enough to judge."

"I know, dearest." Looking flustered, Sophy said, "And that must change, Penelope. Far too long have I allowed my selfishness to rule. The season is in full swing, and we shall accept every invitation we receive. It's high time you met eligible bachelors—"

"Gilbert Bromfield is a most eligible *parti*," Penelope murmured. "He has vast holdings in Norfolk, owns a mill in Lancashire, a hunting box in Leicestershire—though a man less likely to shine on the hunting field I cannot imagine!—and an elegant house in town."

"And you would no more marry him than I would receive him as my nephew-in-law. One pompous bore is enough in any family!"

"Auntie! How can you speak thus of your own son!"

"Very easily," Sophy said tartly, "for truth will out. But you, Penelope," she continued, tenaciously pursuing her original thought, "you won't add to your consequence if you're seen in Mr. Rutherford's company. You are—" She frowned, adding the years Penelope had spent at Belmont House, then gasped. "You're three-and-twenty!"

"In fact, quite on the shelf."

"And all my fault!"

Alarmed by the stricken look on Sophy's face, Penelope went to kneel beside her aunt's chair. "I was only funning you, dearest." She took one of Sophy's hands between her own, gently chafing the trembling fingers. "If it'll make you feel better, I shall promise to attend balls, routs, Venetian breakfasts, and even Almack's assemblies just as soon as Julian and I have solved the mystery of the thefts."

"The season may well be over by then!"

"There'll be the little season in November. Aunt Sophy, please don't worry about me. I'm having a great time, and surely you don't wish me to quit now. Just consider, Auntie! Maria will most likely go into a decline if Benjamin Rugby is retained in Newgate Prison."

"But Mr. Rutherford is so . . . so overpowering, Penelope!" Sophy withdrew her hand and gazed at her niece with concern. "I have seen you look at him, my dear. It's the same look you had for—"

"For Harry Swag, Auntie?"

Penelope rose to her feet. "I was not quite seventeen then. Surely I know better now. Surely," she said, whirling and stepping briskly to the hearth, "you do not fear that I may elope with Mr. Rutherford?"

"Penelope!"

"Well, I would have eloped with Harry had he not learned in the nick of time that my inheritance was tied up in court, while Miss Polly Higginbottom and her fortune were ready and waiting for his plucking."

Penelope gripped the poker, aiming a mighty thrust at the logs in the grate. Sparks flew. She took a quick step backward, then, laying down the poker with great care, turned to face her aunt again.

Sophy had been watching Penelope with distress. "Dearest," she said, "you're not wearing the willow for Mr. Swag, are you?"

"Not at all," said Penelope, dusting off her hands. "I was merely indulging myself in a show of violence that would have been more appropriate when Harry was still around. I apologize. But you didn't answer my question, Auntie. *Do* you expect me to repeat my foolish mistake?"

Sophy drew herself up. "No, I do not, Penelope. For one thing, Mr. Rutherford, despite his profession, is truly a gentleman. Not for a moment do I believe that he would take advantage of your infatuation."

Shaken, Penelope sat down again. "Your confidence in me overwhelms me, Auntie."

Sophy paid no heed. "I don't know why it won't come to me," she murmured. "Ever since you told me Rutherford's name . . . there's something I should remember. Now what could it be?"

"You probably met his father when you visited Lady Margaret at Howe Court, dear. I believe he is Lady Margaret's vicar."

"No. That's Mr. Evercrest you're thinking of." Distractedly Sophy pressed her fingertips to her temples. "Oh, I wish the gentlemen would come! But, no doubt, they'll sit over their wine until the tea tray is brought in."

The gentlemen did not, however, leave them waiting quite that long. Barely had Sophy finished speaking when the drawing-room door opened and Maria, followed by Mr. Rutherford and Dr. Ludlow, stepped into the chamber.

Penelope rose at once and flew to her friend's side. "I meant to see you after dinner, Maria," she said in a low voice. "But Aunt Sophy was in such an odd humor. I felt I ought to stay with her."

"That's quite all right, Penelope. I needed some time for reflection."

"Come, let's sit by the window, Maria. Julian and I must speak with you. We've been to see Sprott."

Julian waited only long enough to make certain that Peter Ludlow had engaged Lady Belmont's attention before he ushered the two young ladies to a sphinx-legged chaise longue near the crimson-draped windows. When they were seated, he pulled up an easy chair for himself and gracefully deposited his long frame on the soft upholstery.

Maria turned troubled gray eyes on Penelope. "I guessed that you must have gone to see Sprott when Dawson said you had driven out with Mr. Rutherford. I wish you hadn't, Penelope! Fetter Lane is no place for a lady, and besides, Sprott told me he had sold the pearls."

"That, at least, appears to be true enough," Penelope admitted, "but we also learned that he knows your name, and worse, to whom the necklace belonged!"

Maria's hands clenched in her lap. "Yes. I should have told you that, Penelope. It just didn't seem to matter. Not when Benjamin is in prison—for me!"

"Hush! Keep your voice down, I beg you, Maria. Aunt Sophy must not learn of the part you played in the disappearance of the pearls. She is . . . not quite herself at the moment."

"I was there when Dr. Ludlow came to see her," Maria said quietly. "I quite understand, Penelope, and I give you my promise that she will hear nothing from me that might further distress her."

"Miss Hilbert." Julian uncrossed his ankles and leaned forward in his chair. "You have had time to reflect now. Is there anything else you did not mention to Penelope? Anything at all, even if it doesn't seem important to you?"

Maria's gaze fell. "No," she whispered. "I don't believe so. I can't . . . remember."

"You see, Miss Hilbert," said Julian, "it has me in a

puzzle that all the subsequent thefts were carried out at roughly the same time of the month as, ah, the mishap with the pearls. Did Sprott, perchance, ask you about the habits of the other ladies?''

''No! It . . . it has to do with the Italian dealer who comes to Sprott's shop on the twentieth of each month.''

Julian frowned. ''Sounds deucedly harebrained to me, if they meet like clockwork on the twentieth.''

''But don't you see, Mr. Rutherford? Sprott generally deals in small items, such as clothing, books, a few silver spoons, or candlesticks.''

''Ah!'' said Julian. ''I'm beginning to understand. Those are items anyone might pawn or sell if he finds himself with pockets to let. Nothing to incriminate Sprott as a fence. And then, once a month, he accepts those goods that the Bow Street runners would recognize as stolen.''

''Yes. He has a string of footpads and thieves spread across the country, and every month, shortly before the Italian buyer is expected, they unload their goods in Fetter Lane. That way Sprott has to store them only for a night or two and runs very little risk of being caught.''

''How do you know all this?'' Penelope asked. Much as she tried, she couldn't prevent an accusatory note from creeping into her voice.

Maria gave a start. ''He . . . Sprott . . . was desirous of having a . . . someone in London.''

''He suggested that you work for him? *Steal* for him?'' Penelope said in disbelief.

Julian watched Maria through half-closed eyes. ''Are you trying to tell us, Miss Hilbert, that a wily cove, a professional criminal, disclosed so much about his operation simply to persuade you to work for him?''

''No,'' breathed Maria.

She looked desperately toward the fireplace, but no rescue was forthcoming from that quarter. Lady Belmont was engrossed in animated conversation with Dr. Ludlow and had not so much as a glance to spare for her other guests.

Maria's eyes filled with tears as she faced Penelope. ''You see,'' she whispered, ''for a little while I believed that was what I must do. Steal for Sprott.''

Penelope wanted to get up, but her knees had turned to jelly. Maria's proximity on the chaise longue seemed unbearable suddenly.

Penelope had pitied Maria when she confessed to having taken Lady Spatterton's necklace in desperation. That she had, however briefly, contemplated joining the dastardly Sprott in his plans to rob cold-bloodedly and systematically all those who had befriended her in the past, Penelope could not tolerate.

"Why," she said harshly, "if you could not come to me, did you not go to Benjamin Rugby right away? How *could* you have considered Sprott's offer—even for a moment?"

The last vestige of color seeped from Maria's face. Julian started to speak but thought better of it and merely leaned back in his chair as though to indicate his temporary withdrawal.

"No one knew about Susannah, save for my family," Maria said tonelessly. "How could I approach you or Benjamin? I couldn't drag either of you into my affairs. At least, that was what I believed at the time."

"And I believed you my friend, Maria! Don't you have any faith in our friendship?"

"Penelope," Maria pleaded. "Please try to understand. An illegitimate child . . . the scandal! I was afraid Lady Belmont would not let you see me again."

"I am old enough to decide—" Penelope broke off, changing the subject abruptly. "Never tell me Sprott meekly accepted your change of heart after having so far betrayed himself to you!"

Maria shook her head. Her slender frame trembled as she remembered Sprott's grimy, clawed hand stretching toward her to shake on the "deal" as he called it. "I threatened to go to Bow Street. Turn myself in and give evidence against him. Then an old woman came into the shop with a fob watch she said she had found in the street, and I ran away."

"You went to see Mr. Rugby?" asked Penelope.

"No. Benjamin found me. On the docks. I have no recollection of how I got there, but Benjamin was overseeing the unloading of one of Mrs. Welby's ships, and he saw me and took me into one of the offices."

Maria looked pleadingly at Penelope. "Believe me, I had no intention of telling him, but he was so concerned, so warm . . . it all just spilled out. And then," she finished on a sob, "Benjamin said he'd take care of me and Susannah. Oh, Penelope! That was when he proposed to me!"

Instinctively Penelope encircled Maria's waist with her arm, giving a comforting squeeze. The tears Maria had been fighting started to run down her cheeks. With shaking fingers, she fumbled in the pocket of her skirt for her handkerchief. As she pulled it out, a folded sheet of paper fell onto the carpet.

Julian picked it up and, while Maria wiped her eyes and blew her nose, unfolded it and quite unashamedly perused its contents. His mouth pursed as though he were about to whistle, then curved into a reassuring smile at Penelope, who had not missed the little episode.

"Miss Hilbert, have you shown Penelope this letter?" he asked.

"Susannah's letter!" Snatching it from his hands, Maria pressed the sheet of paper to her bosom. "You read it," she said accusingly.

"Dashed right, I did." Julian leaned forward, his feet firmly planted on the floor, his hands on the arms of his chair. "For Penelope's sake I was prepared to fight to clear your name and save your fiancé from his own folly. Now my efforts will be doubled—for your own sake and that of your little girl. But let us have no more prevarication, Miss Hilbert," he said sternly. "Penelope is your friend, a far better friend than you deserve. You should have shown her that letter the moment you entered the house this afternoon."

Maria met Julian's hard look unflinchingly, and Penelope noted that some of her forthrightness and pride began to emerge again.

"My daughter's state of health does not excuse my behavior, Mr. Rutherford," Maria said quietly but firmly.

Penelope held out her hand. "Let me be the judge of that."

Maria looked at the letter, then, hesitantly, handed it to Penelope. The letter was dated December 15, 1817. *Dearest*

Mama, it started in a wide, childish hand. *Dear Dr. Ziegenfeld says I'm ever so much better! Yesterday...*

Penelope skimmed over an account of Christmas preparations, which, in Switzerland, appeared to involve the making of many tiny marchpane and sugar confections as well as the cutting and pasting of many-colored decorations.

A paragraph at the bottom of the page, written in bold, masculine strokes, caught Penelope's attention.

Miss Hilbert. In regard to your letter of November 25, which I only received this morning, I must admit to a feeling of surprise and misgiving. Of course, I do remember our correspondence two years ago, but circumstances have definitely changed for the better. There is no longer a question of releasing the little Susannah so that she may return to England and die, having known a brief period of her mother's love. The child has, during the past twelve-month, improved greatly. If you remove her now, at this tender stage, the consequences must be fatal. Miss Hilbert, I most strongly urge you to leave Susannah in the sanatorium until she has reached her fourteenth year, at which time, I feel reasonably certain, Susannah will be able to spend at least the summer months with you in your damp country. . . .

The words blurred before Penelope's eyes. "She will!" she said with fevor. "Don't you worry any longer, Maria. Everything will be all right."

Seeing that her aunt had risen to ring for the tea tray, Penelope added hastily, "Just one more question, Maria. Which one of Lady Elizabeth's footmen told you about Sprott?"

"I don't recall his name. He only stayed two or three weeks last autumn, and there have been so many since then. Is it important?"

"Sprott would have to learn from someone when a house would most likely be deserted," said Julian. "A footman makes a good informer."

"I remember he was a brash kind of fellow, rather forward with the maids, and his speech was unmistakably cockney."

Julian rose. "That description fits at least two-thirds of the footmen in London. If you recall anything else, let me know immediately, Miss Hilbert.'' Turning to Penny, he said, ''It might be better if we waited awhile before returning to Fetter Lane to visit the locksmith shop. If we show up again so soon, Sprott might get wind of it and move his place of business.''

Penelope awoke the following morning to overcast skies. Gusts of wind tousled the foliage of the plane trees in the square, and the air smelled damp. A day made for a gallop in the open countryside!

With a sigh, she turned away from the window. To gallop in Hyde Park was unthinkable; a canter would have to suffice. A short while later, Penelope mounted Sable, her long-neglected mare, and trotted toward the park with Hunter following at a discreet distance on old Turk.

Sable, after several days confinement to the stable, was dancing and prancing, eager to run. She pretended shyness at the approach of noisy drays and vendors' carts, and made a perfect nuisance of herself over a basket of watercress and parsley the herb woman offered for sale.

A bubble of mischief grew inside Penelope. It would not be surprising at all, she mused, if Sable insisted on having her head once they were through the park gates. After all, Hunter would never be able to catch up to the mare to check her gallop.

And thus it was that Hunter, no sooner than he had passed through Grosvenor Gate, was treated to the sight of Miss Penelope charging along at a full gallop on the turf beside the carriageway.

''By Jupiter!'' he muttered. ''If only I had a horse betwixt me legs instead of this here tired nag, I'd give her a race!''

When he caught up with Penelope, however, he only said reproachfully, ''Ye shouldn't have done it, Miss Penelope! What if someone seed ye?''

''There's no one here but you and the ducks on the Serpentine,'' Penelope said rather curtly, and pulled ahead again.

Her joy and exhilaration in the forbidden exercise had been short-lived. There was no fun in it when she couldn't share her pleasure; when, instead of a glint in gray-green eyes, she encountered only reproach in the eyes of her groom.

Sobered, Penelope slowed Sable to a walk. She must not grow dependent on Julian's company. He would leave her life just as suddenly as he had entered it once they found the thief and handed him and Sprott to the Bow Street magistrate. And Sophy, newly awakened to her responsibilities as an aunt, was determined to launch Penelope into the fashionable whirl of society—and to find her a husband!

Julian's ruggedly handsome face crowned by the shock of unruly black hair flashed through Penelope's mind.

She glared at a footpath leading off the major drive into a tangle of blooming shrubbery. High-pitched giggles and a soothing male voice emanated from that hidden area, a well-known trysting place of lovers.

If there was a less eligible suitor for her hand than Julian, Penelope didn't know of him. Julian was a nobody, a reporter of all things; she a Langham of Langham Place in Kent. She could never marry him, even if he were to ask her.

In what she considered an objective manner, Penelope thought back over their various encounters, trying to determine whether Julian was flirting with her or, as she had once or twice suspected, wooing her. She found to her chagrin that she could not tell. She hoped, for his sake, that he was merely flirting, because if he were not, he would be hurt.

Her chest constricted as though a sharp blow had knocked the breath out of her. The stab of pain, she realized with dismay, was not for Julian alone.

Penelope returned from her ride feeling rather chastened but more determined than ever to make the most of her time with Julian. Afterward, there would be time aplenty to make the acquaintance of more eligible gentlemen. Men, no doubt, of Gilbert Bromfield's stamp.

She did not, however, see much of Julian during the next few days. He had made it his objective to investigate the Misses Twittering and spent most of his time in Hans Place where the two elderly ladies owned a small house. Julian was far too busy questioning comely serving maids of Miss

Barbara and Miss Helena's neighbors, Penelope thought wryly, to spare a thought for her.

She did not even have Maria to keep her company for long. When Sophy came home from a visit with Lady Elizabeth one rainy afternoon, she swept into the front parlor where Penelope and Maria were embroidering and alternately reading Miss Austen's *Emma* to each other.

"It's all settled, Maria!" Sophy cried gaily, depositing herself and her shawls on a chaise longue. "Elizabeth has given up her foolish notion of finding a 'more suitable companion.' Her words, of course. Not mine."

Penelope, whose turn it had been to read aloud, closed the book with a snap. "No doubt she has realized that she cannot find someone to be at her beck and call from morning till night, and all for starvation wages, and dinner in the servants' hall as an added bonus!"

"Well, this time Maria will eat in the dining room," said Sophy, feeling quite smug. "I made it clear to Elizabeth that she has been treating her companion most abominably."

"I will go," Maria said quietly, "but only to help her with the task of interviewing applicants and training a replacement. Benjamin will be released soon, and we shall be married as soon as the banns can be read." She folded her embroidery and placed it neatly in her work basket. "If you will excuse me, I'll go and pack my trunk, Lady Belmont."

"Let me help you!" In a whirl of flying petticoats Penelope rushed after her friend. "Remember, Maria," she said as soon as the door to the parlor had closed behind her. "You must ask the servants if they know the name of that brash footman who pointed you to Sprott. It must be your first order of business at Lady Elizabeth's!"

"But if I'm not to eat in the servants' hall, I shan't have time to question the staff, Penelope. Once Lady Elizabeth learns that I shall stay for a very short time only, she'll line up dozens of applicants for the position."

"Hang the applicants! Dash it, Maria! What's more important? To find the thief or to find a companion for Lady Elizabeth?"

Stopping on the upper landing, Maria cast a hurt look at

Penelope. "Surely you have no need to ask me that, Penelope. And if you believe that footman might be Sprott's thief, you are well and far off. Sprott would never have a stupid man work for him."

"Oh," Penelope said, disappointed. Then she brightened. "But perhaps he was only pretending to be short of a sheet."

"He was so foolish he could not even find his way around town for all that he grew up here! I sent him once to pick up a new hat Lady Elizabeth had ordered from Balena's, and he didn't return until three hours later. He'd lost his way!"

Penelope planned to tell Julian that Lady Elizabeth's former footman might as well be stricken from the list of suspects, but when he finally came to see her, striding into the library where she had once again been chasing the elusive shillings, her first thoughts were, *How well he looks! And how I missed him!*

"I missed you, Penny," said Julian, his deep voice a caress. And when he turned her hand over and pressed his lips against her wrists, all sensible notions quite slipped from her mind.

"I thought you had forgotten our little pact to catch the thief," she said breathlessly.

His mouth curved into a smile that made her silly heart turn somersaults. "There were times when I wished I could. The inhabitants of Hans Place are a tedious lot. But I could never forget *you*, Penny, my love."

Penelope strove for composure. "That's what I call emptying the butter boat, sir. Out with it! Do you have some disagreeable task that you wish me to perform?"

Julian pulled a chair closer to the desk and sat down. "Disagreeable? I think not, unless you are quite different from any lady I know. I want you to go look at hats, Penny."

"Hats?"

"Balena hats."

Penelope's eyes widened. *Balena's again . . . Maria's footman.*

For a moment she sat stock-still, hardly daring to breathe while her mind tried to sort her wildly tumbling thoughts.

"Balena," she said finally. "*Ba*rbara and He*lena*!"

chapter TWELVE

Julian rewarded her with his lopsided grin. "Knew you'd be a worthy partner," he said. "Sharp as a pin."

"That explains Miss Barbara's expensive gown. Their sudden affluence." Penelope's face lit up. "I can strike them off the list of suspects. Oh, I'm so glad!"

"Not so fast, Penny," Julian said gravely. "The Misses Twittering have owned the shop for three years, but, as far as I could discover, Balena's Hat Shoppe was not much patronized by the fashionable world until recently."

"That's true. No one spoke of the place until Sally Jersey sported a daring Balena confection at the races in New-market. All white silk and gauze. Overnight Balena hats were all the rage."

"It takes a bit of capital to maintain a shop just off Oxford Street. Their house in Hans Place is heavily mort-gaged and, according to some informed neighbors, the Misses Twittering sold their last silver spoon a long time ago. Their house is bare. Have you seen it?"

Penelope shook her head. "I don't think anyone has seen their home recently. It has always been understood that they don't entertain. No one calls on them because we're afraid they're so poor they couldn't afford tea and coffee."

"But they attend the card parties given by Lady Spatterton?"

"They're invited everywhere. That is, I've seen them wherever I went with my aunt. But they always come late. Sometimes as much as two hours late."

"Time enough," murmured Julian.

Their eyes met.

"It appears that Maria's footman once 'lost his way' when he was sent to fetch a hat at Balena's," said Penelope.

"If Miss Helena and Miss Barbara are our thieves, they won't need a footman to inform them of their friends' whereabouts."

"Talking pays no toll, Julian. We must act," Penelope said firmly. "We shall go to Balena's."

She pushed back her chair and started to rise, but at Julian's next words she slowly sank onto the seat again.

"I'm afraid I shan't be able to accompany you, Penny. I'm expected in Bow Street to put the finishing touches on the next issue of the *Hue and Cry*."

Disappointment was evident in her face, but she nodded. "I understand, Julian."

"Do you?" His voice sounded harsh. Then he smiled and said with a quizzical lift of his dark brows, "It would not do, you know. You're bound to meet a handful of society ladies at Balena's, and you wouldn't wish to be seen with me hanging on to your sleeve, telling you how charmingly this or that hat would become you."

Hang the society ladies! Penelope thought irritably, but, a scarce half hour later, she stepped briskly along Davies Street with only her maid to keep her company. It did not matter, she told herself stoutly. She could perform the mission just as easily without Julian, but it was too bad that he should suddenly have decided to be careful of her reputation.

"We should 'ave taken t' carriage, Miss Penelope," grumbled Nancy. "We'll be soaked afore we get 'ome. Mark me words!"

"We shan't melt," said Penelope.

She glanced at the overcast sky. The air felt moist against her face and gusts of wind nipped around the corners of buildings to tug at her skirts and her hat. They passed few pedestrians, and those who did venture out on foot had armed themselves with large umbrellas.

Penelope swept left-handed into Oxford Street, then, waiting until a carriage had passed, crossed over to the far side, with Nancy following petulantly in her wake. A heavy raindrop splattered onto Penelope's nose and the wind howled at her around the corner of Orchard Street. Gripping her skirts with one hand and her wide-brimmed hat with the other, Penelope lengthened her stride.

"What did I tell ye! Now we're in for a real soakin'." Huffing, Nancy caught up with her mistress. "If only ye wouldn't be so headstrong, Miss Penelope!"

"It's but a few more steps. Run, Nancy!" Suiting the action to her words, Penelope dashed along the deserted sidewalk.

"Miss Penelope! What if someone seed ye!"

"They'd congratulate me on my good sense, you goose."

Laughing, Penelope whirled into Quebec Street and came to a stop before a narrow door in the corner building just as the rain started to come down in good earnest.

Balena's. It was but a small shop, but it boasted a show window facing Oxford Street and a second one in Quebec Street. Penelope pushed open the door and entered the small salesroom, partitioned off from the workshop in the back by smoke-gray velvet drapery.

Only four customers were inside. An elderly matron, whom Penelope recognized as one of Mrs. Welby's friends, stood with two of her daughters before the Oxford Street window. She was scowling at the rain-streaked glass pane, but turned and greeted Penelope with a smile when one of her young companions nudged her ample midriff.

The fourth lady, her straight, narrow back toward the door, was seated before a large, gilt-framed mirror, while the sales assistant held a silver and emerald silk turban at readiness above the dark, elaborately coiffed head.

Oh, bother! thought Penelope. *She'll take forever.* Forcing a smile to her lips, she directed a greeting at the stiff back. "Good afternoon, Lady Elizabeth. Is Maria not with you?"

Cold, dark gray eyes met Penelope's in the mirror. "I dropped her off at Miss Barrow's agency," Lady Elizabeth said in clipped tones, then addressed the shop assistant. "Lilibeth! I don't have all afternoon to waste!"

"Ready, my lady."

As the girl bent to adjust a hairpin, Penelope saw her face clearly reflected in the glass. Penelope blinked and looked again. There was no mistake! No rouge cheapened the exquisite beauty of the girl's features this time. The golden curls were dressed simply, held together by a slim blue velvet ribbon, and her shapely curves were demurely covered by a gown of pale gray cotton. A startling change from the scarlet taffeta she had worn outside Sprott's house!

Blue eyes fringed by darkened lashes widened briefly as they met Penelope's in the mirror, but instantly a courteous smile covered Lilibeth's confusion.

"Please have a seat, miss. I'll be right with you."

Penelope tore her eyes away from the blond head bent so attentively over Lady Elizabeth's dark one. This was worse than she had feared! Lilibeth provided a real link between Balena's Hat Shoppe and Fetter Lane. Between the Misses Twittering, the locksmith, and Sprott.

Movement at the Oxford Street window caught her attention. The downpour had ceased as suddenly as it had started, and the two young girls picked up a hat box each. One of them hurried to open the door for her mother, the other lingered briefly, smiling and mouthing a thank-you to Lilibeth.

When the door had closed behind the three ladies, Penelope looked consideringly at Lady Elizabeth. The dowager was fingering a plain white turban, but the emerald and white creation still adorned her head. And then there was Nancy, fiddling with the ribbons of a pretty little cottager hat.

"Nancy!" Penelope searched her reticule for a snippet of silk and some coins. "This may take longer than I anticipated. Please go to Miss Leete's and find me a ribbon to match this blue. And you need not come back here, Nancy. I shall take a hackney home."

"But, miss—" began Nancy, outraged.

"There's enough money for a hackney for you as well if it should start raining again," Penelope said hastily before the maid could draw Lady Elizabeth's unwelcome attention with the remonstrations she was undoubtedly about to deliver. "Now hurry! I want to wear the blue silk tonight and I have not a ribbon to match it."

When the girl had left, Penelope wandered around the shop. Apparently absorbed in a study of the displayed hats, she made her way slowly toward the gray velvet curtains, but no matter how hard she strained, she could hear no sound in the workshop behind the partition. Not Miss Helena's high voice that went so well with her last name, nor Miss Barbara's deeper tones.

Penelope glanced impatiently at Lady Elizabeth. Would she never make up her mind?

As though she had felt Penelope's eyes on her, the older lady looked up. "Didn't you bring your maid, Penelope?" she asked sharply.

"I sent her on an errand. That is a delightful turban you chose, ma'am. The green would match your emeralds."

"Yes. That's why I considered it. I plan to wear the emeralds with my new gown. Come here, Penelope. Tell me what you think," demanded Lady Elizabeth. She held up a swatch of heavy silver brocade. "Céleste is making up the gown. Should I have used the brocade for the turban as well?"

"No. The green and white will be perfect," Penelope said decisively.

Lady Elizabeth turned to the salesgirl. "You may have the turban delivered to me tomorrow. The weather is too unstable today. Don't want to risk the silk getting wet."

"If you're plannin' to wear it tomorrow, my lady, I could take a hackney when I close up and bring it by personally," Lilibeth offered.

Lady Elizabeth rose. "No need to waste money on a carriage, girl. I don't plan to wear it before the concert at the Argyll Rooms." Drawing on her gloves, she turned to peer out the window. "Is that my coach? I told my coachman to be here at four o'clock sharp, and it's already a quarter past. Servants are all the same, and my new coachman's no better than the last."

So grumbling, she went slowly to the door, which Lilibeth held open for her. There she stopped, addressing Penelope over her shoulder. "No doubt I'll see you and Sophy at the concert, Penelope. The last one of the season, you know."

Lady Elizabeth raised a hand in careless farewell and without waiting for an answer stepped out into the street.

Lilibeth closed the door. "Would you like to try that on, miss?"

Penelope looked down at the dashing little riding hat à la Hussar in her hands. She couldn't remember picking it up, but it was a very fetching hat and would go well with her habit.

"Yes," she said, sitting down before the mirror. Did Miss Barbara design it or Miss Helena?"

Wide, guileless blue eyes met Penelope's in the looking glass. "Miss Helena does the designs, but it's Miss Barbara as comes up with the colors. Can I show you another hat, miss?"

"I'll take this one, thank you. Are the two ladies here, Lilibeth? I'd like a word with them."

"No, miss. They went home early today. Will you be takin' the hat with you, miss?"

"Y—no," Penelope amended hastily. "Have it delivered tomorrow morning. Or can you not get away then?"

"We have a delivery boy, miss. And where shall I send the hat?"

"Belmont House in Berkeley Square."

Although Penelope watched the girl closely, she could detect no uneasiness in her manner. On the contrary. Lilibeth's smile was quite saucy.

"Thought you'd been in here once before, miss. You're Lady Belmont's niece. Miss Langham, right?"

Penelope set her own hat atop her light brown curls. "Actually, we've met twice," she said, placing a hairpin with precision. "Do you not remember Fetter Lane?"

The saucy smile wavered. "I haven't forgotten, miss, but I thought you'd be too embarrassed to mention it. I was wonderin' at the time what a lady like you was adoin' in a place like that."

Penelope rose. "I daresay you were, Lilibeth. As I was wondering about you. What were *you* doing there?"

Lilibeth's eyes narrowed. When she spoke, it was as though each word were dragged from her against her will. "I was meetin' my betrothed, miss."

"The handsome Erskin. I wish you joy, Lilibeth. Well, I must be off. Don't forget to have my hat delivered tomorrow morning."

Outside, Penelope allowed herself a grim little smile. Lilibeth had not liked it that she had been recognized in Fetter Lane. Was it purely because she had been caught looking like a piece of Haymarket ware?

For a moment Penelope stood on the sidewalk, looking up and down Oxford Street, but for once there was no sign of one of the old, ponderous hackney coaches. She should have remembered that in inclement weather they were at their scarcest.

While Penelope still hesitated, a closed carriage turned from Park Lane into Oxford Street, slowed, then stopped not three feet from her. A man, his face shadowed by a high beaver hat, appeared at the window and stared at her.

Indignant, Penelope spun on her heel, prepared to retreat into the hat shop, when a familiar voice hailed her. "I say, Penelope!"

"Gilbert!" Her first reaction was annoyance. What a great to-do he would make of the situation! Only practicality made her turn and speak pleasantly. "What friendly fate brought you out on such a day? Can you take me up?"

A footman sprang down from his perch at the back of the carriage and, on Gilbert's impatient instructions, opened the door and let down the steps for Penelope.

"Ah, this is better," she said, snuggling into the well-upholstered seat opposite Gilbert Bromfield's cloaked and muffled bulk. "Can you take me to Hans Place, please?"

Gilbert nodded to the footman but waited barely until the man had shut the door before addressing Penelope in an outraged voice. "I could not believe my eyes, Penelope! Where is your maid?"

"I should have known! No *friendly* fate would have sent you!"

She clasped the strap set into the paneled wall of the carriage as the coachman, with much jerking and backing, turned the vehicle around. "Come now, Gilbert. There's no reason for you to fly up into the boughs. I sent Nancy to buy some ribbons, and I planned to take a hackney to Hans

Place to see the Misses Twittering. All above board and respectable, you know.''

"There can be nothing respectable about a young lady standing *alone* at the corner of Oxford Street! You looked like the veriest—"

"High-flyer?" she asked when Gilbert broke off in some confusion. "Straw damsel? Fancy-piece?"

His chest puffed out and his eyes started from their sockets. "Penelope! Your language! Most unbecoming in a female."

"I'm surprised you stopped the carriage if you find me so much sunk beyond the pale." Penelope threw a quick glance out the window. "We're nearing Tattersall's. I'll easily find a hackney there. You had best set me down, Gilbert.''

"Oh, no! Not at all," he said, stammering a little and adjusting the muffler around his throat. "What I mean is— Dash it, Penelope! If you don't put words into a fellow's mouth! But it curls my liver to hear you talk of—hmm. What I mean to say—"

"I assure you, Gilbert, there's no need at all to say any more. Look, we are even now turning into Sloane Street. In a few moments you'll set me down in Hans Place, and then you can be comfortable again."

Gilbert relaxed. "Now, Penelope," he said, a superior smile appearing on his round face, "you know very well I can't just set you down. How will you get home?"

"Find me a hackney, Gilbert, and have it wait."

"I shall do no such thing. Why, if you must know, I set out this afternoon with the particular aim to pay you a visit. I—"

"Gilbert," Penelope said firmly, "I have no wish to know why you did such a harebrained thing. Undoubtedly you're coming down with something, but I warn you—"

"Harvey protested most strenuously against my venturing outside in the rain, but I wouldn't be swayed from my purpose."

"—that I'm in no mood to listen to any of your lectures today," Penelope continued ruthlessly, "and I can only advise you to leave whatever you mean to tell me for another day."

Gilbert stared at her for a moment, then nodded. "Yes. You may be right at that. You're much too brittle-tempered. I shall call on you in the morning. Will you and Lady Belmont be at home at eleven o'clock?"

"Aunt Sophy will be home, but I cannot promise—"

Gilbert cut her off. "And I must request," he said, "that you deny yourself to any other callers, Penelope. I have something of the utmost importance to discuss with you."

She looked at him suspiciously. "If you're planning to propose—" Penelope broke off when the coachman opened the panel and asked where in Hans Place Miss Langham wished to be set down.

"Number two," Penelope directed, and before she had time to complete her interrupted warning, the coach drew to a halt. "Thank you, Gilbert," she said hastily. "Don't forget to send the hackney."

He rose, bowing rather awkwardly within the confines of the coach. "You'll forgive me, I know, for not getting out. My delicate constitution . . ." His voice trailed off under her steady gaze. He blushed and stammered, "Shall do myself the honor to wait on you in the morning. Matter of the utmost importance, m'dear."

Penelope accepted the footman's arm and stepped down. A fresh rainshower sent her scurrying for shelter under the portico of the narrow, two-story terrace house owned by the Misses Twittering.

She raised her hand to the knocker, but it was not necessary to announce her presence. The front door opened, revealing Miss Barbara in an elegant silk gown of muted dark green, cut and draped in such a way as to disguise her angular shape. A pair of magnificent pearl drops and a long rope of pearls, twisted into a knot on her bosom, further softened the somewhat "sharp" appearance she generally gave.

"Come in, Penelope," Miss Barbara said calmly. "Helena and I were just sitting down to a cup of tea in the front room, and we could not help but notice your arrival." She stepped back, motioning Penelope toward an open door on the right.

Penelope entered a spacious chamber. At least it appeared

spacious since the only pieces of furniture were four straight-backed chairs around a small table by the window and a wooden settle placed against the wall opposite the narrow fireplace.

The polished floor was bare of rugs. Pale outlines on soot-darkened walls showed where formerly paintings or tapestries had hung. The drapes on the window looked gray, and only in the very depth of their folds could Penelope detect a hint of the royal blue they must once have been.

As she stepped farther into the room, Penelope's eyes were drawn by a splash of color in the corner beyond the settle. A gown of deep lavender satin lay across a stool, as though hastily flung down, and a box with tissue paper spilling out peeked from underneath.

Penelope quickly averted her eyes from the evening dress, for Miss Helena came tripping toward her, a yellowed lace shawl draped around her thin shoulders and only inadequately disguising the fact that her gown was horribly faded and worn.

"My dear!" The younger Miss Twittering could not hide her confusion and dismay as she greeted the unexpected visitor. "What a surprise! We do not often, in the general way, have the pleasure of entertaining. Not that our friends wouldn't wish to come, of course, but— Oh, dear! I do hope nothing's amiss with dearest Sophy?"

"My aunt is doing very well, thank you."

Gently Penelope extricated herself from Miss Helena's trembling embrace. She sat down on the chair indicated by Miss Barbara and slowly stripped off her gloves. What could she say? Her suspicions seemed preposterous now that she faced the two ladies who had grown up with her aunt. Yet she had seen Julian's findings confirmed before her own eyes. Besides, she could not simply get up, apologize for having made a mistake, and leave.

Penelope accepted the tea Miss Barbara had poured for her from a plain earthenware teapot, such as she had seen Mrs. Dawson use for the servants at Belmont House. The cups and saucers, admittedly, were of finest china, but each piece had a chip or a crack.

Impulsively Penelope decided to be at least partially

truthful about the reason for her visit. "I have only just learned that you're the owners of Balena's Hat Shoppe."

"Oh! And you have come to congratulate us, you dear child!" Miss Helena beamed, then turned to her sister. "Didn't I tell you we need not be ashamed of our lovely hats? Oh, I wish we had not been so secretive. Whatever will dearest Sophy think of us when she finds out!"

"Does your aunt know?" asked Miss Barbara, always forthright.

"No, but I daresay she will be quite jealous when she finds out. She once told me that she and Miss Helena had always dreamed of having a small hat shop of their own."

Miss Barbara snorted. "A girlish fancy! There's nothing romantic about being engaged in a trade. On the contrary."

"Oh, but our troubles are over now! Or could be," said Miss Helena, cocking her head to one side and looking just like a ruffled bird as she eyed her sister's finery. Then, with a little bounce, she turned in her chair. "More tea, Penelope? Oh! There is no more. Well, no matter. I shall go and ask Molly to pop the kettle on again."

Clutching the heavy teapot to her bosom, Miss Helena tripped off to the kitchen.

Acutely uncomfortable, Penelope hardly dared look at Miss Barbara, but the older lady was not a whit discomposed by Miss Helena's veiled accusation.

"Now that we're making a bit of money," she said frankly, "my sister wants to pay off the mortgage and refurbish the house."

"But you don't," Penelope said with a smile.

"There's no telling how long the ladies will continue to patronize Balena's. I am six-and-fifty, Penelope. I want some of the fineries my mother always told us should be ours by right—if only Papa hadn't gambled or shown such a poor head for investments."

"But why didn't you tell Aunt Sophy, or Lady Maragret, or any of your friends, that you had the hat shop? They could have helped bring Balena hats into fashion years ago."

Miss Barbara drew herself up. "And have Elizabeth Howe condescend to us as she does to poor Gertrude?"

Then she seemed to shrink, and despite her large-boned, angular frame and deep, booming voice, she looked vulnerable. "But I daresay it would be for the best if our friends knew."

"Indeed, Miss Barbara. They could avert a sudden waning of Balena's fame."

" 'Twould be a good thing, for a steady income is what we need. Helena deserves her happiness, too, and she, poor dear, cannot be happy until we own this house again."

"And perhaps you could get more help for your shop," Penelope suggested. "Lilibeth must have her hands full since Lady Jersey has set her stamp of approval on Balena hats."

"That girl!" Miss Barbara's deep voice reverberated through the bare room. "If she weren't such a jewel with the customers, I'd dismiss her instantly. Such a flibbertigibbet as she has become!"

Penelope remembered the low-cut, crimson taffeta gown, the bright spots of rouge on Lilibeth's cheeks when she had stepped out of the locksmith shop in Fetter Lane. Yet at Balena's it had been a high-necked, demure cotton frock and businesslike reserve.

"Aunt Sophy thinks her quite clever and eager to please."

"Yes, she has a wonderful way with the ladies. Knows exactly what color and shape will suit them. Knows, too, how to talk them out of purchasing something quite unsuitable. And then"—Miss Barbara shook her gray-streaked dark head—"I've seen her when her young man comes to meet her at night, and you'd think she had no taste at all. Looks no better than a lightskirt!"

"She is betrothed to the young man, I believe."

"Betrothed to a slibber-slabber here-and-thereian! A scattergood, wasting his money on flashy waistcoats and fobs. And where he gets the money, I don't dare inquire."

"He's not employed, then?" asked Penelope.

"That young scamp is not one to hold down an honest position for long. Was all rolled up this past winter, and Lilibeth begged us to let him make our deliveries."

Penelope, who could not picture the dapper Erskin from

Fetter Lane in any such menial position, interjected in astonishment, "He's your delivery boy?"

"*Was*, my dear. He came crawling to us without references. Had been dismissed by Henrietta Spatterton—or was it Margaret?"

"Perhaps Lady Elizabeth?"

Miss Barbara shrugged. "I daresay. Dismissing her servants appears to be one of Elizabeth's favorite pastimes. But how on earth did we get on this topic?"

Her dark eyes narrowed. "You said you had only just learned that we're the owners of Balena's. Why did you come, Penelope?"

"Yes, dear. Why?" echoed Miss Helena, carrying the heavy, towel-wrapped teapot in her hands. Her soft-soled slippers had given no warning of her approach, and both Penelope and Miss Barbara turned with a start.

"Here, let me pour," Miss Barbara said gruffly. "Did you scald your hands? Should have let Molly carry the teapot."

Miss Helena dabbed her pink face with the dishtowel. "Her gout's acting up again. You know she can't manage the stairs when she's that way."

"Gout! You mean she's wasted part of her wages on Blue Ruin again."

For a moment they sat glaring at each other, the tall angular Miss Barbara and the dainty, mousy-blond Miss Helena, and no one would have taken them for sisters had it not been for their eyes. Small, dark, and piercing, the two pairs were identical.

Then Miss Helena turned to Penelope and asked sweetly, "Well, my dear? Why did you come to see us?"

chapter
__THIRTEEN__

Penelope took a sip of tea. It was too hot, burning her tongue and the roof of her mouth, but fear of hurting the sisters' feelings was more acute than the momentary discomfort to her mouth and insides.

"You may have heard," she said, carefully choosing her words, "that Mr. Rutherford and I—he's the reporter from *The Times*, you know. Well, we're trying to discover who stole Aunt Sophy's opals."

"Oh, dear!" Miss Helena perched on the edge of her chair, peering closely at Penelope. "Sophy did say something at Gertrude's musicale, but I didn't realize it was Mr. Rutherford who is helping you, or I would have dropped a word of caution in Sophy's ear. He's not at all the thing, dearest Penelope!"

"I understand that, Miss Helena, but, after all, I'm only meeting him . . . on business, you might say."

"But he's known as a libertine, and no matter what the purpose of your association, I fear you cannot be safe in his company."

"Rubbish!" Miss Barbara said forcefully. "Julian Rutherford knows better than to seduce a young lady of quality. Besides, the days of his disgraceful *affaires* seem to be over. Haven't heard a word against him these past three years."

Puzzled, Penelope asked, "Do you know him well, then?"

"Known him for years. Liked him, too. Basically, he's as sound as the next one."

"Oh, but there's that scandal!" Miss Helena lowered her

voice confidentially. " 'Twas five years ago. Or was it six? He—"

"Helena," interrupted Miss Barbara sharply, "don't you go stirring up that old tale! In all likelihood it was blown out of all proportion the first time it was told, and the boy has been punished enough."

"He's hardly a boy any longer."

"He was then." Miss Barbara overruled her younger sister curtly, and Penelope tried to make herself as inconspicuous as possible while the forceful older woman defended Julian.

"A mere stripling of three-and-twenty. And Melanie Somers!" said Miss Barbara. "What did you expect but that the two of them made a hash of it. I always said Melanie was a pea-goose!"

"Such a sweet girl," Miss Helena murmured

"A ninnyhammer!" Miss Barbara shot back.

"She's the Marchioness of Ellsworth now."

The softly spoken pronouncement appeared to clinch the matter.

Disappointed, Penelope ventured to probe a bit further. "I wouldn't want you to repeat old gossip if it distresses you," she said to the elder Miss Twittering, "but I've often wondered about Jul—Mr. Rutherford. He seems such a contradictory character."

Miss Barbara drew her dark brows together. "Contradictory? Now that's something I've never found him to be. On occasion he may exhibit a certain degree of levity that I cannot condone, and he has an undeniably stubborn streak in his makeup, but—"

"He's so unsuitable," Miss Helena interposed on a sigh.

"Since I don't intend to marry him, Miss Helena, his suitability, or rather his *un*suitability, is of no account to me."

Penelope would have said more. Indeed, she longed to ask a great many questions about Julian, but Miss Barbara regarded her with such a knowing look, steady and unsmiling, that she felt embarrassed and guilty.

"To the point," Miss Barbara said briskly. "If you and Mr. Rutherford are investigating the theft of the opals, why come to us?"

"Penelope, my dear, surely you don't suspect us?"

Penelope's face stung. "Everyone was suspect at first, Miss Helena. You see, there are also Lady Arbuthnot's paintings, Mrs. Welby's money, and Lady Margaret's silver service."

"Not to forget Henrietta's pearls," said Miss Barbara.

"Ah, yes. Julian and I are presently making inquiries about some of the servants and . . . and I decided to ask you about Lilibeth. How long has she been with you?"

"Why, ever since we started our little venture, dear. We couldn't open our shop without an assistant since Barbara insisted that we must keep it all a deep, dark secret." Miss Helena smiled cheerfully. "And now we're discovered after all. Tell Sophy, dear child, that she may help me with my designs if she wishes."

Penelope shook her head. "I shall leave it to you and Miss Barbara to tell your friends about Balena's. But about Lilibeth, does she show a great interest in when and where the ladies will wear the hats they purchase?"

"I see what you're getting at," said Miss Barbara, looking alert. "But no, I've never heard the gal ask impertinent questions. As long as she's in the salesroom, she's quiet and reserved—however flighty she may be outside the shop. But I've said too much on that subject already."

"Oh." Penelope swallowed her disappointment and started to draw on her gloves. "Thank you for the tea. It was most kind of you."

Miss Helena, who had been staring in some abstraction at her empty cup during this last exchange, suddenly looked up. "You're not happy with what you learned here. But only think, my dear. Have you ever known a lady *not* to volunteer where and when she'll wear the hat or grown she is purchasing?"

"No, indeed!" said Miss Barbara. "And she's a crafty thing, that Lilibeth. No doubt she has her ways of prodding without appearing unduly curious."

Remembering Lilibeth's offer to deliver Lady Elizabeth's turban and the dowager's reply that she wouldn't need it until the concert in the Argyll Rooms, Penelope bounced off her chair to enfold first Miss Helena, then Miss Barbara in a grateful hug. "I must go. Thank you ever so much!"

The Misses Twittering accompanied Penelope to the door. "Is that your hackney, Penelope?" Miss Barbara pointed to the dilapidated old coach and the drooping horse waiting in the wet street. "You didn't come in one."

"Mr. Bromfield was kind enough to take me up in his carriage."

"Now there's a suitable and most eligible gentleman," Miss Helena said happily.

As the lumbering vehicle conveyed Penelope to Berkeley Square, she remembered Gilbert's insistence on seeing her on the morrow. No doubt he, too, would stress his eligibility and try to convince her that they were well suited.

Never! Penelope pounded the carriage seat with her fist, but a cloud of dust rising from the musty-smelling, faded upholstery forced her to desist in her emphatic denials. Gasping and choking, she tugged on the stiff window until a two-inch gap allowed a breath of fresh air into the stuffy interior of the hackney.

Undoubtedly she had been too kind and gentle on the previous occasions when he had proposed to her. She must be firmer with Gilbert. Give him her answer with no bark on it. And if he complained to his grandmama—so be it! Aunt Sophy would not hold it against her niece if Henrietta Spatterton cut up stiff over the rejection of her precious grandson.

And, most assuredly, the upcoming interview with Gilbert could be no more trying than her tea with Miss Barbara and Miss Helena had been!

Julian and Melanie.

Penelope did not know Melanie Somers, the "sweet girl," or the "ninnyhammer," depending on which of the Misses Twittering was speaking, but she fancied her a tall, willowy blonde with an English wild-rose complexion and melting blue eyes. The type of young lady most admired by gentlemen.

Had Julian tried to abscond with the Marquis of Ellsworth's bride-to-be? Or had Melanie thrown Julian over for a title? After all, the marquis would one day be the Duke of Wynchfield.

Penelope had met the marquis once, over six years ago, at one of Lady Arbuthnot's soirees. It had been the very first—and the last—grand evening entertainment she had attended at her aunt's side, and she could not help but be dazzled by it all. There had been hundreds of candles in glittering chandeliers, flowers, and heavenly scented and jeweled ladies in elaborate coiffures and gowns.

However, Lady Arbuthnot, a youngish widow, had surpassed all with her fiery hair, a black lace gown, and starry diamonds scattered all over her person. The Marquis of Ellsworth, a man rarely found in town, had never been far from Lady Arbuthnot's side. He had not been married then, not even betrothed. Sophy and Gertrude Welby had been convinced that the middle-aged, portly peer was courting Sylvia Arbuthnot.

Obviously, he had changed his mind and chosen the sweet ninnyhammer over the voluptuous widow.

A frown appeared on Penelope's forehead. If her conjectures were correct, she and Julian had much in common. He had been dropped for the marquis, and she had been abandoned—at just about the same time—for Miss Polly Higginbottom and her ready cash.

On an impulse, she opened the small panel behind the driver and shouted, "To Bow Street! Set me down at the magistrate's house, please."

Julian tipped back Sir Nathaniel Conant's chair and propped his booted feet on a corner of Sir Nathaniel's desk. To all outward appearances he was a man deeply engrossed in checking the still-wet printer's proofs of the *Hue and Cry*, but his mind was far removed from reports of crimes and the happenings at diverse magistrate's courts.

Julian saw instead Penelope's face, the disappointment mirrored in her brown eyes when she learned that he did not plan to accompany her to Balena's.

He had called only infrequently at Belmont House during the previous week, giving as his excuse the investigation of the Misses Twittering when, in fact, he had learned all he needed to know during his first two visits in Hans Place. The neighbors had been most eloquent on the sisters' habit of leaving their home in the morning and not returning until ten or twelve hours later, on their poverty, and on the second mortgage the two ladies had taken out on their property three years ago.

A blowzy maid scrubbing the area steps of the neighboring house had been happy to exchange the time of day with him and to let drop that a friend of a friend had assured her the two old ladies owned a hat shop off Oxford Street. Consequently, Julian had spent a few mornings in the city and in the coffee houses and chop houses where merchants and tradesmen congregated, and had received all the information he'd ever want on Balena's Hat Shoppe.

In truth, Julian could have enjoyed every afternoon in Penelope's company. He had instead gone to the offices of *The Times* and shown himself so disagreeable and short-tempered that his superior had advised him to finish his article in support of the Second Factory Act in his lodgings, or else resign his position as a reporter.

"Damn you, Peter!" Julian crushed the copy of the *Hue and Cry* in his hands and tossed it to the floor.

Peter Ludlow's questioning of his conduct had shaken Julian to the core. When Julian first met Penelope, he had wished for no more than a pleasant flirtation with the aloof young lady. The more he got to know her, the more he felt drawn to her, and when Maria Hilbert was arrested, Julian's uppermost thought was to help Penelope in her distress.

Then he had kissed her.

Julian's feet hit the worn floorboards of Sir Nathaniel's sparsely furnished office with a crash, followed by that of the front chair legs hitting the floor. He got up and paced, one hand stuffed into the pocket of his coat, the other balled into a fist and pounding his thigh.

Penelope's response to his kiss and his own reaction to the feel of her lips, her soft body pressed against his, should have been a warning. He had disregarded it. He had blithely continued his flirtation, not acknowledging that, in fact, he was wooing Penelope.

Until Peter had asked him why he wished to keep his identity a secret from her.

"Damn you, Peter," he said again, but without heat this time. "I suppose I should be grateful to you."

Clearly, blindingly, Peter's question had revealed to Julian that he wanted Penelope to fall in love with him. With Julian Rutherford, lowly reporter of *The Times*.

If Penny loved him—and Julian knew enough about women to be quite certain that she was not indifferent to him—if she agreed to marry him, not knowing that he was heir to a viscountcy, he could be certain of her love. He could be certain that none of the Cheltenham tragedy Melanie had enacted would be repeated.

Then Peter had spoken of the scandal that had tarnished Julian's name when he had cried off from the betrothal with Melanie, sparing her the ignominy of being called a mercenary jilt.

With a groan, half of frustration and half of anger, Julian stopped before the empty fireplace behind the magistrate's desk. Would he never be finished paying for his act of chivalry toward Melanie? It had turned his mother into a lachrymose malingerer, who could not spend two minutes in his company without tears and reproaches. His father, admittedly, had recovered from his shock and appeared to lay the blame in the right quarters, but not once since the scandal had he come to town to spend time at his favorite club.

Society had turned against Julian, and not even Melanie's advantageous marriage to the Marquis of Ellsworth a few months later had softened the tongues of gossiping matrons and dowagers. Not that it had bothered him to be banned from Almack's or from the homes of families with nubile daughters. He had never been one to attend balls and routs. But it had hurt when even some of his cronies had started to shun his company.

One thing was clear: a man of his reputation was not fit to hand Penelope into her carriage, let alone propose marriage to her!

It was a wonder Lady Margaret had not instantly dragged him from Belmont House when she found him there, Julian reflected wryly. But the old lady had always had a soft spot for him, and she had never cut their acquaintance. Not even at the height of the scandal.

Well, he'd do all he could to prove himself worthy of Lady Margaret's trust. He would not drag Penny down with him.

With awful precision, Julian aimed a kick at the iron grate. The pain shooting from his toes to his knee was exquisite, yet it was easier to bear than the pain evoked by the knowledge that the delectable Miss Langham could never be his wife.

"Hard at work, eh, guv'nor?"

At the sound of the rumbling voice, Julian swung around. Theobald Dare had entered the magistrate's office and was looking from the crushed sheets of the *Hue and Cry* to Julian, nursing his sore toes.

Julian glared balefully at the Bow Street runner. Then, as he caught a flicker of excitement in the other's expression, his eyes narrowed. "Why the sudden interest, Theo? Are you getting bored with playing least in sight?"

Grinning, the runner advanced into the room. He pulled a straight-backed chair to the desk and straddled it. "Can't blame a man for obeying strict orders," he said comfortably. "But now we've got the proof we was lookin' for, and I'm at liberty to discuss the matter with you."

It crossed Julian's mind that Theobald Dare might be referring to the pearls Maria Hilbert had sold to Sprott. "What matter?" he asked, resuming his seat in Sir Nathaniel's large, worn leather chair.

"The matter of Mr. Benjamin Rugby." Obviously enjoying himself, the runner placed his folded hands on the back of his chair as a rest for his pugnacious chin. He quirked a bushy gray brow. "Don't tell me, ye wasn't wonderin' why Miss Hilbert was set free all of a sudden."

"She told us her fiancé turned himself in and confessed to the crimes."

Theobald Dare chuckled. "Aye. And from yer long association with Bow Street, ye knewed as we're all gullible and would fall for a likely tale."

"Stubble the gammon, Theo. I'm in no mood for games. You must have checked Rugby's story, for you kept Miss Hilbert two days *after* he'd turned himself in."

The runner scowled. "If it hadn't been for Sir Nathaniel and his obsession with the Habeas Corpus Act, both of 'em would be in Rumbo still. It's Lombard Street to an eggshell that Miss Hilbert's in it, too. Only we can't prove it."

"But you can, ah, prove Mr. Rugby's guilt?"

"Just found the last piece of the puzzle, ye might say."

Theobald Dare sat up, patting the bulky pocket of his old-fashioned frock coat where he kept his occurrence book. "And it's put the noose around his neck right 'n tight."

Julian experienced a sinking feeling in the region of his stomach. "A previous conviction?"

"Aye. For a score of break-ins, pickpocketing, and pilfering from the Covent Garden and Billingsgate markets. Mind, he was only a nipper of ten at the time. A rare little hellion!"

"And his childhood offenses are to be held against him?" Julian said scathingly. "Damn it, Theo! The man has been a model of propriety and honesty for the past seven years that he's worked for Mrs. Welby."

"Rugby has a large bank account. Are ye telling me he didn't feather his nest while he worked for the old dame?"

"If you can prove that, I might believe you."

The runner stuck out his chin belligerently and scowled, but he said nothing.

"Did Rugby escape from prison, or how did he manage to get the education necessary to act as Mrs. Welby's agent?"

"He was on one of them prison hulks on the Thames. Waitin' to be transported, but his papers got lost or something. He was there five years, then he caught the attention of some old geezer, a phi-lan-thro-pist," Theobald Dare spat out disdainfully. "T' geezer, Mr. Benjamin Weatherall, bought his release and sent him to school."

Julian's startled eyes met the runner's contemptuous look.

"Aye," Mr. Dare said heavily, "that's how the scaly rascal picked his name. Wasn't known as nothing but Pockets on the riverfront, and as Number 449 in the hulk. An' if you think he got more education at some fancy school than during five years in the hulks, you ain't the man I took ye for."

No, Julian didn't believe that the years on the riverfront, in the slums, and in a prison hulk could be wiped out by a few years of schooling.

He began to understand, however, why Benjamin Rugby had not turned from Maria in disgust when she confessed to him the theft of the pearl necklace. And whether he was guilty or innocent of the four later thefts, Benjamin Rugby had acted nobly when he turned himself in to the Bow Street magistrate to facilitate Maria's release from Newgate Prison.

"Theo," Julian said, tipping the heavy chair back again and putting his feet on a corner of the desk, "mayhap you have your thief and mayhap you don't. Miss Langham and I have done some investigating of our own, and I would advise you to hold off on any action until I've spoken with you tomorrow."

"It is my dooty to report to Sir Nathaniel," the runner said in his blustering way. "I—" He broke off when he heard the door swing open behind him. Hastily abandoning his straddle position on the chair, he jumped up and turned around.

"Butterwick!" he exclaimed in indignation as Sir Nathaniel's cadaverous-looking clerk stuck his head into the office. "When will ye learn to knock, man!"

"I'll knock when I know Sir Nathaniel to be in," Butterwick said haughtily, then, addressing Julian with a slight bow, he added, "A young lady to see you, sir."

Julian saw Penelope's light brown curls peek around the clerk's shoulder, and once again his feet and chair came down with a crash. "Penelope! Come in. Nothing went wrong, I hope?"

Smiling widely, Penelope darted into the office. "It couldn't have fallen out better had we planned it! Julian, I believe I've found a way to catch the thief!"

"Penelope," Julian said warningly. "You remember Mr. Dare, don't you?"

"Oh. How d'ye do?" Penelope nodded to the runner, then closed the door in the affronted Mr. Butterwick's face. "Mr. Dare may be interested in this as well," she said, looking around for a chair.

Instantly the Bow Street runner offered the one he had just vacated. Julian resumed his place of authority behind the magistrate's desk while Theobald Dare stood, feet planted apart and arms crossed over his wide chest.

"I may have solved the mystery, Julian! The girl from Fetter Lane, the one who went to see Sprott with her young man, why, she's no other than Lilibeth, the shopgirl at Balena's!"

Penelope then proceeded to relate those parts of her

conversation with the Misses Twittering that pertained to Lilibeth and concluded, "So you see, we need only conceal ourselves in Lady Elizabeth's house on the sixteenth, which is the date of the Philharmonic Society's last performance, and I daresay we'll catch our thief red-handed!"

Mr. Dare was the first to find his voice. "Very irregular!" he said. "And I must inform you, Miss Langham, that it is my dooty—"

"Yes, yes, I know. To inform Sir Nathaniel of what you learned. But surely you can inform him *after* we catch the thief!"

"There's more to it, Penny." Julian stepped around the desk. Sitting down on the edge of the scratched and cluttered desktop, he possessed himself of Penelope's hands. "Theobald Dare has news as well," he said quietly. "Unfortunately, his is more convincing than yours. Tell her, Theo."

Quietly Penelope listened to Mr. Dare's report on Benjamin Rugby. She gave no sign of distress, save when Julian suddenly let go of her hands and moved away from her to stand leaning with his back against the window. Her eyes followed him, then fell before his stern gaze.

When the Bow Street runner fell silent, it took her a moment to collect her wits. When Julian had excused himself from coming to Balena's with her, she had felt his withdrawal. She had told herself that he had to attend to his business, but just now, when he dropped her hands, she realized that he was keeping her at a distance. Had she done something to affront him?

Theobald Dare was staring at her with a question in his sharp eyes. She must pull herself together, must respond. Penelope rose, irked suddenly that both men were standing and looking down on her.

"Well, gentlemen, if you prefer to wait around to see if a theft will take place this month, it is your privilege to do so. I don't see that the evidence against Mr. Rugby is overwhelming. *I* would prefer to take some action!"

A reluctant grin tugged at the corners of Julian's mouth. He looked at the Bow Street runner. "Theobald?"

"I ain't sayin' the little lady don't have a point, but"—he pulled the stub of a pencil from his coat pocket and scratched his grizzled head—"I don't like it one bit. For one thing, Sir Nathaniel will insist on getting permission from . . ." He raised a questioning brow to Penelope.

"Lady Elizabeth Howe."

The runner nodded. "Right. Sir Nathaniel ain't a cove as wants to fall afoul of the nobs, but Lady Elizabeth don't strike me as one who'd let us into her house while she's gone. A right old harridan I judge her to be. If you'll pardon me saying so, Miss Langham."

Penelope kept a straight face. "Yes, indeed, Mr. Dare. And just think what might happen if Sir Nathaniel denied you permission to conceal yourself in Lady Elizabeth's house! Julian and I would be there on our own, without your guidance and counsel."

"Besides," said Julian, "we don't want just the thief. We want the fence, the locksmith if he supplied the keys to the houses, and, if possible, the foreign buyer. We need several of your men to stand guard in Fetter Lane. What do you say, Theo?"

But Theobald Dare was not so easily swayed. "What locksmith? And what's all this talk of Fetter Lane? Heard Miss Langham mention it earlier. Upon my soul, Mr. Rutherford, if I don't smell a bubble here! What have you been up to?"

"Now don't get into a taking, old fellow! I've done nothing you wouldn't have done yourself. I investigated some of the more notorious fences—"

"Do ye think I didn't?" Mr. Dare said, looking mightily put out.

"—to see if I could find any of the stolen articles. In Fetter Lane, outside Sprott's house, Miss Langham spotted the young woman Lilibeth and her, ah, fancy man. And in the basement of the same building happens to be the shop of Lady Belmont's locksmith."

Incredulous, the runner could only sputter. "Ye mean to tell me ye took Miss Langham to Sprott's? In Fetter Lane?"

Julian glanced at Penelope, but she only raised her head and looked adorably mulish. *The deuce take Lady Margaret and the old scandal,* he thought. *I may only have six more days with my love.* He pushed away from the window and went to stand beside Penelope.

"Meet my partner, Theo," he said, placing his arm around her waist and pulling her closer. "Penny and I are sworn to catch the thief. He brought much unhappiness to her aunt when he took her opals."

Responding to Julian's warmth, Penelope smiled first at him, then at the Bow Street runner. "Please, Mr. Dare, will you help us?"

The runner stared at them for a moment. Then he capitulated. "And I daresay Miss Langham is to be one of the party on the sixteenth?"

"Yes," she said.

"No," Julian said at the same time.

They turned toward each other, and when their eyes met, Theobald Dare knew he didn't exist any longer. He felt as though he stood outside a magic circle that no one could enter and no one could break. They seemed as one, bound together by a firm promise.

Afraid to move, yet more reluctant to stay, Theobald Dare forced his feet toward the door. Quietly he let himself out. Quietly he closed the door, but not before he saw them draw even closer.

"I could've gone home," he muttered, "if only he'd told me how many of my men I should brief."

Theobald Dare trudged down the corridor to the clerk's tiny office. Butterwick might be a nuisance, but he always proved generous when it came to sharing a drop of something to while away the time.

chapter
FOURTEEN

A_s Julian's mouth came closer, Penelope was aware of a deep need to feel the touch of his lips again. Standing on tiptoe, she locked her hands behind his neck and raised her face to his kiss. His mouth was warm and firm. Once again the heady scent of his skin and his shaving soap engulfed her, and then she had no strength left for rational thought. She was pulled into a whirlwind of sensations. Every fiber, every nerve of her body was alive, yearning for the touch of his hands and his lips.

Gradually she became aware of a gentling of those breathtaking forces. As her body quieted, her mind took over and she realized that Julian was slowly pulling away from her. They still stood breast to breast. She could feel his heartbeat echo her own. She could still taste his essence on her lips.

The distance widened. They stood apart. Penelope looked at Julian, a question in her eyes. He raised a hand to her face and slowly, tenderly traced the shape of her mouth with his thumb. Then, when she would have spoken, he bent down and kissed her. Infinite tenderness. Infinite love.

Arm in arm they left Sir Nathaniel's office. Neither one paid attention to Theobald Dare, who followed them out into the street, calling after them, "And how many men will ye be needin', guv'nor?"

Julian handed Penelope into his curricle, then jumped in and pulled her into the shelter of his arms. Night was falling rapidly, and by the time they reached Berkeley Square, it was completely dark. They had not spoken, but the feeling of belonging between them more than made up for the lack of paltry words.

As they pulled to a halt before Belmont House, Dawson, obviously on the lookout, opened the door wide. Under the butler's watchful eye, Julian raised Penelope's hand to his lips for a last salute. Only then did he break the silence.

"Tomorrow," he said.

But his eyes, she thought, said much more.

Then Sophy, resplendent in a dinner gown of dark lavender lace over satin, appeared beside Dawson, and Penelope hurried into the foyer.

"Don't scold, dearest Auntie." She whirled past and

started up the stairs, still speaking. "I forgot you were giving a dinner, but I'll be changed in the twinkling of a bedpost, you'll see."

"Penelope!"

The high pitch of her aunt's voice made her stop. Slowly she turned. "Yes, Aunt Sophy."

"Come down, Penelope. I must speak with you."

As Penelope descended, Sophy impatiently advanced to the bottom step. Penelope noted the bright spots of red high on her aunt's cheeks and heard again the note of hysteria in her voice.

"First Nancy comes home without you! Then Barbara and Helena say that you should have been here long ago!"

A flicker of resentment kindled in Penelope's breast, but she suppressed it. She *should* have sent word, no matter that never before had Sophy asked for an accounting of her movements.

"Then you know about Balena's. Did Miss Helena invite you to help with the designs, Aunt Sophy?"

"Where were you, Penelope? I was ready to send the Bow Street runners looking for you!"

"Oh, Auntie. I am sorry." Penelope leaned down from her superior height on the third step and embraced Sophy. "That's exactly where I went. To Bow Street. Mr. Rutherford then brought me home."

"You're still chasing after the thief, Penelope?" Sophy's face crumpled. "I don't know what I was about to let you follow your hubble-bubble notion. Oh, it is so mortifying! I am such a bad aunt! So much that I neglected while I was taking that . . . that elixir. All the hey-go-mad things I permitted you to do!"

"Now that is nonsense, and you know it," Penelope said sternly. "You have always been the best of aunts. It is only that I was bored, and this wretched thief gives me the excuse to have an adventure. Oh, I wish I could make you understand, Aunt Sophy!"

Recovering some of her poise, Sophy said, "What I understand is that it's high time for you to be married and start a family. Then you won't have time to feel bored."

Penelope drew in her breath sharply. If she couldn't have

the man she loved, she wouldn't marry at all. The man she loved—Julian! She barely heard her aunt's next words.

"Gilbert sent word that he will call on you at eleven in the morning. He asked my permission to speak with you privately. Is he going to propose again, do you suppose? Not that I would ever pressure you to marry *him*, but you can't afford to throw away your chances. Will you think about it, Penelope?

"Penelope!" Sophy said sharply when her niece continued staring off into some far distance.

"What? Oh, yes. Gilbert. Auntie, I had best go and change. Colonel Wringer and his nephew are always early, and I know you wouldn't wish to have to entertain them by yourself."

"No, by God! I wouldn't!" Sophy said with feeling. "If I've heard his tales of Bengal once, I've heard them a thousand times. Don't stand there laughing! Hurry, child!"

Penelope leaned down and touched her cheek to her aunt's powdered and scented one. "I'll be down before the cat can lick her ear. I promise."

A scant twenty minutes later, Penelope was dressed in a gown of cornflower silk, embroidered all around the hem and neckline with feather stitching in palest blue and ivory. Her short curls were arranged á la Sappho and held together with the new blue ribbon Nancy had procured at Miss Leete's haberdashy. Colonel Wringer, a tall, reed-thin octogenarian, pinched her cheek and told her that she was a pretty puss and wished that he, or at least his nephew, were a few years younger so he could pay court to her.

Lady Margaret, sailing into the room just then, snorted and told the colonel to stop making a cake of himself; Penelope undoubtedly would pick and choose her own admirers.

All in all, Penelope reflected, the evening could be no more trying than any other she had spent in the company of her aunt's friends, and yet this night there seemed to be a difference. She had to force herself to be patient and keep smiling when Mrs. Welby was scatter-brained during the after-dinner game of whist. She had to grit her teeth when the colonel's nephew, a sixty-year-old confirmed bachelor, who liked to think of himself as a dashing ladies' man, paid her fulsome compliments or fondled her fingers in an obvious fashion when he accepted his teacup from her.

Why? she asked herself when she got ready for bed later that night. Why did her aunt's friends, whom she had known and liked for years, seem so tedious all of a sudden? Had she changed so drastically with the knowledge that it had not been her fault Aunt Sophy had taken too much laudanum?

Penelope sat before her mirror, brushing her hair, but she did not see her reflection in the glass. Instead, she saw the events of the past weeks parade before her mind's eye, and she realized that somehow, very subtly, she had started to change when Julian Rutherford entered her library for the first time.

Had she never met Julian, she might still be the quiet, poised, perfect lady despite having had that weight of guilt over Aunt Sophy removed from her shoulders. She might still contemplate marriage to Gilbert Bromfield as an alternative to being left alone, an eccentric old maid, when Aunt Sophy was gone.

Had she not met Julian, she would feel no excitement, no bubbling, heartwarming happiness. And no sadness, no pain. Julian had changed her. He had made her come alive.

She could not possibly return to a staid pace, to a humdrum existence.

"And that, Penny, my love, means that you must make some decisions!"

The hairbrush clattered onto the dresser top when Penelope realized what she had just said. Her eyes, dark and mysterious in the candlelight, stared back at her from the mirror.

And he hasn't even called me "my love" anymore.

But he loved her! She could not be mistaken. His kisses, his glances, his touch—everything had been a message of love.

She rose, doused the lights save for the small lamp on her bedside table, then climbed into her four-poster. Wide-awake, Penelope lay thinking about Julian.

She couldn't be certain about his family background since Aunt Sophy had denied that he was the vicar's son from Lady Margaret's parish in Kent. The Misses Twittering knew of some horrid scandal in his past. And he was working as a reporter.

He was clearly ineligible to marry Penelope Landham of Langham Court.

But it doesn't matter!

She loved Julian, and to be married to him was above all things what she wanted. She *would* marry him. Just as soon as he asked her. Aunt Sophy might not cry with joy at Julian's proposal of marriage to her niece, but she would understand. She would not cast them off. After all, she had remained a staunch friend to Gertrude Welby, who had married into trade.

"And the rest of society may go hang!"

Turning over, Penelope went instantly to sleep. She awoke to bright sunshine peeking through her drapes and a feeling that something absolutely wonderful was about to happen.

Julian!

Humming, Penelope went downstairs for breakfast, then descended to the kitchen quarters to discuss the day's menu with Maurice and to settle diverse household matters with Mrs. Dawson while keeping one eye firmly on the clock. As the hands crept past ten and closer to eleven o'clock she grew impatient.

Where was Julian?

"Pardon, Miss Penelope." Dawson, a knowing smile on his seamed face, entered the kitchen. "Mr. Bromfield requests the honor of seeing you. I've shown him into the front parlor."

Penelope looked at him in consternation. She had forgotten all about Gilbert. "Thank you, Dawson. If Mr. Rutherford calls, I want you to show him in without delay."

"Now Miss Penelope—" the butler protested in outraged tones.

"Without delay, Dawson!"

Smoothing her skirts, she quickly left the nether regions and Dawson's disapproving frown. Without a check she swept into the parlor.

"Gilbert," she said, giving him her hand in greeting. "How punctual you are."

Red-faced and beaming, Gilbert bowed over her hand. "Indeed. It is but one of my virtues. Of course, as a lady you're not expected to adhere quite as strictly to—"

He was interrupted by eleven noisy booms from the marquetry clock in the corner of the parlor and by the chimes in the hall, which were, as usual, just a little bit behind.

"There," Penelope said with satisfaction. "I was sure I wasn't late."

"Oh, no. Didn't mean to imply that you were late," Gilbert assured her hastily. "I only meant to point out—but that's neither here nor there. May we not sit down, Penelope?"

Choosing a chair over the chaise longue, Penelope invited him to take a seat. "What can I do for you, Gilbert?"

He drew a large handkerchief from his pocket and mopped his glistening brow. "Dash it, Penelope," he said ruefully. "I had a speech all prepared, but those infernal clocks have clear driven it from my mind."

"Perhaps you shouldn't speak at all," she said gently.

"No. No. Made up my mind to it yesterday, only you were out. Saw you myself. In Oxford Street. Yes, and that only convinces me that it's high time I popped the question. No doubt I've left you dangling long enough, and now you're upset. That's why you've been behaving in such a hurly-burly fashion of late, isn't it?"

"What!" Penelope exclaimed. "Have a care what you say, Gilbert!"

Gilbert Bromfield, however, had the bit well between the teeth and could not be stopped. "No need to poker up, m'dear," he said. "I pride myself on my understanding of the fairer sex, and I know that you're afraid I've changed my mind. You're not getting any younger. In fact," he added judicially, "neither one of us is getting any younger. So we might as well take the plunge together."

Speechless with growing indignation, she could only sit and stare at him.

"We'll get married," he said, enunciating carefully as though he were addressing a backward child. "Have I quite taken your breath away, m'dear? Well—" He chuckled and heaved himself out of his chair. "I'm not usually one to rush my fences, but I daresay my haste in this case may be excused."

Arms held wide, he approached Penelope. "You've made me the happiest of—"

"Oh, no!" Penelope rose with rather more haste than grace and whisked herself behind the chair. "Now listen to me carefully, Gilbert. I do not intend to marry you."

"I *have* rushed you." He stopped in his tracks, a puzzled frown creasing his broad forehead. "But I thought my hints to you yesterday and my note to Lady Belmont made it perfectly clear. Felt sure you had sufficient time to consider the matter."

Keeping her voice steady, Penelope said, "Gilbert, I've had more than enough time for consideration. I'm deeply appreciative of the honor you're doing me, but I will *not* marry you."

He stared at her, his face darkening. "I warn you, Penelope! I'm done with playing games. I see I've been far too indulgent."

"I'm not playing games, Gilbert."

Heedless of the signs of rising temper on her stormy countenance, he went on, "And where did it lead? To disgrace! If anyone other than I had seen you yesterday, flaunting yourself in Oxford Street, your reputation would be in shreds! See if anyone would have married you then!"

"You're mad! Utterly mad!" Burning with anger, Penelope stepped around the chair and confronted him. "If I were a man, I'd mill you down for that, Gilbert. What right have you to censure me? What right to accuse me of leading you on? Four times you proposed to me. Four times I said no. Can I help it that my answer didn't penetrate that thick skull of yours?"

His hands shot out, clamping painfully onto her upper arms. "What right? From the moment I came to town, you've singled me out! You never so much as looked at another man. You accepted my escort. You've driven out with me. Why, you've lived in my pocket for years!"

"Let go!"

Penelope aimed sharp fingernails at his face, but he easily held her off. She kicked, but only succeeded in hurting her toes on his boots. She wanted to spit at him, but when she raised her head, she saw such a look of horror in his eyes that her fury abated.

"See," she said, trying to keep her voice level. "See

what a hellion you would have to contend with if you married me? Admit you're horrified that I want to scratch and kick. You've always prided yourself on your good sense and even temper, but I make you lose it.

"And what about your health, Gilbert? I'd want to ride in wind and rain. You'd want to sit by your fireside and have Harvey, or a like-minded wife, brew you a hot posset."

She had obviously struck the right note, for Gilbert let his hands drop from her arms. He stared at her as though seeing her for the first time. And, perhaps, he was. She had certainly never acted like this in his company before.

"But what about—" Confused, Gilbert shook his head. "You *haven't* looked at another man for as long as I've known you," he said accusingly. "You know you haven't! I believe that you meant to have me in the end, Penelope!"

"I'm sorry you should feel yourself misled, Gilbert. It was not my intention. Pray think back! Your grandmama and my aunt do not mix with any of the younger set. I have never met another man!"

Her face stung as, irrepressibly, Julian intruded in her thoughts and gave her words the lie. She pushed the thought aside. Gilbert would never understand about Julian.

"But," stammered Gilbert, "but that's not true. There have always been men. There's—" He broke off, frowning.

"Colonel Wringer? His nephew?" Penelope asked softly. "Old Lord Beaseley with his creaking corsets? Why, yes. I daresay I could have flirted with them."

Gilbert merely looked at her, realizing the truth of her argument. Penelope stood before him, once again calm and poised, with just a faint blush staining her cheeks, and he felt a pang of regret. Then he remembered her outburst of temper, the nails going for his face, dark eyes flashing in her white face. With a barely repressed shudder, he congratulated himself on his narrow escape. *She* would be the one to rue this day!

He bowed abruptly. "I shall not inflict my unwelcome presence on you any longer than necessary, Penelope, but I feel it my duty to point out that you're making a grave mistake. This day's work cannot be undone, I fear."

"I promise not to carry a grudge," she offered handsomely.

Gilbert scowled. "I was thinking of Harvey."

"For heaven's sake, Gilbert! What does your man have to do with it?"

Again they confronted each other like antagonists. "Harvey," Gilbert pronounced in ringing tones, "has taken particular care over the selection of my raiment this morning. We pride ourselves in having struck a felicitous mixture of the somber and the exultant, exactly right for a man bent on soliciting the hand—"

A knock, followed by Dawson's announcement of Mr. Rutherford's arrival, put Gilbert to the rout. He would have collided with Julian in the doorway had Julian not reacted with a swift sidestep.

"I hope he didn't leave on my account. It's Gilbert Bromfield, isn't it?" said Julian, looking over his shoulder after the departing man.

"Yes. Do you know him?"

"We met once, I believe."

Julian appeared to study her closely, but if he had heard Gilbert's last words, he made no reference to them. Penelope wished now that she had asked Dawson to show Julian into the library. She didn't want to entertain him in the same room where Gilbert had behaved so abominably.

"Let's go to our—to the library, Julian. That's where I keep our papers. We may need to refer to them."

"Very well." He held the door wide, allowing her to pass, then followed her to the first floor.

Julian had seen the signs of distress in her eyes when he first entered the parlor, and he had heard enough of Bromfield's blustering speech to guess what had happened. He wanted nothing more than to take her into his arms and kiss away the marks of strain around her eyes and mouth. He wanted to tell her it was only right that she refused that boorish knave.

Penny belonged to *him*. She had broken through his guard, and turned his flirtation into a deep and lasting love. He wanted her at his side. Day and night. Forever.

He wanted her as his wife.

Julian caught his breath on a stab of pain. Penny was his life, his love—but he must not ask her to marry him. He cared for her as he had never before cared for a woman.

He must protect and shelter her. Penny's name must not be coupled with that of a jilt.

He felt Penelope's eyes upon him, questioning and slightly apprehensive, as she took her seat behind the desk. He mustn't let her down now. She needed him.

"I saw Theobald Dare again this morning," he said, settling himself in his customary chair. "He will join us inside Lady Elizabeth's house. Two runners will be concealed outside, and four of his best men will be in the vicinity of Sprott's house."

"Could I have been mistaken, Julian? Perhaps Lilibeth was not trying to draw out Lady Elizabeth."

"Changed your mind?" He raised his brows quizzically. "It's a lady's prerogative, of course. Would you rather not be involved, Penny?"

Her heart cried, *Why don't you say "my love" anymore?*

Aloud she said, "Just think what it would do to the headline of your article! And besides, I wouldn't dream of letting you have all the fun by yourself." She put all her love into the look and the smile she gave him, but the smile she received in return was slightly mocking.

"What happened to the proper young lady I met in this very room not so long ago? Demure as a nun's hen you were then. Now you're more of a madcap than I am."

"I'm an apt pupil. Is there anything else you'd care to teach me, Julian?"

The sudden gleam in his eyes made her pulse race, but his words were like a spray of cold water.

"Have a care, Penny. That's dangerous ground you're treading now."

Julian took the lists of dates and suspects from her hands and fanned them out on the desk. "Shall we cross off Miriam?" he asked. "If Lilibeth and her lover are the culprits, Miriam won't be needed as a go-between to the locksmith shop."

Penelope lowered her gaze to the sheets of paper as though she, too, were studying them. Where was the closeness she had felt between them yesterday? Had Julian had second thoughts?

Yet that had not been the message conveyed in his look when he warned her to have a care.

Julian drummed his fingertips against the desktop. "I'm convinced," he said, "that the books have no connection to the other thefts. Why would anyone steal books when a silver bowl could be sold much easier and fetch a better price?"

Suppressing a sigh, Penelope concentrated on the matter at hand. "Then who *is* stealing the books?"

He grinned. "Mayhap Miriam is only borrowing them."

"To read medical and philosophical works? Pray be serious, Julian." Turning, she reached for the bell pull behind her. "I'll send for Miriam. Surely it will do no harm now to ask her about the books, even if her great-grandfather is involved in the thefts."

"Go ahead and question her. Just be careful, Penny. We don't want her to find out that we suspect Samuel Abel of wrongdoing."

Ben, who came to answer the summons, shook his head when Penelope asked him to send Miriam to her. "I'm mighty sorry, Miss Penelope, but Miriam's gone already."

"Gone? It's not her day off, is it?"

"No, miss. Didn't ye know she planned to go to Fetter Lane?"

Penelope shook her head. "No," she said, her voice sounding hollow. "I didn't know."

"'Twas only about fifteen or so minutes ago. Miriam came to Mrs. Dawson. She was nabbin' her bib something awful, and wantin' to take a leave."

"Miriam was crying? But why, Ben?"

"It appears that her great-granfer, him that be our locksmith, has fallen sick. Miriam said she be the only one as can nurse him, Miss Penelope."

"Did a message come for her?" Julian asked.

"That be just what Mrs. Dawson was wonderin' because none of us has seen anyone come an' tell Miriam that her great-granfer be sick."

Penelope's and Julian's eyes met across the desk. "Thank you, that will be all, Ben," she said.

They sat without speaking until they could be certain that Ben had left the first floor. Then, in one accord, they got up and quietly left the library. Penelope led the way along the corridor. At the far end, a narrow door opened onto the back stairs.

The stairwell leading into the attics was dark and steep. After proceeding a few steps, Julian groped for Penelope's hand only to find that it had already been extended to him. His fingers closed warmly around hers.

At the top of the stairs, two doors were set at right angles. One, Julian surmised, leading into a part of the storage area, the second one, which Penelope opened, into the maids' sleeping quarters. It was brighter up here, and after they had turned sharply to the right into a narrow hallway, Julian noted two small, dusty skylights set into the roof.

The servants' attic was not, as he had half expected, a dormitory. It had been partitioned into five rooms—no more than cubicles, and each decreasing in height with the slope of the roof. Penelope opened the last door and entered. Julian, following her, had to duck his head to enter and was obliged to keep this awkward position even inside the small chamber.

There, on a tidily made-up cot, lay several leather-tooled volumes.

"All but the plant books and *The County Housewife's Family Companion*," said Penelope after a quick inspection of the titles. "And Dr. Johnson's dictionary. I do not see it here."

chapter
FIFTEEN

"*The* illustrated plant books are priceless," Penelope said in a tight little voice when they had returned to the main part of the house. "If you know where to sell them. Sprott, I daresay, will give her no more than a groat apiece."

"Miriam would hardly have left the other books on her bed if she meant to sell them." Julian halted outside the library door. Placing a finger under Penelope's chin, he firmly pushed her face up until she had to look at him. "Now put it from your mind," he commanded.

She intended to tell him that no one would normally enter Miriam's small chamber; the maids each cleaned her own room. Lady Belmont never ventured into the attics, and Penelope only when Mrs. Dawson insisted that she inspect the results of the great spring cleaning. With the feel of his hand under her chin, his closeness, everything flew from her mind. She could only think of him and how much she wanted him to take her in his arms again.

For an instant her feelings were mirrored in Julian's eyes. Then his look became remote. His mouth tightened, and he removed his hand as though he had burned himself.

"You had best get your parasol, then," he said, stepping away from her. "We'll walk to Brook Street. Just to see the different approaches the thief could make."

Perturbed by this renewed demonstration of aloofness, Penelope hurried off to fetch the pretty white and cherry-red sunshade that matched her striped gown. She felt hurt, but more than that she was determined to find out what caused him to withdraw from her.

When she rejoined Julian she took care to show none of her thoughts. Smiling, she dipped into a curtsy. "Shall we, sir?"

"My pleasure, ma'am."

Twirling her parasol and with her free hand resting lightly on Julian's arm, Penelope strolled with him across the square. After the recent period of cooler weather, the sun had come out in full force. The air was sultry and redolent with the sweet perfume of the plane trees.

"How pleasant this is!" exclaimed Penelope. "I must say your employer is very generous, Julian. I'm glad, though, for how could you make time to see me otherwise?"

He looked into her upturned face framed by the frivolous, octagonal piece of muslin and lace the ladies called a parasol. His heart swelled with tenderness. "And so am I, Penny."

Well, she thought, *this is promising.*

"Lady Margaret knew you as a child," she said, trying to make her voice sound diffident. "Did you grow up near Cleve Court?"

"Lived there all my life."

"And then you came to London to become a reporter. How long ago was that?"

"To be precise, Penny, I didn't come to London straightaway."

"That's right. Dr. Ludlow said you were wounded while serving in the army. Which was your regiment?"

He seemed to answer readily enough. "I was with Sir John Moore's troops in Spain first, and for a little while I served under Wellington."

"With Sir John!" she exclaimed. "You must have been very young!"

White teeth flashed in his rugged countenance. "No younger than most of the lads who're army mad."

Penelope twirled her sunshade a little faster. It was uphill work, trying to learn something about this man she had fallen in love with. Or, mayhap, she was not going about it the right way.

They were in New Bond Street, and she observed several gentlemen nodding to Julian. He returned their greeting but showed no sign of wishing to stop and talk or to introduce them to her. Were they friends or merely acquaintances? They all had the look of a Corinthian about them with their well-tailored coats and gleaming Hessians.

Penelope proceeded in silence until they came to Brook Street. "That's Lady Elizabeth's house." She pointed to an imposing edifice complete with Gothic windows, with columns and portico, and situated about halfway between Hanover Square and New Bond Street.

Slowly they walked past it, turned, and retraced their steps.

"Let's hope there are no lights on the sides of the house," Julian said as they crossed the street to view it from a distance. "Else Theobald will find himself hard-pressed to hide his men."

"I have never noticed any lanterns or flambeaux except those near the front door. The tradesmen's entrance is on the right-hand side, toward the rear of the building. I know it is not lit. Once Maria had to take Lady Elizabeth's pug out late at night, and it worried her."

"Not very pleasant for Miss Hilbert but fortuitous for us. Do you think she could get us a key to the house?"

"She must." Penelope looked over her shoulder for a last glimpse of Lady Elizabeth's house. If the thief showed up on the sixteenth, she mused, Benjamin Rugby was clearly innocent and must be released from prison. "I shall see to it tomorrow."

They left Brook Street behind and retraced their steps to Berkeley Square. Not wishing for a speedy parting, Penelope slowed down to a mere snail's pace.

"I should, perhaps, draw a plan of the house for you and Mr. Dare," she offered.

"Theo would like that. He's worried, you know. Thinks his days as a runner are numbered."

"What could possibly go wrong?"

"The thief could *not* show up. We'd look proper fools if anyone caught us in the house." A thought struck him and he came to a sudden halt. "My God, Penelope! If that happened, your reputation would be in shreds. I can't let you come!"

"Pah! So much for my reputation," she said, snapping her fingers at him.

"You won't say that once you've lost it. Believe me, Penny," he said, his voice tinged with bitterness. "I know what I'm talking about. A tarnished reputation is like a millstone around your neck. You can't shake it off. It'll drag you down and dash all hope of future happiness."

Her eyed widened. *Of course! The scandal in Julian's past!* That was the reason he tried to stay aloof. He believed himself ineligible! His code of honor would not allow him to propose marriage to her.

She started walking again. Now that she knew what kept Julian at a distance she would find a way to fight it.

Slanting a glance at his set face from under her lowered

lashes, she said, "I daresay you know all about scandal. Miss Helena fears you have the reputation of a libertine."

Against his will, he chuckled. "I can hear her say it. Poor soul! She must have been in a regular flutter when she learned of your association with me. But," he said, turning serious again, "I *am* considered shockingly loose, and I daresay my critics are right, for I didn't even think to ask you to bring your maid."

"I didn't have a maid yesterday when I saw you at the Bow Street office. So you see, I am just as shockingly loose as you are."

"Penny, this is no joking matter. I—"

"Don't be tiresome, Julian," she interrupted. "If you believe you can talk me out of going to Lady Elizabeth's house, you're far off the mark. Nothing," she declared, "can make me cry off!"

"Very well," said Julian, making a vow to protect her and her reputation at all cost. If Benjamin Rugby was the thief after all and they were discovered empty-handed in Brook Street, he'd just have to pretend that he kidnapped Penelope. And Theobald Dare could make the arrest, thereby saving his skin as well.

They had reached the corner of Bruton Street and were waiting for a lull in the traffic before crossing when he saw Maria Hilbert step out of a tea chandler's on the opposite side of the street.

Penelope saw her, too, and waved her parasol. A horseman swore roundly when his mare snorted and reared in fright at the flashing red and white object, but the horse's startlement provided opportunity for Penelope and Julian to dart across the busy street. They caught up with Maria in front of a confectioner's shop.

Maria's face broke into a smile. "Well met, Penelope. I was just bemoaning Lady Elizabeth's long shopping list, for I did so want to see you today." She glanced shyly at Julian. "How do you do, Mr. Rutherford."

"You look positively radiant, my dear." Penelope embraced her friend, then stepped back to look into Maria's glowing face. "Has Mr. Rugby been released?"

"No." Maria's joy dimmed. "But I know he will be,"

she said firmly. "If you see me fairly dancing with happiness, it's because of Susannah. Oh, Penelope! Dr. Ziegenfeld wrote that she may come to stay with me next month! For five whole weeks!"

Julian allowed the two young ladies a few moments to embrace again, then said, "That's marvelous news, Miss Hilbert. And I can promise you that Penny and I will do our best to have Mr. Rugby at your side when your daughter arrives."

"But we need your help, Maria." Briefly Penelope outlined their plan, ending with a request for the key to the house.

"How I wish Lady Elizabeth were still her clutch-fisted old self!" exclaimed Maria. "She would not then have asked me to accompany her to the concert, and I could have let you in."

"It's much better if you're not there, Miss Hilbert," said Julian. "Can you get us a key?"

"I don't know." Distractedly Maria chewed on her lower lip. "I may not be able to take the key to the front door. There are only two. One in Lady Elizabeth's desk, and one in the housekeeper's possession. But if you don't mind the key to the service entrance . . . ?"

"What about the servants, Miss Hilbert? Wouldn't the back door lead us through the kitchen quarters?"

"And Pug," Penelope interjected.

"Oh, Pug was sent into the country after the Bow Street runner arrested me. And you need not fear the staff, Mr. Rutherford. The moment Lady Elizabeth steps into her carriage, they'll be off to their own amusements. And that reminds me! Penelope, you asked me about the footman who told me about Sprott."

"We may not need him any longer, Maria, but if you know his name, you may as well tell us."

"It's Erskin."

Julian heard the rattle of a coach approaching on Brook Street. He withdrew deeper into the darkness beneath the double set of marble stairs and listened. Like two others that had passed a few minutes earlier, it did not slow or stop.

Pulling his hat low onto his forehead, he peered out of his

hiding place. From this vantage point he had a full view of the street in front of Lady Elizabeth's house, of the massive, carved door illuminated by two flickering lanterns, and, if he craned his neck, of the side of the house. There was no sign of Theobald Dare's two men stationed in the dark area around the service entrance.

Theo and Penelope had disappeared in Lady Elizabeth's home some time ago, but Julian had elected to remain outside. He wanted to witness the thief's arrival and entry and, if necessary, cut off his retreat.

The sound of approaching footsteps drove him back into the shelter beneath the stairs. A man's steps, he guessed from the steady rhythm. Not wearing boots, but light evening shoes. And on *his* side of the street.

Julian held his breath as the nocturnal stroller came into view: a young dandy, his evening cape draped negligently across his shoulders, displaying a dark coat and pantaloons, a vest that shimmered pale blue or turquoise in the uncertain light and was embroidered in deep, rich hues. In one hand he carried a small, elegant traveling case.

Almost abreast of Julian, the young man stopped. He set down the leather bag, pulled a watch from the pocket of his waistcoat, and flicked it open. Something in his stance, the way he touched his free hand to his tall hat and tugged at it, the way he held his head, told Julian that he was not checking on the time but watching the street and the house across the street.

Unhurriedly, he restored the watch to his pocket, and during that instant Julian caught a glimpse of his face profiled against the light of the street lamp. Sharp features that reminded Julian of a fox.

Julian had seen Lilibeth's lover once, and then only briefly, but he had no difficulty recognizing him now. *Erskin the thief*, he thought, *the link between Lilibeth the informer and Sprott the fence*.

Erskin stood motionless, as though listening, and Julian wondered if his breathing and the thudding of his heart could be heard above the distant rumble of traffic in New Bond Street and Hanover Square.

Erskin bent to pick up the bag. Swiftly, yet without

seeming to hurry, he crossed the cobbles and mounted the stairs to Lady Elizabeth's front door.

Julian saw the flash of crimson lining as Lady Elizabeth's uninvited visitor threw back his cape and inserted a hand into his coat pocket. The cloaked back obscured Julian's view of the door lock, but almost immediately the door swung noiselessly open, and Erskin slipped inside, closing it behind him.

So unobtrusively done! So cleverly executed! The innocent appearance of a young gentleman returning to his home!

In a flash Julian was across the street. His ear against the carved wood of the door, he slowly pressed down the handle. The door opened a crack.

There was only silence in the house, yet Julian dared not follow closely on the thief's heels. A shaft of light from the outdoor lanterns might alert him to the presence of a pursuer.

Julian stiffened. Someone was tugging on the door from the inside! Letting go of the handle, he crouched into a stance of attack that Gentleman Jackson himself could not have faulted.

But it was Theobald Dare's chubby countenance that peeked at him through the widening gap. "Upstairs," the runner whispered.

Penelope was hidden upstairs! Julian whisked inside and made for the stairs, leaving Theobald Dare to close the door and resume guard of the downstairs apartments.

Keeping close to the balustrade, Julian advanced cautiously. The fifth and the eleventh step had a tendency to creak in the middle, Penelope had warned him.

And then he saw her on the landing, an indistinct blob of gray pressed against the wall beside an open door. Only the pale oval of her face was clearly visible.

Penelope saw Julian almost the same instant. Her finger flew to her lips in an instinctive gesture of warning. Her heart raced in exhilaration, and when Julian joined her on the landing, she took his hand and squeezed it. The answering pressure, warm and firm, was all she needed to make this adventure perfect.

Through the open door of Lady Elizabeth's drawing room came soft clinking noises as of china or porcelain pieces touching against each other. For a moment, they stood side by side, listening, then Julian tugged on her hand and guided her along the landing into the recess of another doorway.

His arm encircled her waist, pulling her closer. She leaned her back against him, her heart threatening to burst with happiness when his chin came to rest on the crown of her head. His other arm closed around her chest, drawing her even closer.

If only Julian didn't take her trembling for fear! 'Twas naught but the excitement of the chase and his nearness that made her shiver and shake like a blancmange.

The sounds in the drawing room ceased. She could feel Julian tense. Penelope's eyes started to water, so hard did she peer through the gloom. Finally she saw a dark shape glide noiselessly toward the stairs.

Was he leaving? Or did he intend to ransack the lower apartments as well? She held her breath, but all she could hear was the rapid beat of Julian's heart against her ear—as, undoubtedly, he could feel hers against his arm!

When Julian moved, she was not prepared for the sudden loss of support. She stumbled, catching her toe in the hem of her gown. There was a ripping sound that broke the stillness of the house like a thunderclap. Then Julian gripped her elbows, steadying her.

Again they stood motionless, wondering if the thief had been alerted. The click of the front door closing reassured them. They ran downstairs, to be met by Theobald Dare's gloomy voice.

"Locked the door again, he did. The scaly scum!"

Penelope, holding up her ripped skirt, spun on her heel and led the way to the back entrance. Precious minutes were lost as they negotiated the steep stairway leading into the bowels of the house. Countless sharp corners, hazards to elbows and foreheads, had to be turned as Penelope guided them through pantries, sculleries, and kitchens.

As they emerged through the back door, one of Theobald Dare's men came running down the area steps. Panting, he made his report. "Made his getaway to Hanover Square. Brown's close on his heels."

"Not too close, I hope," Theobald Dare grumbled, then set his bulk in motion.

Brook Street lay deserted before them. Penelope and Julian broke into a run, soon leaving Mr. Dare and the second runner behind them.

"Did you get a look at him, Julian?" Penelope asked eagerly. "I didn't see him. The house was too dark."

"It was Erskin. I'd wager my bays on it."

She wanted to cheer, but hitched her gown a bit higher and increased her pace instead.

At the corner of Hanover Square they were stopped by runner Brown. "Have a care, sir," the man warned. "He's barely turned t' corner into George Street."

Julian nodded. "He's probably going for St. James's where he can be certain of finding a hackney." When a breathless Theobald Dare joined them, he said, "Miss Langham and I will use my curricle now. I'm certain he's for Fetter Lane, but try not to lose him until we've caught up with you again, Theo."

The curricle was quickly recovered from the sturdy young boy watching it in Shepherd Street, just out of sight of Hanover Square. Penelope donned her pelisse and hat, which she had left under the seat, and Julian flung his caped driving cloak across his shoulders before taking up the reins.

Traveling south at a good clip, they passed Mr. Dare's two assistants teetering along the sidewalk in a fair imitation of two drunks bent on shattering the night's peace with raucous songs and ribald laughter. Theobald Dare himself was ambling along some distance ahead of his men. Somehow he had obtained a stout walking stick with a silver knob, and this he twirled in the self-assured fashion of a respectable, well-to-do merchant. When they passed him, he gave a little nod and raised his cane.

They turned into Old Bond Street. Instantly, Julian slowed the horses to a walk, for there, mere yards ahead, strode Erskin. The weight of the portmanteau did not noticeably slow him down.

"Let's hope he doesn't recognize you," Julian said as they drew nearer. "You were rather conspicuous in Fetter Lane."

"He won't." An impish smile curled Penelope's mouth.

She moved closer to Julian and placed both her hands against his upper arm while raising her face to his—away from Erskin.

"La, sir," she said in carrying tones and an exaggeratedly refined accent, "I do declare this is most exciting! But I dare not think of what my dear mama will do if she finds out that we've left my maid behind. I shall be in the most dreadful hobble!"

After one startled look at Penelope, Julian rose magnificently to the occasion. Transferring the reins to one hand, he slipped his arm around her waist.

"Don't you fret, my pretty," he said silkily. "I shall more than make it up to you if you find yourself in the basket. How would you like some trinkets and baubles? A set of garnets, mayhap?"

"I vow and declare, sir," Penelope said shrilly as they passed Erskin. "My dearest mama *was* right!"

She saw Erskin dart one disinterested glance at them, then look toward Piccadilly again. He shifted his traveling case into his right hand and stepped out with renewed vigor.

"You are a rogue, sir," she continued, "and a skinflint to boot! If I heard you say it once, I heard you a dozen times. Rubies, sir! You promised me rubies, not garnets!"

Julian pinched her cheek. "Jade!" he said appreciatively. "I wonder where you learned your bargaining?"

Penelope cast a quick look behind them, but Erskin was well out of earshot now. The little game was over. Or it should be.

"In the markets of Bombay, Madras, and Constantinople, sir," she said, unable to resist the temptation of carrying the game one step further. "Gentlemen of the East know how to value a female."

"Devil a bit, Penny! What sort of books have you been reading?"

"I speak from firsthand knowledge, Julian!" She removed her hands from his arm and sat facing forward again. She was gratified, however, that his arm retained its firm grip on her waist.

"I traveled extensively with my parents," she explained. "And Mama was a devout believer in speaking the unvarnished truth. No matter how unsuitable a question her daughter posed.''

"And which maharajah or sultan valued you sufficiently to give you that ruby pendant you wore the other night, my delightful Scheherazade?''

"Alas, Papa had to purchase it," she said primly. "Unlike young ladies of the East, English girls are gauche and gawky at age fifteen.''

Julian guided the horses into Piccadilly. "One gawky English girl at least grew up into a most charming young lady," he said gallantly, but Penelope could not help feeling that his mind was on other matters.

He pulled the curricle into a gap between two carriages in front of Burlington House, from which position they'd be able to see Erskin emerge from Old Bond Street. "If he doesn't take a hackney," Julian muttered, "we must go on foot as well, else he'll notice us for certain.''

Penelope shivered, a condition only partly induced by apprehension and dislike of the dark streets into which they would venture. Excitement welled up in her as well as anticipation of Sprott's and Erskin's arrest.

Suddenly Julian's arms went around her, drawing her against his chest. "Keep your face hidden," he whispered.

She sensed his tension and obediently buried her nose in his lapels. This was it, she knew instinctively. The chase was on!

chapter
SIXTEEN

"*H*old on, Penny, my love," whispered Julian.

The caress of his words stayed with her after he took his arms from her shoulders. He picked up the reins an guided the bays into the steady stream of carriages rolling along Piccadilly. Not until he had passed several slow-moving vehicles and had fallen in behind a hackney carriage turning into Haymarket did Julian speak again.

"There's our thief," he said, pointing with his whip.

It was not at all difficult to follow the hackney as long as they traversed the busy, brightly lit thoroughfares of St. James's, but when they reached that area of town east of the Covent Garden district, streetlights were few and far between and they lost sight of the hackney.

Penelope tensed, peering into the darkness. What if it had not been Erskin? What if the thief did not plan to take his bounty to Sprott?

The curricle hit some hard object lying in their path. The horses reared and snorted as the wheel locked against the obstruction. The light sporting carriage seemed to teeter on one wheel, and Penelope was flung against the side of the seat.

"Penny!"

Julian's hand shot out, clutching her cloak, while he struggled to keep control over his maddened pair. With a thud, the curricle righted itself. The wheel scraped past the obstruction, and the bays, docile again when they found themselves unopposed, set off at a trot.

Penelope's heart seemed to be lost somehwere in her half boots, but after a moment she managed to say, "I'm quite all right, Julian. You can let go of me."

With a shaky laugh, Julian removed his hand. "Damn, but you gave me a scare, my girl! And why the deuce they can't install adequate street lighting is beyond my understanding! Now we've lost Erskin for sure. Thank God, we know where he's going."

Penelope listened, but above the clatter of the curricle and pair she heard not another sound. Not many vehicles, and even fewer pedestrians, ventured at night into these dark streets and the rabbit warren of adjoining alleys. Those that did, went to great lengths not to be seen or heard by others.

They swung into Fetter Lane, even darker and more foul smelling than Penelope remembered it.

Julian pulled up before the Wild Boat Tavern. A volley of shrieks, shouts, laughter, and snatches of songs hit the night air as the door of the tavern opened and a short, unkempt man stepped out. He approached the curricle as fast as his bandy legs could carry him. What portion of his face was visible above a moth-eaten muffler of indefinable hue looked grimy and mean, thought Penelope. She stared at his small, close-set eyes, and hoped Julian wouldn't entrust this unprepossessing individual with his valuable bays.

Julian, however, tossed him the reins without hesitation. "How long since a hackney turned in here, Simms?"

"Less 'n two minutes, guv'nor. Stopped right on target. Orrie 'n his men be waitin' down there."

Julian sprang lightly to the ground. Holding out his hand, he said, "This is it, Penny. We can catch thief and fence together. Are you game?"

Was she game! She cast one last dubious glance at the villainous-looking, short man, one of the men Mr. Dare had sent into Fetter Lane. Responding to the runner's gap-toothed grin with a wide smile, Penelope allowed Julian to hand her from the curricle. Then she had no time left to speculate. Julian clasped her elbow in a firm grip and hurried her toward Sprott's house.

Thankful for his support, she closed her mind to the stink of refuse and questionable substances that squished underfoot. Mustn't miss Sprott and Erskin. If it had been Erskin! If they failed... if their timing were wrong, they'd scare Sprott and would never have an opportunity to clear Benjamin Rugby.

"Where's Mr. Dare?" she asked breathlessly when Julian slowed down one building short of Sprott's house.

"He'll be along. Listen!"

In the distance she heard the sound of hooves striking cobbles and the rattle of a heavy coach. Then the clatter ceased.

"Must be Theo," Julian murmured. "Stopped at the entrance of Fetter Lane."

Julian moved slowly now, carefully. Penelope raised the hem of her gown a little higher and followed on tiptoe. Behind them, she heard the occasional scuff of a boot or a deep-voiced, muffled exclamation. Not very subtle, if that was Theobald Dare following them with his men; but then again, an unintelligible curse might not raise any suspicion in Sprott's quarters.

They reached the house. Theobald Dare and his two men joined them at the railing enclosing the area steps, and two more, whom she had not seen before. Orrie's men, Penelope surmised.

She heard Mr. Dare and Julian argue about something in a fierce whisper, heard Julian insisting on breaking down Sprott's door, but her eyes were on the door of the locksmith shop below. Light showed through a crack. Were little Miriam and her great-grandfather sitting up, waiting for their share of the spoils?

Julian took her arm again to help her up the steps and through the doorless entrance of Sprott's house. Penelope clenched her teeth, afraid suddenly of what they would discover upstairs. She'd have to shield Miriam as best she could, just as she was shielding Maria. Theft was a crime—but hanging was too cruel a punishment!

She ascended the slippery, splintering stairs. Once again the foul odors in the building engulfed her, taking her breath away. But she forged ahead, determined to solve the mystery of the thefts and put a spoke in Sprott's wheels.

On the second-floor landing, Mr. Dare stepped forward. Pounding his fist against the heavy door, he shouted, "Open up to Bow Street! In the name of the King!"

Penelope felt Julian tense beside her. He let go of her arm, and just as Mr. Dare whisked aside, Julian thrust himself against the oaken boards of the door. She felt the impact of his shoulder against the wood in her own body and winced as twice more he repeated the assault.

She heard Sprott's grating voice. "Let be, ye ruffians! I'm comin'. Can't ye give a body time to open his door afore ye come bustin' in?"

She saw a sliver of light appear. Then Mr. Dare's men pushed against the door, flinging it wide. Sprott, holding a lantern, stood in the long, narrow corridor. His dark eyes shifted from Theobald Dare to Julian, to Penelope.

"We would like to meet your friend, Sprott." Julian nodded to the room at the end of the corridor where he and Penelope had confronted the fence over Lady Spatterton's pearls.

Sprott gave a smirk that seemed to flatten his broken nose further and made his scraggly beard jut out. "Go right ahead, sir. Meet *all* my friends. We was just sittin' down to a quiet game o' cards.''

Bowing and scraping, he ushered them toward the brightly lit room. Sprott certainly wasn't saving his pennies this night, thought Penelope, remembering the stygian darkness she had encountered on her previous visit. But then Sprott didn't have to examine stolen goods that other time.

Mr. Dare's men remained in the corridor. Three runners stationed themselves by the door. The fourth picked up the lantern and started to examine the other rooms. Satisfied that there would be no escape for Sprott or the thief, Penelope entered the office.

Three people sat around the stout table that served as Sprott's desk. Her pulse raced with excitement, for there sat Erskin, resplendent in a dark evening coat, a white silk shirt, and turquoise vest embroidered in magenta, carmine, and emerald thread. He stared at her through narrowed eyes.

Penelope believed she saw him turn a little paler, but then he returned his attention to the cards in his hand, as though nothing were the matter.

Next to him, in the chair under the boarded-up window, Lilibeth smiled brightly at Penelope. "We meet again, Miss Langham. Won't you sit down, please?"

She fluttered her cards in the direction of the chair Sprott had obviously vacated. Sprott's cards lay facedown on the scratched tabletop.

"No, thank you, Lilibeth. I shan't be staying long." Penelope let her eyes travel the length of Lilibeth's gown of spangled tulle.

Like the crimson taffeta gown the girl had worn when she came out of the locksmith shop it had a low-cut, sleeveless bodice, but the wide, tiered skirt draping Lilibeth's nether limbs and her chair more than made up for any lack of material on the top.

"Tell me," said Penelope. "Were you able to deliver Lady Elizabeth's turban in time for tonight's concert?"

"What concert, miss?" Lilibeth asked with a toss of her saucy curls. The bright spots of rouge on her cheeks were lost in the angry flush that stained her fair skin.

Smiling, Penelope turned to the third person, a thin man

with an olive complexion and slicked-down, oily black hair. An Italian, she hazarded. The foreign buyer? His Adam's apple bobbed like a buoy on a rough sea, and his eyes did not meet hers.

"Erskin," Julian said harshly. "We want to see your bag."

Erskin looked mulish, but Sprott rubbed his hands and bowed. "Of course. Immediately, sir. If ye just let me pass?"

He darted past Julian into the corner behind his desk and brought forth an elegant black traveling case. "Is this what ye wanted to see, sir? Is this why ye followed the poor boy here? Because he found himself at low ebb and must pawn his last silk shirts?"

"Not quite his last," Julian said with a glance at Erskin's attire. "No, Sprott. I do not need to hold that case in my hands. I can see from here that it is empty. And no doubt we shall also find several silk shirts among your collection of old clothes in one of the other rooms."

"If you'll pardon me, sir." Theobald Dare pushed forward. "Now then, Sprott," he said severely. "We have evidence that this young sprig here"—he pointed to Erskin—"entered the premises of Lady Elizabeth Howe and came away with a bag full of stolen goods. It is my dooty to search this here, ah, establishment."

"Snuffboxes," said Penelope, remembering the chinking sounds she had heard from the drawing room in Lady Elizabeth's home. "Erskin stole the late Lord Howe's collection of Sevres snuffboxes. Lord Howe didn't have one for every day of the year like Lord Petersham, but they're all priceless pieces, some of them jeweled."

"I musta be going." The oily-haired, thin man jumped up, in his haste toppling over his chair. "Good-bye, Signor Sprott. I will see you on the tomorrow, *si*?" he said, inching his way toward the corridor.

"Stop!" boomed Theobald Dare.

The thin man started nervously, but stopped.

"No one leaves the premises until a proper search has been conducted. It is my dooty also to search your person. If you'll step next door, sir?" Mr. Dare stuck his head out the door. "Orrie! Search this man!"

Penelope looked at Julian. "Would they've had time to hide the snuffboxes elsewhere in the house?"

"Time yes, but Orrie had a man hidden on the third floor. He would have heard if someone left these rooms. Don't worry, we'll find them. You're certain we are looking for snuffboxes, Penny?"

"They were the only porcelain items in that room, Julian. And since Erskin was footman there for a while, he'd know, of course, that the snuffboxes are Lady Elizabeth's most valuable possession—within easy reach."

Sprott and Erskin followed the Bow Street runners from room to room while the men searched diligently for over an hour. Not a shelf was missed, not a trunk overlooked. Old clothes were shaken, but not a single snuffbox came to light.

Orrie, who searched Sprott, gave a grunt of satisfaction when he inserted his hand in Sprott's coat pocket. He found a snuffbox all right, but it was of horn, inscribed "Frost Fair, 1814." Penelope shook her head. It was not an item Lord Howe would have cared to possess.

"Well now," said Sprott bitingly. "I hope y'are satisfied with this night's work. Disturbin' an old man's peace! Insultin' his guests! What more d'ye want?"

"We'll search again." Julian walked around the refectory table to look once again through the drawer where Sprott had hidden the pistol. "Pardon me," he said to the pale-faced, sweating Italian, who had sat down next to Lilibeth after he had been searched. "Would you kindly move your chair?"

The man complied hurriedly. Lilibeth threw him a contemptuous look. Throughout the search, while Sprott and Erskin had been dodging the runners' every step, she had sat composedly, with her arms crossed under her bosom, watching the proceedings as though she were attending a rather boring play.

Lilibeth was almost too composed, thought Penelope. The girl hadn't moved, except to place her hand of cards in her lap and cross her arms. The cards lay precariously atop the ballooning tiers of stiff, spangled tulle.

Penelope caught her breath. "Julian!"

Swiftly she moved toward Lilibeth, and before anyone in

the room could even guess what she was about to do, she lifted a layer of the tulle overskirt.

Lilibeth screamed and tried to get up, but Penelope pushed her down. During the struggle, two snuffboxes slipped from Lilibeth's lap. One, a small, gold-painted and jeweled box, broke into tiny shards.

"No!" Erskin hurtled at Penelope like a shot released from a sling.

Julian lunged across the table. His arms clamped around Erskin's midsection just as Erskin was about to tackle Penelope. Both men crashed to the floor.

Torn between her desire to watch Julian and her sense of duty, which told her to stop Lilibeth from rising and smashing all Lady Elizabeth's snuffboxes, Penelope reluctantly attended to Lilibeth. She clung to the girl's shoulders, forcing her to remain in the chair, until Orrie and Brown relieved her of the task.

When she turned around, the fight between Julian and Erskin was over. "Oh!" Her eyes widened in distress. "He cut your lip, Julian.''

He dabbed at the cut with the back of his hand, then grinned. "It's nothing. The bleeding will stop in a minute, my love.''

The endearment brought a flush to her cheeks, but she only said, "We have the evidence, Julian! Benjamin Rugby is innocent!''

Moments later, Erskin, Sprott, and the Italian were handcuffed and guarded by two of Theobald Dare's men, while Theo himself counted the snuffboxes as one by one Orrie transferred them from Lilibeth's lap onto the table.

"An' here's the key, too!'' Theo tossed the large brass key on the palm of his hand. "How did ye get it, Erskin?''

"Tell him, Erskin!'' shrieked Lilibeth. "Tell him about the old bloke downstairs. How he made the keys, then had you go out an' steal for him!''

Erskin's face, decorated with a purplish bruise over one eye and a swollen jaw, lit up with interest. Before he could say anything, Sprott spoke up.

"Ye're a baggage, Lilibeth, and no doubt about it! But you leave Samuel out of this, d'ye hear? Only mistake old

Samuel ever made was ter apprentice Erskin, and then ter let the two of ye in his kitchen for a tankard an' a game of dice at night.''

Theobald Dare took a step toward Sprott. "Are ye saying Erskin himself made the keys?"

"Aye! After *he*"—Erskin pointed his bound hands at Sprott—"tol' me Lilibeth was goin' ter run out on me iffen I didn't bring 'ome some more of the ready."

"And that," said Julian, "clinches the matter nicely. Well, Theo, is there any more work to be done by Penny and me?"

Theobald Dare touched a finger to his forehead. "Not at all, Mr. Rutherford. Seein' that me an' me colleagues must take the prisoners an' the evidence before Sir Nathaniel, I'd advise ye to take your young lady home."

His beetling brows pointed directly at Penelope as he said, "Very irregular to have a lady present tonight, but I'm obliged to ye, Miss Langham. Much obliged. And I don't mind sayin' that I'm mighty pleased to have made yer acquaintance."

"Thank you, Mr. Dare." Penelope lowered her lashes to hide the teasing twinkle in her eyes. "But I did no more than my duty."

His deep, rumbling belly laugh followed them down the two flights of stairs. Outside, Penelope hesitated. She looked at the basement door. The light still showed through the crack. "Could we see Mr. Abel and Miriam?"

"Still worried about your maid?"

"Not worried. Curious."

Cautiously they proceeded down the area steps. Julian rapped on the door, and after a moment it was opened by an old, stooped man. His face had an unhealthy, yellowish color and it had a pinched look, as though he were in constant pain.

"Mr. Abel? I'm Penelope Langham. I'm sorry to bother you so late at night, but could I please have a word with Miriam?"

"Aye, Miss Langham. I reckernize ye. Come in. Miriam, she be in t' kitchen."

With slow, shuffling steps he led the way through his shop

and workroom to the back of the house. "Miriam!" he called. "Here be yer mistress."

The young girl, standing by a trivet over an open hearth, dropped her spoon and whirled around. "Miss Penelope!"

Cheeks glowing as much from pleasure as from her exertions over the fire, Miriam pulled a stool from under the white-scrubbed kitchen table. "Sit ye down, Miss Penelope. Ye should never have come into Fetter Lane, miss. It's not fittin'!"

Penelope sat down, her eyes on a book lying open on the tabletop. She recognized it. *The Country Housewife's Family Companion* from the library at Belmont House.

Samuel Abel picked up the book. "I be right grateful to ye, Miss Langham. Since Miriam learned her letters, she's been lookin' after her ol' granfer. Brewin' possets, mixin' fomentations and ointments. Right clever she's been."

He tugged one of the braided loops dangling over Miriam's ears and looked at her with such love and pride that Penelope was touched. "Please sit down, Mr. Abel. I heard you're not well."

Miriam led her great-grandfather to an upholstered armchair standing by the window. "It's the stones, miss. They be plaguing him right bad these past months. An' sometimes it be his liver actin' up as ye can see in his face. That's why I had to ask Mrs. Dawson for leave when I found these recipes." Taking the book from Samuel Abel, Miriam placed it before Penelope.

Penelope glanced at the open pages. *A guaranteed cure for stones. Remedies for the sufferer of jaundice.* Her eyes widened as she skimmed over the ingredients. She swallowed hard and closed the book.

Mr. Abel and Miriam were looking at her expectantly. "Wouldn't it be better to call in a physician?" Penelope said.

"Nay, miss. The physicians can do nothin', an' I ain't likely to have a surgeon in an' cuttin' me up."

Penelope turned a helpless look on Julian, who stood with his broad shoulders resting against a kitchen cupboard. The corners of his mouth curled upward, and there was a look in his eyes that told her he was quite content to let her handle the situation.

"Well," she said, rising, "I had best be going, then. Let Mrs. Dawson know if you need anything, Miriam."

"Thank ye kindly, Miss Penelope. And, miss—" Miriam took a hesitant step toward Penelope. Her eyes were wide and anxious in her thin face. "I didn't do wrong, did I? Studyin' these books, though I hadn't told you about 'em?"

"No, of course you didn't do wrong, child." Penelope reached out and gently touched Miriam's cheek. "How many books did you read before you found the recipes?"

"Two, miss."

"Next time you wish to study a subject, tell me about it. I can probably direct you to the right volume, and you can save yourself some time."

"Yes, Miss Penelope." Miriam bobbed a curtsy, then looked up at Penelope mischievously. "But it was a lark, miss, readin' all them medical books."

With laughter in her eyes, Penelope waved to the old locksmith. "Get well soon, Mr. Abel. Else you'll see your great-granddaughter turn into a bluestocking."

Miriam took down a small lantern from its hook beside the kitchen door. "T' area steps be dark, Miss Penelope. Let me show you out."

The girl stood, holding the lantern until Penelope and Julian had climbed into the curricle, which Simms had thoughtfully brought down from the Wild Boar Tavern. "Good night, Miss Penelope!" Miriam turned and disappeared into the basement.

"Tell me, Penny," said Julian, setting the bays in motion with a flick of the reins. "What the dickens did you read in that confounded book to make you look positively green for a moment?"

"Oh!" she said with a shudder. "You won't believe it, but Mr. Abel is taking—for his stones, mind you—'a powder, a decoction, and pills.'"

"That doesn't sound so awful."

"The powder, Julian, is made of eggshells and calcined snails, the decoction of herbs boiled with soap and . . . let me see now. Yes, and burned swines-cress. And the pills are made of snails, a variety of wild seeds, spiderwebs, hips, haws, honey, and a good dollop of 'Alicante' soap!"

"After that, I hardly dare ask what he takes for his jaundice."

"Every morning he's supposed to swallow... *nine live lice*!"

"Do you think he does?" Julian asked in awed tones.

They looked at each other; and despite the darkness, Penelope knew that the corners of his mouth were turned up in a grin. She stifled a giggle. "Miriam means well."

"I don't deny that. Yet meaning well and doing well are two different matters," Julian said, thinking of his broken betrothal.

Sensing that their brief moment of shared amusement had come to an end, Penelope leaned against the squabs. She felt restless, dissatisfied, despite the success of their night's work.

There was no reason now why Julian should see her—unless he wanted to!

Julian's arm curved around her waist. "What a night!" he said. "I congratulate you, Penny. You caught the thief!"

"But I didn't find Aunt Sophy's opals. I kept hoping, when we searched Sprott's place tonight, that they would show up."

"Theo will find out where the Italian sells his stuff. As soon as I know that, I'll have some inquiries made, and who knows? We may yet surprise your aunt with her jewels."

We! One small pronoun—yet how uplifting!

The night changed subtly. Penelope noticed the sickle face of a waning moon smiling at them, even a few stars dipping in and out of clouds and layers of sooty haze that habitually drifted above London. It was a lovers' night.

"Will you ask me to supper at the Piazza, Julian?"

She felt him start. For a long moment he looked at her in silence, scrutinizing her face as though he wanted to see through her, see to the very core of her heart.

She knew his thoughts, his every doubt. To show herself in Julian's company at this fashionable hour when the theaters emptied and the *ton* gathered at the Piazza for a late supper was an open declaration. The mean-spirited would say that Penelope Langham, afraid of being left an old maid, had set her cap at a reporter, a libertine whose name had been tainted by scandal in the past.

"Are you going to turn me down, Julian?"

"My love—" His voice was ragged. He shook his head. "Believe me, I'd like nothing better. But I cannot ask you tonight."

"Why, Julian? I want to celebrate with you. I—"

I love you, she wanted to say, but a lady could not throw herself at a gentleman. The declaration must come from him.

But Julian did not speak.

The last few minutes of the drive passed in silence. When they arrived in front of Belmont House, Julian got down and held out his arms to her. "You'll sleep well tonight, I wager. You need not fear for your friends any longer."

"And you, Julian?" She rose from the seat and turned so he could help her down. "Will you sleep well?"

There was an almost imperceptible pause before he replied. "Yes, indeed," he said with a careless smile. "After all, I can write my article now. *'Lady and Reporter Catch Thief'*!"

"Ah, yes. Your article."

Julian gripped her waist as she tried to step down. Penelope had forgotten about her torn gown. Her foot caught in the ripped hem, and she pitched against his chest.

The impact of her fall set Julian rocking on his feet. Tightening his arms around her, he took a step backward to regain his balance. "Are you all right?" he said hoarsely.

Penelope gripped his cloak and murmured against his chest, "Yes, quite all right. Thank you."

She felt his hands move on her back in soothing circles. The warmth of his body so close to hers penetrated the material of her pelisse and gown and kindled a responding fire in her. Slowly she raised her face to his.

Julian looked ghostly pale in the light of the gas lanterns. He bent his head toward her, but when she thought he'd kiss her, he merely brushed his lips across her forehead.

"Good night," he said.

Stubborn! Mule-headed!

She let her hands drop and stepped away from him. "Good night, Julian," she said, turning on her heel. Head held proudly erect, she mounted the marble stairs to her aunt's house. Blindly, she groped for the knocker.

A lady couldn't possibly propose to a gentleman! It just wasn't done!

chapter SEVENTEEN

*B*enjamin Rugby was released from Newgate Prison. He and Maria came to Belmont House armed with assurances of undying gratitude and the news that they were to be married by special license, which Sir Nathaniel had helped them obtain from his friend, the Archbishop of York before Susannah was due to arrive from Switzerland.

Penelope offered her felicitations, but it was hardly surprising that a tiny stab of envy pierced her breast when she saw Maria's happiness.

A day later, Lady Elizabeth announced that she would host a ball to celebrate the recovery of her snuffbox collection and the upcoming marriage of her companion to Mr. Benjamin Rugby.

"Dear Elizabeth," murmured Sophy. "So generous."

Lady Elizabeth, seated across the tea table from her hostess, smiled thinly. "I could hardly do less since Gertrude is giving them a vulgarly lavish wedding reception."

Sophy looked indignant. "None of Gertrude's entertainments are vulgar! She is very fond of Mr. Rugby, and she will welcome Maria and her poor little relation who's coming on a visit from Switzerland. I wish I could say the same of you, Elizabeth."

"I'm giving Miss Hilbert a ball, Sophy. Is that not quite sufficient? Margaret"—she turned toward the dowager marchioness seated on her left—"what do you think? Should I ask some of the members of the Philharmonic Society to play, or should I make do with the string quartet I engaged last year?''

''By all means make it the Philharmonic Society.'' Lady Margaret stirred a second spoon of sugar into her tea. ''But I wonder, Elizabeth. Did you send an invitation to Julian Rutherford?''

Penelope, who'd had her fill of tea and had removed to the window seat of her aunt's sitting room, pricked up her ears. She hadn't seen Julian since Sprott and Erskin had been arrested. Four interminable days. She should never have walked away from him without eliciting his promise to come and see her.

''Do you take me for a feather-brain, Margaret?'' Lady Elizabeth gave a bitter laugh. ''What could I do after *The Times* printed his article about the lady and the reporter catching the thief and finding my snuffboxes? Of course I invited him!''

Excitement gripped Penelope. She would see Julian!

''If word gets out that Julian will attend your ball,'' said Lady Margaret dryly, ''you can count on the affair turning into a veritable squeeze.''

''It *will* be a squeeze. My footmen have been running all morning delivering invitations, and already acceptances have poured in, despite the short notice. Here, Sophy, Margaret—'' Lady Elizabeth pulled gilt-edged envelopes from her reticule. ''Since I knew I'd be seeing you today, I carried your invitations myself.''

Penelope slipped off the window seat. ''Has Mr. Rutherford accepted, Lady Elizabeth?''

Lady Elizabeth raised a brow. ''No, but neither did he decline yet. My footman told me that Mr. Rutherford is out of town. Do you know where he is, Penelope, and whether he's likely to return in time for my ball?''

''No, I don't, Lady Elizabeth.'' Penelope hoped that her voice betrayed none of her perturbation. Had Julian left to avoid another painful meeting with her? Or—optimism flared high in her breast—was he investigating the whereabouts of her aunt's opals as he had promised?

''He'll come to the ball,'' said Lady Margaret with assurance. ''If only to kick up a lark.''

Penelope smiled. Surely Julian was past the age of kicking up larks, but just as Dawson still saw Penelope as a madcap schoolroom miss so Lady Margaret regarded Julian as a young, mischievous boy.

Penelope sank down onto the window seat again, watching a curricle drawn by a pair of magnificent bays enter the square. She leaned closer to the windowpane until she realized that the driver could not possibly be Julian. He'd never wear a driving coat that boasted upward of a half-dozen capes, or sport a nosegay the size of a cabbage, nor would he tie a Belcher kerchief around his neck!

An angry exclamation from Lady Elizabeth caught her attention. "Don't speak to me of the pleasure of entertaining, Sophy. Not only must I play hostess to my companion and Gertrude's agent, but I am forced to invite that disreputable Julian Rutherford! I wish Penelope had never taken up with him. How could you have allowed it, Sophy?"

"Don't talk such fustian," cut in Lady Margaret sharply. "There's no harm in the boy."

"No harm! The *ton* may come flocking to my ball to see the disgraceful man, but I vow, if he expects from then on to be invited to all the best houses, I'll never hear the end of it."

"That is rubbish!" With a flounce of her skirts Penelope swept past the three speechless ladies and whisked herself from the room.

How dare Lady Elizabeth call Julian disgraceful! How dare she say that he would encroach on anyone's hospitality! If that was the attitude Julian would be shown during the ball . . . well, it was not to be borne. Julian had more honor in his little finger than all of the *ton* combined.

Penelope came to a sudden halt just inside her bedchamber. It was his code of honor that kept them apart. It was the reason he had refused her request for supper at the Piazza— and why he wouldn't propose to her.

If she wanted to fight Julian's code of honor, she must use the strongest weapon she had. Her love.

She would propose to *him*! At Maria's betrothal ball. And the devil fly away with the conventions!

* * *

Penelope hummed a lilting waltz tune while Nancy helped her into her ball gown. Heavy silk, the color of champagne, had been fashioned by Madame Céleste's clever fingers into a fitted bodice and shapely skirt. Around the hem and on a narrow sash were sewn hundreds of tiny, ruby-red rosettes. A gauze shawl, also trimmed with rosettes, a beaded reticule, and French dancing slippers completed the outfit.

She was ready, except for some jewelry. A smile flitted across Penelope's face as she bent over her trinket box. She handed Nancy the maharajah's ruby pendant. "Will you fasten it for me, please?"

"Cor, ye look lovely, miss!" Nancy rushed to open the door. "Ye'll turn every gentleman's head."

"One head will be quite sufficient, Nancy."

Impatient to be off, Penelope decided to pay her aunt a visit and speed her on, if necessary. "Auntie!" she exclaimed, stopping in the doorway to Sophy's bedchamber. "What a heavenly gown! The blue deepens the color of your eyes and makes you look ten years younger. You'll cast even Sylvia Arbuthnot into the shade, dearest."

"Flatterer," said Sophy, but rather pleased. "It was high time I wore something other than lavender." She rose from her chair before the dressing table where Sweetings had put the finishing touches to her coiffure. Her eyes widened as she got a full view of Penelope, radiant in her finery and with a glow of excitement about her that was quite contagious. "How charming you look! Doesn't she, Sweetings?"

The dresser's dour expression did not change, but she nodded. "Aye, my lady."

Sweetings collected shawls, fan, and reticule, then followed the ladies from the room. "But handsome is as handsome does," she muttered darkly to herself. Miss Langham might have done right by her ladyship for once when she called in that nice Dr. Ludlow, but she couldn't pull the wool over *her* eyes. Sweetings could tell from the look on Miss Langham's face that some madcap notion lurked behind the young lady's smooth forehead.

Penelope's keen ears had caught the dresser's mumbling. Wouldn't Sweetings be gratified to see her prophecy fulfilled! Chuckling, she accompanied her aunt downstairs, where Dawson was waiting to see them to the carriage.

The short drive to Brook Street seemed to drag eternally. But then she couldn't expect otherwise with old Sands instead of Hunter handling the reins, Penelope reflected wryly. Additional delay was caused by those carriages already lined up to disgorge their passengers at Lady Elizabeth's house. Penelope tapped her foot in impatience. 'Twould be faster if they walked, but she knew any such suggestion would be met with a scandalized look from her aunt.

Finally the carriage door was flung open by a liveried footman, who handed them down onto the strip of red carpet that ran from the street to Lady Elizabeth's front door. Step by step they inched their way into the house and up two flights of stairs.

Ahead and behind them, elaborately gowned ladies and gentlemen in elegant evening attire chattered and laughed. Sophy had fallen into conversation with Lady Arbuthnot and her latest admirer, the tall, silver-haired Baron von Oberndorf, a satellite of the Russian ambassador. The baron bowed to Penelope and tried, in his halting English, to make himself agreeable to her, but the closer she moved to Lady Elizabeth's ballroom, the quieter Penelope became.

What if Julian had decided not to attend?

What if he were upstairs already?

The ladies' perfumes that had tantalized her nose, changed to cloying, stifling odors. She felt first hot, then shivered with cold. She couldn't go through with it! She'd never have the courage to propose to Julian.

Someone took her hand—Lady Elizabeth greeting her. Hastily Penelope dropped into a curtsy, moved to Maria and embraced her, then gave her hand to Benjamin Rugby.

As she left the receiving line, she came face-to-face with Julian.

No more than six feet separated them, yet she could not take a single step to bring her closer to him. His dark evening clothes were fitted to his muscular frame by a master's hand; the snowy whiteness of his shirt and cravat accentuated the deep bronze of his skin. Penelope had known he was handsome and charming, but here in the ballroom he was devastating.

She felt as shy as a schoolgirl, her heart and pulse racing and her knees growing weaker as Julian stepped closer and she saw the warmth of his smile and the glint of admiration in his eyes.

"Finally!" he said, raising her hand to his lips. "I thought you'd never arrive."

Apprehension, doubts, shyness, they all were forgotten when Penelope looked up into his face. She smiled. "If you were that impatient, I wonder you didn't call at Belmont House."

"Had to go out of town for a few days, but I didn't forget my promise to check into the matter of your aunt's opals. Sprott's buyer—" He broke off as the sound of violins drifted down from the musician's balcony. "Come," he said softly. "Let's find a chair for your shawl. I much prefer to waltz with you while I give you my news."

Moments later they were circling the dance floor. Julian seemed to have forgotten that he wanted to speak to her. He merely gazed at her as though he were memorizing every feature of her face. He held her close as though he feared she'd run off.

Penelope felt the telltale warmth of a blush steal into her cheeks. "What about Aunt Sophy's opals?" she prompted.

"Ah, yes. Let's get that business out of the way before we concentrate on pleasure." Briefly Julian told her that Sprott's Italian buyer had connections to a shop in Verona. He had also located a friend, who planned to leave for Italy the following week and had promised to look for Lady Belmont's opals. For this purpose Theobald Dare had furnished a detailed description of the jewels.

"And now," said Julian, smiling into her upturned face, "let me tell you how beautiful you are." His voice grew husky. "I wish I could dance with you all night, my little Scheherazade. You fit into my arms as though you were made for me."

Penelope was mesmerized by his voice, intoxicated by his nearness. "Then let's. Let's dance together all night long."

"Are you sure?"

"Yes."

The familiar emerald glint appeared in his eyes and his

hand on her back pressed her closer as they whirled. They danced the next quadrille, a country dance, a reel, and two more waltzes. Penelope knew that curious eyes were turning on her and Julian, eyebrows were raised, and most of the ladies were whispering behind their fans.

Let them stare now; later they would goggle, when her betrothal to Julian was announced.

Penelope did feel a tiny stab of compunction when, during their third waltz, she noticed her aunt's eyes upon her. Sophy raised her hand as though to beckon to Penelope, but then Lady Margaret took the chair beside Sophy and engaged her in conversation. When the next turn brought the two ladies back into Penelope's view, she noticed that Lady Margaret was smiling broadly and waving at her and Julian, and that her aunt looked anything but unhappy. A bit puzzled mayhap, but not at all upset.

Dear lady Margaret. She always knew how to set Sophy at ease. Returning her gaze to Julian's face, Penelope said, "There is something I particularly wish to say to you. Perhaps you would not mind sitting out the next dance?"

"Not at all. No doubt it'll be a country dance, and I find that extremely unpleasant emotions are raised in my breast when I have to watch you skip down the room on the arm of another."

Believing this to be a very good omen for the success of her scheme, Penelope allowed herself to be led to an alcove decked out with ferns and white roses from the Belmont gardens. After making certain that she was comfortably established on the upholstered bench, Julian said, "Allow me to procure some champagne. I promise I shan't be gone above a minute."

"Champagne! Oh, yes. We must have champagne to drink a toast."

Penelope settled herself against the squabs of the bench. The scene was set. The alcove granted as much privacy as she could expect at a ball; she and Julian would be surrounded by the scent of roses; and the champagne would add the finishing touch.

Alas, her happy anticipation was short-lived. With dismay, Penelope saw Gilbert Bromfield bearing down upon her. Too late to get up and walk away, pretending she had not seen him. He was too close, and he was moving with unexpected swiftness for a man of his bulk.

"Penelope!" Huffing, he stood before her, wiping his perspiring brow. "Are you lost to all proprietary? Six dances!"

"I have pointed out to you before, Gilbert, that you have no right to criticize me. Now, if you will excuse me, I am expecting someone."

"Rutherford! Didn't believe it possible that you'd hold yourself so cheap. Been setting your cap at him, haven't you? But you'll find that it won't fadge, my girl. Even if he says he'll marry you. He's nothing but a damnable jilt!"

"That's quite enough, Gilbert!" Penelope rose to confront him, her face set and pale with anger. "I am quite familiar with the scandal in Julian's past," she lied, "but if you dare repeat what you just said, I'll scratch your eyes out. Julian is no jilt! He'd never—"

"Oh, no?" Gilbert interrupted her. "And much you know about it! Even old man Steeple cast him off. Would disinherit him, too, I daresay, if he could."

Penelope started. Every now and again Lady Margaret had made reference to her old friend and neighbor, Viscount Steeple. But surely...

"Who?" she said in a faint voice. "What are you talking about, Gilbert?"

"I'm talking about Rutherford's father, Viscount Steeple! Completely disowned his son when the cad jilted that poor little thing and broke her heart!"

"Melanie," Penelope murmured absently.

Her happiness crumbled about her like the walls of a sand castle. *Julian the son of a viscount! The Honorable Julian Rutherford. Eligible to propose to any lady on whom he set his fancy.*

"That's right," said Gilbert. "Melanie somebody or other. She went insane with grief, they say. Married a marquis old enough to be her father."

Penelope paid him scant attention. She didn't give a fig for what was said about Melanie. Julian would never jilt a lady.

He simply didn't propose!

Julian had toyed with her. He had indulged in a flirtation

with her. With an old maid of three and twenty who was gullible enough to fall in love with him.

She felt the blood drain from her face. A sound like an angry sea washing against the shore droned in her ears. And the pain! It filled her belly and her chest until breathing was an agony.

Faintly, she heard the music start up again. Another waltz. But she would not be dancing it with Julian. She must think, but she couldn't do that with Gilbert jabbering in her ear. "Go away, Gilbert," she said, but she wasn't certain that he could hear her. She barely heard herself. "I want to be alone."

"Alone with me?" Julian had returned. A glass of champagne in each hand, he stood just outside the alcove. And he was smiling!

Wrath kindled in her breast. So he still wished to flirt, did he?

Well, she'd show him that Penelope Langham had finally taken his measure! Impetuously she stepped toward him, her palm itching to wipe that grin off his face.

Julian's eyes narrowed. He thrust the two glasses into Gilbert Bromfield's unwilling hands, spilling a goodly amount of champagne down Gilbert's brocaded waistcoat, and when Penelope swung at him, he was quite ready. Catching her wrist in his right hand, Julian pressed his left between her shoulder blades and whirled her out onto the dance floor.

"I suppose I must teach you how to strike a man," he said softly. "Do not alert him by opening your hand and raising your arm before you're close enough to touch him. Instead approach him calmly, and for goodness' sake use your fist."

"Let me go!" she demanded, but she had not the strength to push him away.

Julian merely smiled and pressed her even closer. He waltzed her clear across the ballroom, out the double doors and down the full length of the landing until they came to an open door. Without missing a step, he waltzed her inside, then kicked it firmly shut.

"And now, Penny, my love, we must have a talk." Letting go of her, Julian crossed his arms over his chest and propped one shoulder negligently against a set of shelves filled from floor to ceiling with books.

Penelope was sharply reminded of her tête-à-têtes with Julian in her own library at Belmont House. Surrounded by books, she had first made his acquaintance; it was fitting that they'd part in a similar environment.

Then why should tears come to her eyes? She should be glad that his arms were around her no longer, for his touch had played havoc with her emotions.

Because she still loved him.

Penelope turned abruptly, lest he see her weakness, and walked toward the door.

"You have shown me many a delightful side of your character," Julian drawled. "But I never would have believed you'd cry craven so easily."

"Craven!" Whirling, she confronted him boldly, her eyes filled with a mixture of hurt, pride, and indignation. "It's *you* who's lily-livered, Julian! Hiding behind a profession—a false profession, I shouldn't wonder! Making me believe you won't propose because you're below my touch! Well, you may be an 'Honorable,' but you're not honest, Julian!"

"So that's it." Julian pushed away from the shelves. Slowly he approached her. "Bromfield made it his business to tell you who I am. Told you about my past, too, no doubt. That's too bad since I planned to do that myself before I ask you to be my—"

"Too bad indeed!" She started to back away from him, knowing that if he touched her again, she'd be lost. "It cost you the opportunity to watch me make a cake of myself. Now you'll never be able to boast that Penelope Langham was such a besotted little fool that she proposed to *you*!"

Finding her retreat suddenly cut off by the shelf-lined wall, she raised her hands in a feeble effort to ward off his advance. "Stay away from me, Julian! Don't you dare take another step!"

But of course he dared, even went so far as to place his hands on her shoulders. His eyes alight with laughter, he said in a deep, caressing voice that sent tingles down her spine, "Is that what you meant to do? My poor little Scheherazade. You shouldn't be wearing the sultan's ruby, you know. You're not at all up to snuff, and only a sophisticated lady of the world should wear a jewel like that."

His fingers burned her skin where it was inadequately protected by narrow strips of pleated silk posing as sleeves and melted her anger. With considerable but sadly inappropriate interest, Penelope studied the top button of his waistcoat.

"It's a maharajah's ruby," she said faintly.

"As you wish, my love."

She detected laughter in his voice as well, but hard as she tried, she could not rekindle the wrath that had made her stop in her tracks when she should have run from the book room. Not when he was so near that she could feel his warmth through the material of her gown, and when his fingers traced such delightful patterns on her neck and bare shoulders.

Then his grip tightened, and with a hint of sternness he said, "Why, do you think, I asked if you were sure you wished to grant me every dance, you little pea-goose?"

Her eyes, widening, flew to his face.

"Do you truly believe I would have asked six dances of you if I didn't intend to make you my wife? Do you believe me such a slow top that *you* must propose to *me*, Penny, my love?"

Without quite realizing how it had happened, her hands were gripping the lapels of his coat, drawing him closer. "But why did you wait so long, Julian? Why didn't you tell me who you are? I thought . . . I thought you were ineligible and would think it an imposition to ask me."

Julian grimaced ruefully. "Arrogantly, no doubt, I assumed that everyone in town knew me or had, at least, heard of me. And when I realized my mistake, there seemed no reason to say, 'Pardon me, Miss Langham, but do you know that I am in fact the *Honorable* Julian Rutherford?' "

She couldn't help but chuckle, for his voice had reminded her strongly of Gilbert's pompous tones. "But later, Julian. It seems to me there were several occasions . . . Lady Margaret . . . Peter Ludlow."

"If you could have seen your face when Lady Margaret spoke of my childhood! I promise you, it was irresistible to tease you awhile longer."

He drew her closer still until she was obliged to remove

her hands from his chest to his back. His breath stirred the short curls pinned atop her head.

"Believe me, Penny, when Peter started to talk about my past, I was concerned only that you might learn of the scandal before I had made sure you had fallen in love with me."

"You *wanted* me to fall in love with you?"

"Yes. I already loved you dreadfully, you see."

The rapid beat of his heart under her cheek echoed her own. As she raised her face his head came down, and their lips met with an urgency that set her blood roiling through her veins. Her mouth opened under his demand; her body, with a will of its own, pressed against the lean strength of his, and yet never seemed to get close enough.

It was Julian who pulled away first. "We're playing with fire, my love," he said ruefully. "I should have known better than to take you where you aren't chaperoned. Around you, I lose my head far too easily."

Accepting his words as a compliment, Penelope looked up at him with an imp of mischief dancing in her eyes. "I agree. We must strive to kiss more sedately. Let's try it again."

"A most tempting suggestion, my love. But I wouldn't wish to be accused of influencing you in any way before we have discussed that sordid scandal. Let's sit down and be sensible for a few moments."

Looking around the small room, Penelope said, "But there's only one chair. I have no desire to be craning my neck more than necessary. Why must you be so tall, Julian?"

"One chair will serve the purpose very well," he said, leading her to the object in question. After seating himself, he invited her to take her place on his knees. "This way, you see, you may look down on me."

That, Penelope found, was quite an exaggeration, but at least she could gaze into his eyes without fear of causing a stiffness in her neck. "I like this," she said. "Will you promise to offer me your lap whenever I feel the need to scold you?"

"*Are* you planning to scold me?"

"Yes, indeed. For thinking I would be so foolish as to believe you'd jilt a young girl and break her heart! You abominable-thief-of-female-hearts simply don't propose!"

Penelope took up his hand and nestled it against her cheek. "You still haven't, you know."

"You may not believe I jilted her, but in the eyes of the *ton*—Penny, my love," he said huskily. "I wouldn't want you hurt by spiteful tongues!"

"As though I'd care! Besides, Aunt Sophy will stand by us."

Julian's thumb caressed her cheek. "So will Lady Margaret. And my father. That's why I didn't call on you, love. I was at Steeple. Papa can't wait to meet you, and he's promised to bring Mama to town next week and open up Steeple House for the rest of the season. Mama is eager to discuss wedding plans with you." He looked at her quizzically. "I hope you shan't mind. She's rather difficult, you see. Tends to suffer from nervous spasms and such."

"If she doesn't get her own will. I see." Penelope toyed with the folds of his cravat. "Then I must be glad, I suppose, that she won't be called upon to discuss wedding plans."

His thumb ceased its motion and she could feel him tense.

"It would be very forward in me," she said, her lashes demurely lowered, "to discuss a wedding when you still haven't proposed."

"Jade! I should turn you over on my knee and administer a spanking for giving me such a scare. However, I shall be lenient. Just this one time, mind you!"

And then Penelope was enveloped in a crushing embrace to receive—and accept—a most satisfying proposal of marriage.